36 Hours

When disaster turns to passion

Welcome to an exciting new series of twelve books from Silhouette®, 36 HOURS, where danger is just a heartbeat away. Unprecedented rainstorms cause a 36 hour blackout in Grand Springs and it sets off a string of events that alters people's lives forever...

This month look for:

Nine Months by Beverly Barton—
The passionate stranger Paige Summers had been stranded with was her arrogant new boss! Soon she'd have to tell him that the baby she carried was his!

The Parent Plan by Paula Detmer Riggs—
A strong man and a proud woman put their marriage to the test. They had a child, so were their differences really irreconcilable?

Beverly Barton

has been in love with romance since her grandfather gave her an illustrated book of *Beauty and the Beast*. An avid reader since childhood, she began writing at the age of nine and wrote short stories, poetry, plays and novels throughout school and college. After marriage to her own 'hero' and the births of her daughter and son, she chose to be a full-time homemaker.

When she returned to writing, she joined the Romance Writers of America. Since the release of her first Silhouette® book in 1990, she has been a two-time winner of the National Reader's Choice Award and a RITA finalist, as well as the winner of the GRW Maggie Award and the Laurel Wreath Award. Beverly considers writing romances a real labour of love. Her stories come straight from the heart, and she hopes that all the strong and varied emotions she invests in her books will be felt by everyone who reads them.

36 Hours

When disaster turns to passion

NINE MONTHS

Beverly Barton

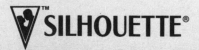

™ SILHOUETTE®

*Silhouette and Colophon are registered trademarks of
Harlequin Books S.A., used under licence.*

*First published in Great Britain 1999
Silhouette Books, Eton House, 18-24 Paradise Road,
Richmond, Surrey TW9 1SR*

© Harlequin Books S.A. 1997

Special thanks and acknowledgement are given to Beverly Barton
for her contribution to the 36 HOURS series.

ISBN 0 373 65015 9

105-9908

*Printed and bound in Spain
by Litografía Rosés S.A., Barcelona*

36 Hours

when disaster turns to passion

For the residents of Grand Springs, the
storm-induced blackout was just the beginning…

Each book stands alone, but together they're terrific!

To our first grandchild, Braden Forrest Waldrep,
Grammy and Granddaddy's pride and joy.
Words alone never could express the love in our hearts.

Prologue

The elevator doors swung open. Since it was after office hours on a Friday, Paige Summers had expected the elevator to be empty. But a lone man occupied the small space. Tall and lean, with an aura of masculine strength surrounding him, the stranger stared at Paige, inspecting her from head to toe. Forcing herself to ignore his interest, she quickly ran her gaze over the handsome cowboy.

His faded jeans fit like a glove, and with one more washing his plaid work shirt would need to go into a ragbag. A sweatband circled the base of his black Stetson.

Although he dressed like dozens of other men in Grand Springs, Colorado, one glimpse told Paige that this man was unlike any she'd ever met.

When she glanced back at his face, he smiled at her and her stomach did an evil flip-flop. He *did* possess a killer smile. A wide, sensuous mouth. Full, tempting lips. And beautiful, perfect teeth, sparkling white against the dark, suntanned skin of his face.

"If you're worried about getting on an elevator with a stranger, I can assure you, you'll be safe with me."

The man spoke with a drawl. Oklahoma or Texas, maybe, she thought.

Paige forced a smile to her lips. "I'm sorry. It's just that I didn't expect anyone to be here still." She stepped inside the elevator, but deliberately avoided eye contact. She was a quiet, private person, who didn't normally find herself lusting after a stranger.

Lusting after? Good grief, Paige, how could you think such a thing? He's attractive. That's all. You've never lusted after a man in your life.

She glanced at the cowboy again, unable to stop herself. His dark brown hair brushed his collar. Strands of gray streaked his thick sideburns. He grinned and tipped his hat at her. Paige looked down at her feet. A guy with his looks and charm could be dangerous.

The elevator doors closed.

Jared Montgomery couldn't remember the last time he'd been instantly attracted to a woman, and never this strongly attracted.

She was lovely, in a fresh, unspoiled sort of way. He liked that she was a good deal shorter than he, and that every inch of her five-and-a-half-foot body was filled out in lush, curvaceous proportions.

The elevator jolted to a sudden halt, shaking Jared instantly from his thoughts and tossing him sideways. Acting purely on instinct, he grabbed the young woman the moment he realized they were both falling. She clutched the front of his shirt, accidently ripping off two buttons. Quickly maneuvering her around, Jared took the brunt of the fall as they hit the floor. The black Stetson flew off his head and landed a few inches from his right shoulder. The impact of his big body sandwiched between the hard surface beneath and the woman on top momentarily knocked the breath out of him.

The red emergency lights came on, coating the interior of the elevator in a rosy pink glow. Paige realized she was lying on top of the stranger, her body intimately aligned with his. Her breasts crushed against his muscular chest. Their bellies pressed together. Their legs entwined.

A fluttering, quivering sensation began in the depths of her femininity. It quickly spread through her entire body, and she became embarrassingly aware that the man lying beneath her was aroused. His hardened sex pulsated against her.

She rolled off his chest and onto the floor beside him. "Are you all right?" she asked, her voice deceptively calm. She shook like a leaf in the wind.

Jared stared up into the woman's big brown eyes, concern evident in her gaze as well as her voice. She hovered over him, her large, round breasts almost touching his chest. God, she was gorgeous.

"Fine." He sat up too quickly and groaned.

"You're hurt."

"I said I'm fine. How about you?"

"Okay, I guess." She wriggled against him. "What happened?"

"Well, I'd say the electrical power went out." He rubbed his forehead, then ran his hand across his stinging cheek. "Ouch."

"What is it?" In an effort to see what was wrong with him, she leaned too close and her breasts brushed his arm.

His body tightened even harder. "I think I bruised my cheek when we fell. No big deal. Are you sure you're all right?"

She scooted away from him. "I'm perfectly all right, thank you. Just...well, just a little unnerved."

"Yeah, sure. Having an elevator go dead in mid-descent is enough to unnerve anybody." Jared placed his Stetson on his head, then stood up slowly. Glancing down at the woman on the floor, he held out his hand.

Paige stared at his hand—an obvious offer of assistance—and hesitated.

"You are the most cautious woman I've ever met," the man said. "Come on." He wiggled his fingers back and forth. "I promise I won't bite you."

"I didn't think you would." Her cheeks flushed. Retrieving her purse off the floor with one hand, Paige reached up with the other. She allowed him to help her stand, then immediately took a careful step backward.

The stranger grinned. The bottom fell out of her stomach. Turning his back to her, he checked the telephone.

"No answer," he told her.

"Isn't there any other way to get help?" she asked. "How will anyone know we're in here?"

Noting the slight panic in her voice, Jared tried to reassure her. "Hey, there's nothing to worry about. The minute the electrical power went out, the emergency generators kicked in to keep the lights and the ventilation working. The maintenance crew should have things going again pretty quickly."

"But it's Friday evening. Don't you think everyone who works in this building has gone home?"

"No. There should be at least one maintenance man on duty twenty-four hours a day."

"What if the outage isn't just in the Wellman Building?"

"There's no way to know," he said. "But one way or another, we'll get out of here, so stop worrying, honey."

Jared stood quietly for a while, silently fidgeting and trying not to look at the woman. But when he glanced at her, he noticed her actions mimicked his.

"Are you sure the air is circulating in here?" She tugged on the collar of her suit jacket. "It feels awfully warm to me."

"The air-conditioning probably isn't on, if that's what you mean," Jared said. "But the air ventilation is working just fine. Relax, honey."

"Would you please not call me honey." The woman glared at him, her chin tilted defiantly, as if she were a schoolmarm scolding a naughty little boy.

"Sorry, but since I don't know your name—"

"Paige. My name is Paige."

"Hello, Paige." He smiled and held out his hand. "I'm Jared."

Paige stared at his hand, but this time she didn't accept it. Instead she crossed her arms over her waist and tapped her fingers up and down on her elbows. Glancing around the elevator, she sought a means of escape. She couldn't stay here any longer, trapped inside this tomb.

She unbuttoned the top two buttons of her suit jacket, clutched her throat and took a deep breath. She couldn't fall apart. Not in front of this stranger. After all, they weren't in any real danger. They had air and light, and sooner or later someone would rescue them. Sooner, she hoped. "Jared, please find a way to get us out of here!"

"I'll do what I can, hon—Paige. Maybe I can open the doors." Pressing his hands flat against the metal surface, he positioned his fingertips along the sealed edges and pushed. "We could be stopped right at floor level."

"What if we aren't?"

"Then we'll either climb up or step down."

"All right." Forcing a smile, she nodded affirmatively. She'd suffered mild attacks of claustrophobia all her life, but she usually managed to avoid situations that might trigger her problem. Unfortunately, using elevators was a necessity. And if she hadn't stopped to call and tell her mother about her new job, she wouldn't be stuck in this elevator—with a rough and rugged cowboy!

"They're opening!" Jared pried the doors apart, then cursed under his breath. "It appears we're trapped between the mezzanine and the first floor. And if I remember correctly, the first floor is about forty feet high."

Paige stared at the solid wall behind the open door. "Then we are trapped, aren't we." She rung her hands together.

"We aren't trapped."

"But you said—"

"Sorry. Poor choice of words. But there's no reason to panic." He took a couple of tentative steps toward her.

Paige backed away from him. "I think I should tell you something."

Lifting his eyebrows, he looked quizzically at her. "Let me guess. You're claustrophobic. Right?"

"Sort of. But I'm only slightly claustrophobic."

"Oh, I see." Hell, it was just his luck to get stuck in an elevator with a young, nervous and shy woman who was only *slightly* claustrophobic.

Paige couldn't help but notice that Jared's devastating smile had vanished and been replaced by an intimidating scowl. "I haven't cried or screamed or anything foolish, but you're angry with me, aren't you?"

"I'm not angry." He was not angry. He was frustrated. And he had to admit that the thought of dealing with a potentially hysterical woman unnerved him.

He tossed his Stetson to the floor and looked up. With his arms held straight above his head, he jumped toward the ceiling.

Paige let out an astonished cry. "What are you doing?"

He jumped again, then again. "I'm trying to reach the emergency hatch up there." He pointed toward the sealed square in the roof. On his fourth attempt, he shoved open the vent.

"Damn!" He cursed loudly.

Paige's gaze followed Jared's line of vision. "Oh, no. I can't climb up there. We must be at least twenty-five feet from the mezzanine level."

Jared saw the panicked look in her eyes and realized he really was going to have a hysterical woman on his hands if he didn't do something to distract her. And in his experience, there were only two ways to gain a woman's complete attention. Either make love to her or make her fighting mad. He decided on the latter.

"I know it looks like a long way, honey, but I can boost you up to the opening, you can grab onto the—"

"Have you lost your mind?" She glared at him in disbelief.

"I know you're claustrophobic—"

"Slightly claustrophobic!"

"But you don't suffer from acrophobia, too, do you?"

"No, I am not afraid of heights!"

"Then what's the problem?" Watching her face turn crimson and her brown eyes sparkle with dark fire, he grinned. "You must be afraid you'll get your beige suit dirty. Is that it?"

"Despite the fact I'm a little upset right now, I am not some silly female who would worry about getting her suit dirty."

"Oh, then you must have another reason for wanting to stay here with me. Could it be that you think if you play the helpless female, I'll play your hero? Honey, if you want me, you don't have to be coy. All you have to do is come and get me."

"Oh!" Paige huffed loudly. "Of all the nerve. You must have a monumental ego to think—"

"My ego isn't the only thing about me that's monumental," he announced. Paige gritted her teeth and Jared could tell that she was too mad to give a thought to being *slightly* claustrophobic. He'd rather have an angry woman on his hands than a hysterical one.

"Why, you egotistical, macho jerk!" Without giving a thought to what she was doing, Paige balled her hand into a tight fist and punched Jared in the stomach.

The blow was totally unexpected, and Jared doubled over from the instant pain.

"Why the hell did you do that?" He straightened up to his full six-foot height, poked his hand through the opening where two of his shirt buttons were missing and rubbed his stomach. His movements loosened his shirt from his jeans, revealing several inches of his washboard-lean belly covered with swirls of dark brown hair.

"You were being hateful and insulting," Paige said, forcing her gaze away from his body and up to his face.

"I was trying to keep your mind off being trapped in this elevator," he admitted. "But I had no idea you had such violent tendencies."

"I do not have violent tendencies." Her voice quivered ever so slightly. Then as the anger, frustration and sense of helplessness overwhelmed her, her eyes filled with tears that overflowed down her cheeks and ran into the corners of her mouth.

"Oh, hell, honey. Don't do that!" Dammit, this was what Jared had been trying so desperately to avoid. Under normal circumstances, he would walk off and leave her. He didn't tolerate any woman's silly, emotional spells. But he was as trapped as she was. "There's no cause for your acting this way."

Paige glared at him through misty eyes. She hated him! Jared Whoever-he-was. She hated him! Why couldn't he be more like her father and act like a gentleman?

Hugging herself as she continued breathing deeply, Paige closed her eyes and leaned her head back against the wall. She would stop crying. She would regain control. And she wouldn't say another word to Jared Whoever-he-was. No matter how long they were stuck in this hell-hole together.

Jared didn't know whether two minutes, twenty minutes or two hours had passed, but it seemed like two days to him. Paige stood on one side of the elevator, he on the other. Neither of them had spoken a word. But he could hear her ragged, sobbing little gulps for air. He glanced over at her and cursed himself for a fool.

What the hell! he told himself. What would it hurt to

comfort her a little? Maybe if he put his arm around her and soothed her, she'd stop that noise. If necessary, he might even apologize. Anything to quiet her.

"Paige?" He took a few steps forward, stopping just short of touching her. When she looked at him with her dark chocolate eyes and bit down on her bottom lip, all soft and pink, he felt as if he'd been poleaxed again. He wanted this woman!

Paige sucked in a deep breath. Jared was looking at her as if... No, surely not, she thought. He couldn't possibly want her. She was letting her imagination run wild. She tried to break visual contact, but it was as if she were hypnotized by his seductive stare.

Reaching out with both hands, he used his index fingers to wipe away the tears from her cheeks. Paige's breath caught in her throat as Jared traced the planes of her face with his fingertips.

"Don't cry anymore, honey." He took her face in his hands, cupping her cheeks tenderly.

"Please...don't." She couldn't bear the way he made her feel. Hot and cold at the same time, her stomach tightening into knots and her breathing quickening.

"Don't what?" Jared whispered the question, his voice compellingly sensual. Touching her had been a big mistake. If she didn't push him away, if she didn't tell him no, he was going to make love to this woman. Here. Now. In the elevator.

"Don't confuse me this way. I don't know how to deal with a man like you," she reluctantly admitted.

"What sort of man do you think I am?" He lowered his head and brushed his lips across hers.

She gasped. "You—you're a master game player and I don't know how to play games."

"Then I'll teach you."

Before she could respond, he engulfed her in a passionately gentle kiss. Paige discovered herself succumbing totally to his tenderness. She dropped her purse to the floor and swayed toward him, her breasts pressing against his hard chest.

Oh, dear God, she felt as if she were drowning in the dark, swirling depths of her own desire. She opened her mouth, allowing his tongue entrance, then moaned when he threaded his fingers through her hair. The neat French twist fell apart under his marauding hand and her mahogany red hair tumbled down her back.

He eased his other hand down her waist and across her hips, pulling her close to him. She wrapped herself around him. Clinging to him. Wanting him. Lost to everything except the all-consuming longing coursing through her.

What was happening to her? Why couldn't she stop...or ask him to stop? In the swirling confusion of her mind, one coherent thought made its way through—she didn't want the incredible experience to end and she'd never felt like this. *But how could she feel like this with a stranger—a stranger she didn't even like?*

Jared was fast losing control, and if he didn't stop now, he was going to take Paige with all the wild desire raging inside him. He ran his fingers down her throat and deepened the kiss. Then he slipped his hand inside her suit jacket and covered her breast, his fingers seeking and finding her nipple. Opening her jacket fully to reveal her beige satin bra, he lowered his head and took her nipple into his mouth, suckling her through the soft material. Paige grabbed at his shirt, quickly undoing the remaining buttons, then spread his shirt apart.

Lifting her up against the wall, he pressed her moist, warm body between him and the mirror behind her. While she clutched his shoulders and succumbed to the desire to place her mouth on his chest, he shoved her skirt upward, bunching it around her hips. She lifted her leg, fitting her calf around his thigh.

"I want you, honey," Jared said, his voice deep and soft and dripping with desire. "Right here. Right now."

"I—I—" She couldn't seem to form her thoughts into words.

"If you don't want this, too, Paige, stop me now."

"No," she whimpered. "No, don't stop."

Her words seemed to end any doubts on his part, sending him into a sexual frenzy. Within minutes, he'd divested her of her shoes, panty hose and bikini panties, then unzipped his jeans and lifted her to straddle his hips. She clung to him as he braced her against the mirrored wall. While she returned his wild, wet kisses, he thrust into her.

Paige threw back her head and cried out from the sheer joy of having him inside her. The tension spiraled upward and outward, a hotter, wilder passion than any she'd ever known.

Jared whispered dark, erotic, almost incoherent words to her as he claimed her. He was lost in the moment, not thinking, only feeling. Paige cried out as fulfillment spread through her and her release triggered his. They clung to each other, straining to hold on to the ecstasy, shuddering as the last quivers shot through their bodies.

When Jared lifted her face to kiss her, he saw tears in her eyes. "Did I hurt you, honey?"

"No. It's…it's just that I've never…I mean it was never like that before."

"Yeah, I know what you mean." He kissed her, softly, sweetly. "I haven't been that wild for a woman since I was eighteen."

Her cheeks flushed. Bending her head, she looked down at where their bodies were still pressed together. She eased her legs down his and tried to stand. When she wobbled, he grabbed her by the waist, then he drew in a deep breath and stepped away from her. She looked like a woman who had been thoroughly loved, and the very sight of her aroused him anew.

Seeing her reflection in the mirror, Paige sucked in a deep breath. Suddenly embarrassed, she tugged down her skirt and buttoned her jacket.

"Are you on the Pill?" Jared asked as he reached down and picked up her panties and panty hose.

"What?" She grabbed the lace bikinis and the panty hose out of his hand and stuffed them into her beige leather purse, which she picked up off the floor.

"I didn't use anything," he said. "I got so carried away, I didn't even think about protection. I'm sorry, Paige, I don't usually do something that stupid."

"Oh. I…"

"If you're protected against pregnancy, then everything else should be all right, shouldn't it?" Hell, how could he have forgotten to use a condom? He never forgot. "What I mean is that I'm always careful." *Until tonight.* "You are, too, aren't you?"

"Yes. There's nothing to worry about at all." Oh, dear God, Paige thought, she had just had sex with a man—a stranger—and hadn't given a thought to protecting herself. She was twenty-five years old and she should have known better.

She tried to smile, but the effort failed. "You certainly found a very effective way to get my mind off my claustrophobia."

He reached out to touch her and she moved out of his reach. "Unfortunately, I've never made love with a stranger before and I find the situation rather awkward."

"Well, if it makes you feel any better, this is a first for me, too." He grinned, then explained. "I've never made love to a stranger in an elevator, either."

Nodding her understanding, Paige smiled weakly. "I—I don't suppose many people have."

Jared tucked in his shirt and zipped up his jeans. Now what? he wondered. Despite how awkward things were between them, they were stuck with each other for the time being.

He picked up his Stetson and set it on his head. "I suppose you live here in Grand Springs, don't you? I'm from Texas. Just got into town today and—"

"Stop it, will you?" Crossing her arms over her chest, Paige leaned against the back of the elevator. "I don't want to talk to you. Do you understand? I want to pretend that what happened didn't happen. We're strangers who will never see each other again once we leave this elevator, so let's keep it that way."

"You're right," he said. "We're both better off not knowing anything about each other. Just a couple of ships that passed in the night."

Jared slumped down on the floor, leaned back his head and drew his Stetson down over his eyes. Paige rummaged in her purse, pulled out a paperback book and began to read.

They ignored each other for quite a while. After checking her watch for the dozenth time, Paige wondered if they were going to be trapped in the elevator all night. The power had gone off around seven o'clock, more than four hours ago.

A rather loud banging caught their attention. The elevator vibrated every so slightly.

"Hey down there!" a masculine voice called out. "How many of you are there?"

Jared glanced up and saw a man at the mezzanine level of the shaft. "Only two of us. Are you maintenance?"

"No, sir. I'm Troy Dodd with the fire department. We'd

have been here sooner, but we didn't know anyone was
still in the building when the power went out.''

"Can you tell us what happened?'' Jared asked as he
stood.

"Well, the whole town's in the dark. Seems the heavy
rainstorms caused a mud slide that buried Grand Springs's
only source of electricity.''

"Will you stop talking and get us out of here!'' Paige
said impatiently.

"Is your name Paige?'' Troy Dodd asked.

"Yes. Why?''

"Your parents called and told us that you were probably
trapped in the Wellman Building.''

She glanced at Jared, who smiled at her. That devastating killer smile.

"I was supposed to have dinner with them tonight,'' she
explained.

"Hey, folks,'' Troy Dodd said, ''we're going to send
down a lift chair and bring you two up, one at a time.''

"Jared, about what happened,'' Paige whispered as they
waited for the chair, ''I want you to know—''

"You don't have to say it, honey. What happened was
a mistake. We lost our heads and went a little crazy.''

"Yes, we did.''

"The best thing we can do is forget about it. Right?
Pretend it never happened.''

"Yes, of course. You're right. It never happened.''

Fifteen minutes later, Paige and Jared stood on the mezzanine level of the Wellman Building and shook hands
with the firemen. After thanking them for coming to the
rescue, Paige said goodbye to Jared. They stared at each
other for one, long, sweet moment, then Paige walked
downstairs and into her mother's open arms.

After thirty-six hours without electricity, Grand Springs
was a flurry of activity on Monday morning. Jared arrived

at his new office in the Wellman Building before any of the office staff. He had planned to be in town for a week before he turned the entire Grand Springs operation over to his manager, Greg Addison. As this Colorado branch of Montgomery Real Estate and Land Development expanded, it would be necessary for Jared to make trips more frequently and stay longer, so he'd told Greg to hire a secretary for him, someone capable of doubling as his assistant.

But the thirty-six-hour blackout upon his arrival had set the tone for the entire weekend, and Jared had decided to cut his visit short. It had been one wild, unexpected event after another. He'd said his goodbyes to Paige, telling himself he'd forget all about her, and left the Wellman Building with the firemen who had rescued them. Discovering how desperately volunteers were needed during the local emergency, he had offered his services. He hadn't gotten a bath or a hot meal until Sunday morning when electricity had been restored and he'd checked into a local motel.

And he had dreamed about Paige. About touching her. Making love to her. For the past two days, he hadn't been able to get her out of his mind.

Since Grand Springs wasn't a big town, the longer he stayed, the greater the odds were that he and Paige would run into each other. He didn't want that, and he suspected neither did she. What had happened between them had been a chance happening, a one-night stand to end all one-night stands.

"Trying to make the rest of us look bad?" Tall, lanky Greg Addison sauntered into Jared's private office and sat down on the side of his desk. "I didn't expect you until later in the day."

"Since I'm going to be here only a couple of days, I want to make the most of my stay," Jared said. "I need to meet your assistant and break in my new secretary. You did hire someone for me, didn't you?''

"Never fear. I hired a highly recommended young lady on Friday afternoon." Scooting off the desk, Greg stood and pointed toward the outer office. "As a matter of fact, Ms. Summers has just arrived. She's outside talking to Kay."

"Kay?"

"My assistant, Kay Thompson."

"Well, I might as well meet them now. I want to brief my secretary on her duties and—"

"What's the hurry? I thought you planned to spend the week."

"My plans have changed," Jared said.

"Blonde, brunette or redhead?" Greg asked.

Jared caught himself before he blurted out "redhead." "I left some loose ends back in Texas I need to tie up, and I have to run down to Florida. Besides, we all can't be playboys like you."

Greg laughed heartily. "Yeah, sure. Tell that to someone who doesn't know you the way I do."

"Introduce me to the people you've hired." Jared quickly changed the subject. "I'm especially eager to meet my secretary. We have a lot to do before I leave town."

"Right this way."

Greg swung open the door and the two men exited Jared's private office.

"Well, here they are," Greg said. "Ms. Thompson, my assistant, and Ms. Summers, your secretary."

"Ms. Thompson." Smiling at the tall, slender brunette, Jared shook her hand, then turned to the other woman. "And this must be—" He stared at the curvaceous redhead who looked at him as if he had suddenly sprung a second head. Dear God, it couldn't be. His secretary was Paige. His Paige…from the elevator!

One

After hurriedly leaving Grand Springs four months ago, L. J. Montgomery was finally returning for an indefinite stay. Paige had overhead Greg Addison telling Kay that he thought it was past time for Jared to return, that he couldn't understand why the boss man had stayed away so long. It wasn't like Jared not to keep his finger directly on the pulse of a new branch office.

Paige couldn't help but wonder if Jared had stayed away because of her. Surely not. He'd made it perfectly clear that their sexual encounter had been a mistake, something he preferred to forget. Easy enough for him. But not for her. Not now.

She supposed if she'd been more experienced and less romantic in nature, she could have gotten over the silly notion that she'd fallen in love with Jared. And as long as she lived, she'd never forget her first morning at Montgomery Real Estate and Land Development.

On the previous Friday afternoon, Greg Addison had hired Paige as L.J.'s private secretary and told her she'd meet her boss on the following Monday morning.

She'd arrived at work that Monday prepared to prove herself indispensable to her new boss.

"There's no need to be nervous," Kay told her. "Greg tells me that Mr. Montgomery is a demanding boss, but a fair one. Besides, he's only going to be here a week this first time, then he'll fly back and forth once we get things set up and running.''

Paige smoothed her hands down the sides of her lavender coatdress and wished she could check her appearance in a mirror just one more time. She wanted to make a good impression on her first day. Since the moment she'd entered the Wellman Building that morning, she'd heard nothing but talk about L. J. Montgomery. How rich he was. How powerful he was. What an eligible bachelor he was. How handsome he was rumored to be.

Obviously the women in the Wellman Building saw L. J. Montgomery as the answer to their prayers. But why would a rich, powerful, successful, handsome man be interested in a working girl when he could have his pick of wealthy, cultured ladies?

Besides, Paige wasn't interested in L. J. Montgomery, other than as her employer. The only man who interested her was a tall, green-eyed cowboy with the most devastating smile she'd ever seen. She had tried all weekend to put him out of her mind, to pretend that what had happened hadn't happened. But she kept remembering. His smile. His touch. The feel of him making hot, wild love to her. Just remembering brought a blush to her cheeks.

He'd told her that what had happened had been a mistake, and he'd let her walk out of his life. Obviously their lovemaking hadn't meant anything to him, nothing more than a diversion to pass the time while they were trapped in the elevator. Perhaps if she was a little older, a little more experienced, that was all it would have meant to her. But their lovemaking had been unique, unlike anything she'd ever known. She'd been in love with Kevin, her college sweetheart, but he'd never made her feel the way Jared had.

''Hey, earth to Paige,'' Kay said. ''Where are you, girl? I've been talking a blue streak to you for five minutes now and you're just staring off into space. Thinking about a guy, huh?''

"What?"

"I said, you must be thinking about a guy."

"Well, to be honest, I was."

"Not weaving fantasies about your new boss, are you? I understand from Greg that L.J. has a cardinal rule about not dating his employees."

"Oh, no, I can assure you that I haven't set my sights on Mr. Montgomery," Paige said. "I was thinking about a cowboy I met Friday night. When the power went out."

"Oh. We'll have to go to lunch together." Kay grabbed Paige's arm. "You can tell me all the delicious details."

The inner office door swung open and two men emerged from L. J. Montgomery's office. Paige looked up to see Greg Addison.

"Well, here they are," Greg said. "Ms. Thompson, my assistant, and Ms. Summers, your secretary."

"Ms. Thompson." The man smiled at Kay.

Paige's stomach tightened into painful knots. She recognized that voice. She looked at the man standing beside Greg Addison, and for one heart-stopping moment, she thought she was going to faint.

"And this must be—" Jared glared at her, his mouth agape.

"Mr. Montgomery?" Paige spoke his name in a strained squeak.

Grabbing Paige's arm, Jared jerked her toward him. "Come with me, please, Ms. Summers."

She allowed him to drag her into his office, leaving behind Greg and Kay. Glancing back over her shoulder, she saw the startled looks on their faces. Jared slammed the door.

"You're my secretary?" Jared settled his hands on his hips and glared at her. *"You?"*

Paige looked at the harsh, stern man and wondered if she had lost her mind. This couldn't be happening. He was the same man she'd made love with in the elevator—and yet he wasn't. Jared, her Friday night lover, had been a cowboy in a Stetson, boots and jeans. L. J. Montgomery wore an expensive suit, silk tie and linen shirt.

"Why were you dressed like a cowboy Friday evening?" she asked.

"I'd just flown in from my ranch in Texas," he said. "Besides, I don't wear suits all the time. What about you? Why didn't you tell me you'd just been hired as my secretary?"

"I didn't know who you were! I had no idea you were L. J. Montgomery."

"Sit down." He pulled up a chair and placed it in front of his desk. "We're caught in a rather awkward situation here, aren't we?"

That was the understatement of the year, she thought as she continued standing there staring at him. He was going to fire her, here and now. She was just about to lose the best job she'd ever had before she even started work. "I'll save you the trouble of asking me to leave. I'll get my purse off my desk and—"

"I'm not going to fire you," he said, then pointed to the chair. "Please, Ms. Summers…Paige, sit down."

Reluctantly, she sat, her back ramrod straight.

"I know that we both assumed we'd never meet again," he said. "But…we have."

"Yes, we have." Paige was torn between her delight at seeing Jared again and her misery over the fact that he had turned out to be L. J. Montgomery. Her boss! One of the wealthiest and most powerful businessmen in the Southwest.

"Look, as far as I'm concerned, there's no reason you can't keep this job." Jared eased his rear down on the edge of his desk and crossed his arms over his chest. "What happened between us Friday night was a one-time-only thing. Under normal circumstances, it wouldn't have happened. And it'll never happen again."

"I'm not sure I could work for you after what happened," she said. *Not now that I think I might already be halfway in love with you.*

"Look, Paige, you obviously need this job or you wouldn't have applied for it." Jared uncrossed his arms and stuck his hands in his pockets. "A job like this one, with all the benefits, doesn't come along every day. It wouldn't be fair to ask you to give it up just because of what happened. And I don't date my employees. It's one of my cardinal rules. One I never break."

"But don't you think it might be a little embarrassing, our working together every day?"

"There's no reason why it has to be. We'll just put the Friday night incident in the past, where it belongs. And it's not as if you'll even see me that often. I probably won't be back to Colorado for several months."

"I know. Mr. Addison explained about your work schedule when he hired me."

"Then there shouldn't be a problem." Jared eased off his desk. "Honey, we're a couple of adults. It wasn't the first time for either of us. These things happen."

They don't happen to me, she wanted to say, but didn't. Instead she said, "You're right, Mr. Montgomery. It would be stupid of me to let what happened between us make me give up a wonderful job."

"Then you'll stay on here at Montgomery Real Estate and Land Development?"

"Yes, I'll stay." As long as he wasn't around every day, she'd be fine. And when he was in town, she'd just have to find a way to manage.

"Then we have a deal, Ms. Summers. We're going to

pretend Friday night never happened.'' Jared held out his hand. ''And you're going to stay on as my secretary.''

She didn't want to touch him. But she had no choice. If she didn't accept his handshake, he'd know she was afraid. Willing herself not to tremble, she put her hand in his. Her insides melted. All she wanted to do was wrap herself around him and ask him to hold her close forever.

That had been the last time Paige had seen him. Four months ago. And in those four months her life had changed forever. She had longed for Jared to return and tell her that his rejection had been a mistake, that he still wanted her as much as he had the night they'd shared such unparalleled passion in the elevator.

Now Paige realized that once she had discovered L. J. Montgomery and her lover, Jared, were one in the same, she should have given up her job as his secretary. She could have found something with another firm. After all, she had a business degree and nearly four years' experience. If only she'd done the smart thing, she wouldn't have had to endure talking to him on the phone, which always prompted her to dream about him. And she wouldn't now be facing the prospect of his imminent return. But jobs that paid the salary she received at Montgomery's and companies that provided such excellent employee benefits were few and far between.

And now that she was in this situation, she desperately needed her good insurance to pay the doctor and hospital bills.

This situation? Paige laughed aloud. Tears sprung to her eyes. She swatted them away as if they were pesky insects. She was not going to feel sorry for herself. She'd gotten herself into this *situation* and it was up to her to take care of herself.

If she had a viable alternative to facing L. J. Montgomery, she wouldn't still be working for his firm. But she needed her job, now more than ever. Her parents weren't poor, but neither were they wealthy. Her father's carpentry work supplemented his army retirement and the family got along just fine. But her parents had one son in his second year at the University of Colorado and a younger one was a senior in high school. They could hardly afford to take care of her.

So far she'd been able to keep her condition a secret from everyone at work, including Kay Thompson, with whom she'd formed a genuine friendship. She wasn't showing—not yet—not so that anyone could tell she was four months pregnant. But sooner or later, her pregnancy would become noticeable, and then what would she tell everyone? What would she tell Jared?

Paige checked her watch. Twelve-thirty. Jared was due at the office at two. An hour and thirty minutes. Maybe she would feel differently about him once she saw him. It was possible that he wasn't quite as wonderful as she remembered. Maybe he wasn't as tall and lean and powerful and sexy as she'd thought he was. Maybe she had imagined his killer smile—those white teeth, that darkly tanned face. Maybe he was just an ordinary, attractive man with a nice smile.

Yeah, sure. And I imagined our wild, hot, passionate lovemaking in the elevator. I imagined that what we shared was earth-shattering, unlike anything I'd ever experienced. And maybe I'm just imagining that I'm four months pregnant.

Paige took a deep breath, squared her shoulders and glanced straight at L. J. Montgomery's big, wide oak desk. Pretending he was sitting in the chair behind the desk, Paige went over her stories—the ones from which she'd have to choose when it became necessary to reveal her pregnancy.

One was a lie. He wasn't the father. The other was the truth. He was the father.

What sort of woman would lie to a man about something so important? But then again, what sort of woman would make love to a perfect stranger in an elevator? She wasn't the type to do either. But she'd already done one and might be forced to do the other.

Once she saw Jared again, she'd know the right thing to do. Maybe, if she was lucky, he'd walk into the office, swoop her up in his arms and declare his undying love for her. But something told Paige she wasn't going to be that lucky.

Jared had convinced himself that for the past four months he'd been far too busy to become involved with someone new. Although he'd made time for a few dates, not one of them had involved more than a pleasant dinner and a chaste good-night kiss. And when thoughts of Paige Summers drifted through his head, as they so often did, he forced them away, determined to put his Grand Springs secretary out of his mind.

In the cold, hard light of day, Jared was completely in charge of his life. He had learned at his wealthy father's knee that power was everything, and despite his inherited millions, he'd been determined to prove himself in the business world—without his father's help. And at thirty-seven, he'd done just that.

But despite his iron will, he could not control his dreams. At night, Paige curled herself around him like a purring kitten and he became powerless against his desire for her. No matter what his good sense told him—that no one, least of all some sexy redheaded working girl, was going to veer him off course and ruin his plans—his body told him the exact opposite—that he should give up everything to possess her.

Years ago, another beautiful secretary had wanted him to play Prince Charming to her Cinderella. If it hadn't been for Grandpa Monty's intervention, Jared would have found himself married to a sexy little gold digger. But he'd learned his lesson well, and in the years following, his romantic liaisons had been confined to brief, mutually satisfying affairs with sophisticated women, who like him, wanted nothing more.

Of course, he would marry—eventually. He was damn near close to accomplishing everything he'd set out to achieve when he'd started his real estate and land development company straight out of college. In another five years—when he had achieved all his goals—he'd find a suitable wife, marry and have children.

But he certainly wouldn't find his life's mate in an elevator. The woman he made his wife wouldn't just have a gorgeous face and great body. And she certainly wouldn't be some unsophisticated, hot-blooded, earthy, emotional redhead. No, when Lawrence Jared Montgomery married, he'd marry a dignified, sophisticated princess who would make him the perfect wife.

And until recently, Jared noted, he'd enjoyed a rich, full social life, with his pick of women wherever he went. Oh, he still had his pick of women, but he'd been too busy to begin a new affair. Besides, he hadn't met anyone really interesting in quite some time. Not since he'd spent an evening trapped in an elevator with a redheaded temptress.

But Paige Summers was *not* the reason he hadn't had sex with another woman in four months. She didn't mean that much to him. Hell, she didn't mean a thing to him! They'd had a one-night stand and that was all there was to it. They had both agreed that what had happened had been a mistake, that they'd forget it, pretend it never happened. All she was to him was an employee. His Grand Springs secretary. A voice on the phone.

They had corresponded on business matters via fax, E-mail and occasionally telephone. He avoided calling her except when it was absolutely necessary. Just the sound of her voice made him hard. It wasn't her fault, of course. She couldn't help that her voice was sweet and soft and so sexy that she could make reading from the phone book sound like an invitation to bed.

Jared had put off returning to Colorado as long as he possibly could, relying on Greg to get the business off to a good start. But he needed to be in Grand Springs himself. He'd never before let a new branch of his company go without his personal attention for such a long time. And Greg was beginning to ask questions. Questions Jared couldn't answer. Hell, what was he supposed to say? I'm scared to come back to Grand Springs because I had sex with my secretary when we were trapped in the elevator and I can't get her out of my system? He'd never forget that Monday morning after they'd made love in the elevator.

Seeing Paige again was a surprise. Finding out she was his new secretary was a shock. He supposed he should have fired her on the spot. But that would have been unfair to Paige. He felt relieved when she agreed to remain in his employ.

"Then you'll stay on here at Montgomery Real Estate and Land Development?" he asked.

"Yes, I'll stay."

"Then we have a deal, Ms. Summers. We're going to pretend Friday night never happened." He held out his hand. "And you're going to stay on as my secretary."

Jared clasped her small soft hand. He wanted this woman. Wanted her badly. And wanted her now. Thank God he wouldn't be in Colorado long. If he knew what was good for him, he'd leave that day. The last thing he wanted was to get involved with some secretary who had stars in her eyes and the wedding march playing in her head. Paige Summers might be the most gorgeous, tempting female he'd ever run across, but she was not the type of woman he planned to marry. He certainly wasn't going to allow his attraction to her ruin all his plans.

He wished she wasn't so damned gorgeous. All round, voluptuous curves, big brown eyes and glorious red hair. Just looking at her aroused him. If he had any sense at all, he'd send her away.

Pulling her hand out of Jared's grasp, Paige smiled weakly. "I'd better go back outside to my desk."

"Good idea. I'm sure Greg and Ms. Thompson are wondering why I whisked you off in here so quickly."

"If Kay…that is, if Ms. Thompson asks, what can I tell her?"

"Tell her that my plans have changed and I'm going back to Texas today, so I needed to brief you on your duties immediately."

"But you haven't," Paige said.

"Haven't what?" He stared at her quizzically.

"You haven't briefed me on my duties."

"No, I haven't." Damn! If he didn't straighten up his act, Paige would figure out what sort of effect she was having on him. Hell, if she took a good look at his crotch, she'd know. Just brief her as quickly as possible, he told himself, and get her out of your sight.

Within an hour, Jared had rearranged his entire weekly schedule and was en route to the airport. He knew that the sooner he got away from Paige Summers, the better. And he'd have to stay away long enough to forget her. Forget about her beautiful face and perfect body. Forget about her sweet lips and warm brown eyes. Forget about her whimpering little cries of pleasure when he thrust into her. Forget about the way he felt when she fell apart in his arms.

How long would it take? A month? Two? Longer? Heaven help him, he'd just have to stay away, no matter how long it took to work her out of his system.

Well, that had been four months ago, and Jared still wasn't a hundred percent sure he had worked Paige Summers out of his system. But whether he had or not, he was returning to Colorado. He had already stayed away too long.

He checked his Gucci watch. Another hour and his pilot would land the Montgomery jet in Grand Springs. He lifted his glass to his lips and took a sip of the half-Drambuie, half-Scotch drink. A rusty nail, as the mixture was called, had been Grandpa Monty's favorite, and the old man had served Jared his first on-the-rocks rusty nail when he'd been fourteen. That night had been a rite of passage in many ways for Jared. His grandfather had been quite a man, not as smooth or sophisticated as his father, the old man's only son, but smarter, tougher and filled with a passion for life few men possessed. The old man had made his millions in oil right after the First World War, but in his heart, he'd never been anything but a cowboy. Jared had cared for Grandpa Monty more than he'd ever cared about another living soul, and even now, fifteen years after Monty's death, Jared still missed him.

He wondered what the old man would think of Paige Summers. He already knew what his widowed mother would think of her. Joyce Montgomery shunned anyone she considered even remotely beneath her.

Of course, it didn't matter what anyone thought. He wasn't returning to Colorado to begin an affair with Paige. Quite the opposite. He was going to stay in Grand Springs as long as it took to get over his obsession with the girl. And that's all it was. An obsession. Once he saw her again, he'd probably realize that his memories of her were overblown fantasies. She couldn't possibly be as lovely as he remembered or her body as alluring. And the sex they'd shared had been just that—sex. He'd had good sex before. Often. His mind and body had played tricks on him, making him remember their lovemaking as something more than it was. It couldn't have been that earth-shattering.

When he arrived at his office, he intended to treat Ms. Summers as nothing more than an employee. If she had been fantasizing about their having a relationship, then she'd have to face reality. He was her boss. She was his secretary. If she harbored any illusions about the two of them, then he'd make it perfectly clear to her that they had no future together.

Two

Paige heard Jared's voice in the hallway. He was here. Her heart skipped a beat. Greg Addison laughed heartily. The door to Paige's office swung open and the two men entered, Kay Thompson following closely behind.

Paige's heart stopped for a split second as she rose from her chair, her gaze riveted to Jared. He was the very essence of a successful businessman, an aura of wealth and power surrounding him. He filled out the double-breasted jacket he wore to perfection, and the brown stripes in his broadcloth shirt matched the dark silk of his hair.

She stepped out from behind her desk and smiled. More than anything, she wanted to run into his arms. She'd been kidding herself if she thought she could see him again and not feel the same magic that had caused her to act so out of character four months ago. She was as drawn to him as metal to a magnet.

When Jared paused briefly at her side, Paige's smile widened. ''Welcome back to Grand Springs,'' she said, amazed that she'd been able to keep the nervous quiver out of her voice, when it was wreaking havoc in her stomach.

''Thank you, Ms. Summers. It's good to see you again.''

His gaze never quite settled on her face. Paige realized that he was looking somewhere over her left shoulder, at the wall behind her. Without another word or gesture of any kind, L. J. Montgomery proceeded to his office. When Kay followed the two men into Jared's office and closed the door behind them, Paige slumped down in her chair. Clenching her teeth tightly in an effort not to cry, not to overreact to Jared's cool, businesslike greeting, she closed her eyes and counted to ten. Counting had always been her mother's solution to problems. When they'd been children, Mama had given Bryant, Austen and her to the count of three to obey her command or else face the consequences. And whenever any of them lost their temper, Mama would caution them to always count to ten before throwing a tantrum.

Paige most certainly wasn't going to throw a tantrum. She wasn't the type. Never had been. But she was upset and hurt. Jared had treated her as if she were nothing more than an employee.

Well, silly, what did you expect? That he'd treat you like a lover—a lover he'd been unable to forget, as you've been unable to forget him? He told you that he thought it best if you both pretended your night of passion hadn't happened. Obviously he's been able to do just that. Forget it.

But how could he have forgotten, when, for her, the experience had been so unforgettable?

How on earth was she going to continue working for him, day after day, growing bigger and bigger with his child, and act as if he meant nothing more to her than an employer? Dear God, Paige prayed, how would she ever explain her pregnancy? She didn't want to lie to him. But he might give her no other choice.

"Ms. Thompson, please ask Ms. Summers to gather up all the facts and figures on the Rocky Springs Ranch development and bring them in to me in about ten minutes," Jared said.

"Yes, sir." Her brilliant smile dazzled the two men

watching her. "And may I say, we're very pleased that you'll be in Grand Springs for a while."

"Thank you, Ms. Thompson, or may I call you Kay?" Jared thought the lovely divorcée was not only a shrewd businesswoman but a charming addition to the Montgomery Real Estate and Land Development staff. He didn't doubt for a minute that, with Kay's years of experience and real estate savvy, he'd be putting her in charge of one of his many branch offices someday soon.

"Yes, please call me Kay."

"Good, but only if you'll call me L.J., as all my associates do."

"All right, L.J."

The moment Kay exited the office, Greg slapped Jared on the back and chuckled. "Are you considering breaking your cardinal rule about not dating your employees?"

Jared snapped his head around. "What?"

"Kay Thompson is a striking woman, isn't she?"

"Yes, she is." Rounding his desk, Jared twisted the lever on the miniblinds covering the huge window and exposed the view from the top of the Wellman Building. "I'm surprised you haven't made a move on her."

"I have, but she declined the offer," Greg said. "She told me that she went through an unpleasant divorce not long ago and she's not quite ready for the dating scene again. But she might change her mind if the big boss asked."

"I don't intend to ask. I'm not going to break my rule for anyone, not even the charming Ms. Thompson." Jared could have added that if he broke the rule for anyone, it would be for Paige Summers, not Kay Thompson. But no one knew about the evening he'd spent with Paige, trapped in the elevator. No one except Paige and him. And that's the way he wanted it. That little incident had created

enough problems in his life without other people knowing
and spreading gossip around the office.

"I don't know how you do it." Greg shook his head.
"You're surrounded by attractive women in every branch
office and yet you're able to resist temptation. I'm afraid
I don't have your willpower."

"Yes, I know." Jared grinned. "That's why you have
a reputation for being the company Lothario. Besides,
there are more than enough beautiful ladies who don't
work for me from which to choose."

"Yeah, you're right," Greg agreed. "But how any man
could resist your secretary is beyond me. Our Ms. Summers is one hot little number, don't you think?"

Jared pivoted sharply, his green eyes boring into Greg.
"What do you mean by that!"

"Whoa! Have I hit a nerve?"

"Explain what you meant by your remark about Ms.
Summers." Had Greg come on to Paige? Had she succumbed to his charm? Had the two of them made love?
Jared hated the unaccustomed feeling of jealousy that suddenly raged inside him.

"Isn't it obvious? I mean, just look at her. She's young,
beautiful and build like a brick—"

"Shut up!" Jared slammed one big fist down on top of
his desk. The force of his blow shifted the telephone and
several items neatly arranged on the smooth oak surface.

"Well, well." Greg rubbed his chin, mocking a medi-
tative gesture.

"I'm surprised your shenanigans haven't gained us a
sexual harassment suit before now." Glowering at Greg,
Jared knotted his hands into tight fists. If Greg had touched
Paige, he'd kill him!

"What's got you so riled up, old buddy? You know
damn well that I never cross the line. Besides, if you'd

just told me that you'd already staked a claim on Paige Summers, I wouldn't have asked her out.''

"You're dating Paige…that is, Ms. Summers?"

"No, but not for lack of trying," Greg admitted. "After the fifth try, I gave up. I had to accept the fact that the lady isn't interested."

"Then she has a boyfriend," Jared said, uncertain whether or not he wanted to believe his statement.

"Well, when I asked if there was someone else, she said that there was."

"I see."

"Do you want to tell me what's going on?" Greg asked.

"There's nothing going on. I just don't want you pestering my secretary. From now on, stay away from her and don't make any more remarks about her…er…physical attributes."

Jared realized, too late, that his reaction to Greg's comment about Paige had been a mistake. Greg was no fool. He knew how uncharacteristic it was for Jared to lash out at him over a woman—any woman. In the past, their common code had been *live and let live*.

"I don't think I've ever seen you so…possessive." Greg stared at his boss, as if seeing him for the first time. "What I can't figure out is why. You've only seen the woman twice. The first day she came to work here and again a few minutes ago. Come on, old pal of mine, fess up. What's going on with you and Paige?"

"Nothing. Absolutely nothing." Greg wasn't buying it, but Jared could hardly tell him the truth. "After I finish with Ms. Summers, we'll need to discuss the particulars of the Rocky Springs Ranch deal. Until then, go get some work done and leave me the hell alone."

Holding up both hands in an "I surrender" pose, Greg whooshed out a breath and backed toward the door. "I'll tell Ms. Summers you're ready for her." Greg grinned, but before Jared could respond, he jerked open the door and exited quickly.

Willing himself into an uncertain calm, Jared stood and waited for Paige to enter his office. A moment later, carrying a stuffed file folder, she appeared in the doorway.

"Are you ready for these now, Mr. Montgomery?" she asked.

He'd been a fool to think that seeing Paige again would break the spell she'd cast over him. In person, she was even lovelier than he remembered. Her dark red hair shimmered with a healthy burgundy glow. Her creamy skin beckoned for his touch. She lifted her eyes and looked directly at him. He'd never forget those huge brown eyes gazing at him with such passionate longing four months ago. But not now. Not today. Her look was cool, distant and wary.

"Yes, please, come in, Ms. Summers." If he acted purely on instinct, he'd reach out and grab her, pull her into his arms and kiss her senseless. Then he'd take her, here, on his desk.

She laid the folder on his desk instead of handing it to him, obviously not wanting to risk their touching. "I think you'll find everything you need in there."

What I need is you, Paige. Naked, lying beneath me and sighing my name as I give you pleasure. You're what I've needed for the past four months. Every day. Every night.

"I'm sure the file is complete," he said. "Mr. Addison tells me that your work here is exemplary. I hope you've found working for Montgomery's challenging and satisfying."

"Yes, I have."

"We reward good work. Performance like yours deserves an increase in salary." The moment the words were out, Jared wished them back. God, how would she interpret what he'd said? Would she think he was referring to their one-night stand instead of her excellent work record?

"I—I... Thank you."

"I understand that Greg...Mr. Addison, has asked you out several times." Jared took a deep breath and swallowed hard. "I want to assure you that he won't bother you again. One thing we pride ourselves on at Montgomery's is a sexual-harassment-free workplace for our employees."

"I understand, and I'm sure all your employees are grateful. But Mr. Addison didn't offend me in any way. He was a perfect gentleman every time he asked me for a date."

Unlike you. Jared heard the words she left unsaid. Greg had always acted like a perfect gentleman, whereas he, on the other hand, had acted like a barbarian. He—a stranger—had taken her, passionately, standing up, in a stalled elevator. And afterward, told her to forget it had ever happened. No doubt Ms. Summers didn't think much of him. And he couldn't blame her. He didn't think much of himself and his actions that Friday evening four months ago.

"I'm glad to know that Greg didn't offend you." Jared picked up the folder, sat down behind his desk and opened the file.. "I want you to be happy here, Ms. Summers. If you ever have a problem of any kind, I want you to come to me. Is that understood?"

"Yes, sir."

"Good."

For the next twenty minutes, Jared went through the motions, putting on his best Big Boss facade. He'd been fooling himself to think getting Paige out of his system would take nothing more than seeing her again. If anything, being around her again made him want her all the more. Hell, if she wasn't his employee and if she wasn't so damned young and sweet, he'd rush her into a torrid affair and let the fire between them burn itself out. But as things stood, he would have to take an alternative route.

Jared decided he'd have to suffer through more withdrawal symptoms and try to find solace in the arms of another woman. Maybe tonight. He sure as hell hoped so. He couldn't go around the office every day blatantly aroused. That was something he couldn't pretend didn't exist.

"Have you got things wrapped up?" Kay asked as she stopped by Paige's desk.

"Just about. Give me another five minutes. Mr. Montgomery is trying to make up for lost time today." Paige didn't admit to Kay that her inability to finish up on time had more to do with her frame of mind than with Jared's workload.

"I know why I don't have a dinner date tonight and am going out with a female friend," Kay said. "But why aren't you dating someone?"

"I—I...uh...there's someone. I mean, there was someone and I'm not quite over him."

"Oh, brother, do I know how that is. As bad as my marriage was, I sometimes find myself thinking about that bastard I stayed with for five years. I loved him so much when we first got married."

"I always thought love—real love—was meant to last a lifetime, even forever."

"Yeah, well, so did I. But when love is one-sided, it can't last. My ex-husband loved me, I suppose. In his own way. The only problem was that he loved half a dozen other women just as much."

"Oh, Kay, I'm so sorry. You've never said before what happened."

"And you were too nice to ask."

"My college boyfriend left me for someone else, too," Paige said. "I guess I should have known it would happen. The whole time we were dating, he kept trying to change me. He hated that I was so emotional and naive. He wanted me to be someone I wasn't. If he had truly loved me, he would have accepted me for who I was."

The outer office door opened and a tall blonde sailed in, swaying her slender hips and smiling warmly at Kay and Paige. The woman was beautiful. She was dressed in the height of fashion, and diamonds and gold accented her ears, fingers and wrists.

"May I help you?" Paige asked.

"Are you Jared's secretary?"

"Yes, I am."

"Then you can help me. Please tell him I'm here." She held out her hand to Paige. "Marcy Dailey. Jared asked me to meet him here."

"Paige Summers." Still seated behind her desk, she lifted her hand and exchanged a cordial greeting with Ms. Dailey. Returning the woman's smile, Paige wondered just who Marcy Dailey was.

"Oh, you're Mr. Montgomery's interior decorator, aren't you? I'm Kay Thompson. You picked up the keys to Mr. Montgomery's house from me a couple of months ago."

"Oh, yes, Ms. Thompson. I remember you."

"I thought you'd finished the decorating job," Kay said.

"I did. I'm not here on business. Jared called earlier today and asked if I was free for dinner tonight."

Paige felt as if someone had hit her in the stomach. His first night back in Grand Springs and he already had a date. With another woman! And not only was the other woman beautiful, she was nice, dammit!

"I'll tell Mr. Montgomery that you're here," Paige said. You are not going to let this upset you, she told herself.

What difference does it make? She already knew that she didn't mean a thing to Jared, that he'd put their night together behind him. As far as he was concerned, it hadn't happened. But it did happen, she wanted to scream. And *I have the living proof growing inside me.*

Before Paige had a chance to inform Jared that his dinner date had arrived, he opened his office door and stuck his head out. "Ms. Summers, could you— Oh, Marcy, hello." He glanced down at his watch. "I'm sorry. I didn't realize it was so late. Give me a minute and I'll be right with you."

"Is there something you need?" Paige asked.

Yes, Jared thought. *I need for you to stop looking at me with those sexy brown eyes of yours. I need to get you out of my mind. I need to regain my equilibrium and put my life back on track.* "No, Ms. Summers. It can wait until tomorrow."

He rushed back into his office and reemerged after putting on his jacket and straightening his tie. Without giving either employee another glance, Jared said, "Good night. See you both in the morning." He took Ms. Dailey by the arm and escorted her out of the office.

Paige jumped up from her desk and ran toward the bathroom. She thought her bouts with morning sickness had ended weeks ago, but she made it to the rest room just in time. She lifted the commode seat, bent over and vomited.

Kay rushed in behind her, wet a paper towel and handed it to Paige. "You haven't had one of these episodes in weeks. Are you all right?"

Paige had thought she'd hidden her morning sickness quite well and had been unaware that Kay suspected anything. Her friend had never mentioned it.

"Thanks, Kay." Paige flushed the commode, then accepted the damp towel and wiped her face with it. "I'm all right now. It's been a trying day. I think the stress of having Mr. Montgomery here in the office just got to me.''

''Stress over L.J.'s presence might have triggered this little bout of nausea, but it doesn't explain the weeks of morning sickness you've been experiencing.''

''Morning sickness? I don't know—''

''I was pregnant once,'' Kay said. ''I was sick for four and a half months. I miscarried the baby. Lucky for all of us, I guess, since my marriage didn't last.''

''Kay, I'm so sorry.''

''Hey, my problems are in the past. What about yours? You're obviously pregnant and unmarried.''

''Do you think anyone else here at Montgomery's suspects?''

''No one suspects a thing. Believe me. I hear all the gossip that goes on not only at Montgomery's but in the entire Wellman building.''

''Kay, I'd rather you didn't mention this to anyone. I know that, sooner or later, my condition will become apparent, but until then—''

''I won't tell a soul.'' Kay wrapped her arm around Paige's shoulders. ''Are you and the father going to get married?''

''No.''

''Is he already married?''

Paige gasped. ''No, of course he's not married.''

''Then what's the problem? Is it that he doesn't want to marry you or don't you want to marry him?''

''He doesn't know about the baby.''

''What? Why haven't you told him?''

Paige closed the commode seat and slumped down, sitting before her trembling legs gave way. ''You and I have become friends these last four months and I trust you, but—''

''Don't tell me anything you don't want me to know.''

"I've told my parents. My mother is the Rock of Gibraltar. My father has murder in his heart." Paige laughed shakily. "They've promised to stand by me and help me get through the pregnancy. My mother's agreed to take care of the baby until he or she is old enough for play school. And with my salary and good insurance, I should be able to get by just fine."

"Why haven't you told the father?"

"Because…" Paige hesitated, wondering just how much she dared tell Kay. "I've had only one other lover. The college boyfriend I told you about, and we'd planned to get married. Things didn't work out after he got a job in L.A. and met the girl of his dreams—the boss's daughter. There hadn't been anyone else since Kevin. Not until four months ago."

"So, four months ago you started a new relationship and accidently got pregnant."

"I didn't start a new relationship," Paige said. "I did something unthinkable. At least, it was unthinkable for someone like me."

"What did you do?"

"I had a one-night stand with a stranger."

"Oh, my God, Paige, you didn't!"

"I'm afraid I did. We got trapped in the elevator that Friday night in June that Grand Springs lost its power."

"You had sex with a perfect stranger in a stalled elevator?"

"Uh-huh." Paige nodded her head.

"Then you have no idea who he is, the man who fathered your child? You never saw him again?"

"I saw him again. The following Monday morning."

"The day you started work at Montgomery's?"

"Yes."

"He works here in the Wellman Building?" Kay asked.

"Yes."

"For heaven's sake, Paige, who is he?"

Paige hesitated a moment. "L. J. Montgomery."

For once in her life, Kay Thompson was utterly speech-less.

Three

Paige was thankful that Jared had left the office for an early lunch and had told her not to expect him back until after two, if then. Despite his totally professional attitude toward her the entire morning of his second day back in Grand Springs, he had seemed nervous and edgy. And once or twice, when he'd thought she wasn't looking, she'd caught him staring at her. Smiling, she had returned his stare, giving him an opportunity to say something—anything—personal. But all he'd done was clear his throat and look away. If he'd wanted to say something to her, why hadn't he? Maybe her wishful thinking had made her imagine the longing in his eyes, or perhaps it had just been a reflection of the longing in her own heart.

How was she going to work alongside Jared day after day, see him walk out of his office with his dinner dates time and again, and then have to order morning-after roses for those women, as she'd had to do today for Marcy Dailey?

"Eating in today?" Kay asked as she entered the employees' lounge.

"Yes, I brought a microwave meal." Paige pointed to the low-fat, low-calorie pasta dish she'd just warmed.

Kay tossed a brown paper bag on the table, pulled out a chair and sat down. "I brought tuna with fat-free mayo on whole wheat and bottled water. I'm watching my figure. What's your excuse for eating that stuff?"

"I'm watching my weight, too," Paige said. "I'm only

five-five and I've gained three pounds more than I should have. Dr. Petrocelli says that since I'm already well-rounded—'' Paige rolled her eyes and sighed ''—I need to watch my weight or I could easily balloon into an elephant by the time the baby arrives.''

"Speaking of Baby Montgomery, have you given any more thought to what we talked about last night?'' Kay unscrewed the lid from her bottled water.

"Shh!'' Paige glared at Kay. "Anyone could overhear you. No one knows I'm pregnant, and I certainly don't want anyone suspecting that Jared is the father.''

"You do realize that sooner or later, you're going to have to tell him.''

"He may not believe the baby's his.'' Paige lowered her voice to a whisper. "He has no reason to believe me. He'll probably think that I'm just trying to trap him because he's rich.''

"Anyone who knows you, knows you aren't the type.'' Kay unwrapped her sandwich.

"That's just the problem. Jared doesn't know me. Except as his employee. He doesn't have a clue as to who I am as a person.''

"Then we'll have to figure out a way for him to get to know you. And we don't have any time to lose. You're going to have to tell him the truth before you start showing.''

"I think it might be better all the way around if, when it becomes necessary, I tell him he isn't the father. That it's my boyfriend's baby.''

"What boyfriend?'' Kay took a hefty bite out of her sandwich.

"The imaginary one who fathered my child.''

Kay chewed and swallowed, then washed the food down with water. "What if Jared wants to meet your boyfriend? What will you do then?''

"I'll cross that bridge when I come to it. My main concern is keeping this job. I need my insurance, and once I have a child to support, I'll need my weekly paycheck more than ever."

"You'll never be able to look the man straight in the eye and lie to him," Kay said. "You're far too honest. Besides, even if by some miracle you pull this off, what will you do when one day L.J. gets a real good look at your kid and notices that it's a carbon copy of him?"

"I can't worry about the future. At least not the distant future. I have to concentrate on the present and on the immediate future, and how I'm going to explain to everyone that I'm four months pregnant and not married."

Jared had left the office an hour ago with no intention of returning today. Spending an entire morning around Paige had been more difficult than he'd ever imagined. He realized now that getting her out of his system was going to be more difficult than giving up cigarettes. He'd quit smoking seven years ago, but he'd be damned if he didn't still miss the old habit.

During his burger-and-fries lunch at The Saloon, a local bar and grill, he had decided that avoiding Paige was the act of a coward. He'd stayed away from her for four months, running from his feelings. Now, dammit, he'd returned to Grand Springs to face those feelings head-on...and conquer them.

Entering Paige's office, Jared found it empty. She had probably gone out for lunch. Fine. He'd grab a cup of coffee in the employees' lounge and get busy on some phone calls he needed to make.

As he neared the lounge, he heard two female voices and immediately recognized them. Paige and Kay.

"...How I'm going to explain to everyone that I'm four months pregnant and not married," Paige said.

Jared stopped dead in his tracks directly outside the half-closed lounge door. It couldn't be! Surely he'd misunderstood what Paige had said. She couldn't be pregnant. She couldn't be!

"Look, I think all your worries would be over if you'd just tell him he's going to be a father," Kay said. "I'll bet money that he'll want to marry you. Something tells me that he's the old-fashioned, possessive kind."

"I don't want him to marry me because of the baby! What kind of marriage would that be for either of us? When a man asks me to marry him, I want it to be because he loves me and for no other reason."

"I understand how you feel, but maybe you should have given that some thought before you had unprotected sex and got yourself pregnant."

Unprotected sex! Good God Almighty! Jared eased backward several steps, then turned and bolted down the hallway, toward the elevators. He wasn't thinking, only reacting, like a hunted animal trying to escape. Escape from what he'd overheard. Escape from Paige. Escape from the possibility that he could be the father of her baby.

Jared wound up back at The Saloon, where he ordered a rusty nail on the rocks, drank it too quickly and cursed a sudden headache. Then he ordered another and wisely sat there nursing the drink.

Paige Summers was pregnant. Four months pregnant. It didn't take a rocket scientist to figure out that the child was probably his. Although he didn't really know Paige, somehow she didn't seem the promiscuous type. As a matter of fact, even though she'd been as hot and wild for him as he'd been for her that evening in the elevator, there had been something almost innocent about the way she had reacted to his lovemaking. As if she had never experienced desire that powerful or pleasure that intense.

But on the other hand, it was possible that there was

another man. Someone before him or after him. He couldn't be one hundred percent sure the child was his.

"Dammit," he muttered under his breath. "You know that baby's yours." He ran a shaky hand through his neatly styled hair. "How the hell did you get yourself into this kind of situation?"

You know how, his inner voice responded. Because you got so hot and bothered over a tempting piece of— No, Paige was not just another easy conquest. He had desired women before but never lost his head so completely that he forgot to use a condom.

Jared had never wanted a woman the way he'd wanted Paige, and heaven help him, he still wanted her. But she was the wrong woman for him. She didn't fit into his plans. She was attractive and sweet and intelligent, but she was hardly the kind of wife who could step into his life and be an asset as his life's partner.

But she was carrying his child. His child! He had no choice. He'd have to do the honorable thing. The marriage would be doomed from the start, of course, since it would be based on neither the love she wanted from a husband nor the suitability he desired in a wife. But even a marriage of short duration would give Paige and their child his name and protection. And it would give him the opportunity to get to know Paige, see her up close, flaws and all. Marriage to her was probably a surefire way to get her out of his system once and for all.

Before he made any definite plans, he'd have to talk to Paige and ask her point-blank if the child was his. His gut instincts told him that she wouldn't lie to him. After all, a simple DNA test after the baby was born would verify the child's paternity.

A nagging little thought persisted in repeating itself over and over in Jared's head. What if Paige, sweet and innocent as she seemed, had known all along who he was?

What if she had set out to trap L. J. Montgomery's millions?

He couldn't confront her at the office with all his questions. They needed privacy. He'd wait and go to her apartment this evening, and if she told him he was the father of her child, he'd tell her all her worries were over. He would do the honorable thing and marry her. She would become Mrs. L. J. Montgomery and be the envy of every woman in the Southwest. But before they said 'I do,' he'd make sure Paige signed a rock-solid prenuptial agreement that would protect all his financial assets.

Paige changed out of her blue knit suit and silk blouse and into a pair of much-washed, comfortable purple sweats. She ate a green salad with low-cal ranch dressing and devoured a small bunch of grapes. Her appetite had increased, not diminished, even with the bouts of morning sickness she'd suffered for weeks on end. Her doctor was right, she was going to have to watch her weight. All she had to do was look at her plump, middle-aged mother to know exactly what she'd look like in thirty years.

She put on four of her favorite CDs—Air Supply, Yanni Live at the Acropolis, Kenny G, and the Tchaikovsky selections of the Vienna Master series. She had eclectic tastes, was a connoisseur of music as a whole and not a slave to any specific type.

Then she sat down at the small worktable in the corner of her living room and picked up the Lucy Peck doll she had been working on the past few weeks. All that was needed to put the finishing touches on the blue-eyed towhead was to dress her in her 1902 frock.

Paige ran a loving hand over the doll's wax head and mohair-stuffed body. This little lady wasn't quite museum-piece quality, but there were collectors who'd more than compensate Paige for her time and restoration efforts. Just as she ran her finger across the 131 Regent St. address stamped across the doll's tummy, the doorbell rang.

Who on earth? Her mother, probably, Paige decided. Always a mother hen, brooding over her chicks, Paige's mama had become entirely too overprotective since Paige had told her she was pregnant. And Paige hadn't called her mother today. She'd been so busy, she'd forgotten.

Not bothering to slip into her shoes, she padded across the wooden floor in her sock feet. Taking the proper precaution, she glanced through the peephole. Gasping, she stepped backward, away from the door. Jared! What was he doing here? At her apartment?

Leaving the safety latch in place, she cracked the door and peered out at him. "Hello, Mr. Montgomery. What can I do for you?"

"You can open the door and let me in," he said. "Or would you prefer we discuss our personal life while I'm standing out here in the hall?"

Our personal life? What was he talking about? She unlatched the safety and opened the door, but blocked his entrance with her body.

"*We* don't have a personal life, Mr. Montgomery. Not together, anyway. You're my boss. I'm your secretary. Anything we need to discuss, we can discuss at the office. Tomorrow."

"That's where you're wrong, Paige." He put special emphasis on pronouncing her name. "We need to discuss an event that occurred four months ago in an elevator."

Grabbing his arm, Paige dragged him into her apartment, then slammed the door. "I thought we agreed to pretend that didn't happen."

"That was before I realized there might have been some consequences to the incident that would make it impossible for either of us to pretend it didn't happen."

Jared glanced around her small living room, quickly noting how homey it was. Typical middle-class style, with stuffed pillows lining the floral sofa, a half-dozen plants dotting the tables and bookshelves, and an inexpensive CD player, VCR and nineteen-inch TV crammed into an imitation wood entertainment center.

"I'm afraid I have no idea what you're talking about." Dear Lord, surely Kay hadn't gone to Jared and told him about her pregnancy, Paige wondered. No, of course not. Kay wouldn't do such a thing. Besides, Jared hadn't come back to the office all afternoon, so Kay would hardly have had the opportunity to tell him anything.

Jared surveyed her from head to toe, then smiled. Even in a pair of baggy sweatpants and loose-fitting top, Paige was a knockout. Soft, feminine and so very tempting. He liked her hair the way she was wearing it pulled back in a loose ponytail, the thick mane falling down her back like a cinnamon waterfall. His hand itched to grab a handful of that silky mass and drag her toward him, just enough to devour her pouty pink lips.

"Could we sit down?" he asked.

She glared at him, her lips indeed pouting. "Yes, of course. Please, come in, Mr. Montgomery, and have a seat."

"Thanks." He walked over, sat down on the sofa and crossed his legs, acting for all intents and purposes as if he were settling in for quite a stay. "And stop calling me Mr. Montgomery. My name is Jared."

"I know perfectly well what your name is, Mr. Montgomery." She sat in an armchair, separated from the sofa by a Duncan Phyfe coffee table that had belonged to her grandmother. "You and I agreed that it was best for both of us if we kept our relationship strictly business. I'm sure you haven't come here to tell me you've changed your mind."

"That depends." Jared slipped his hands into the side

pockets of his gray wool slacks. His unbuttoned navy jacket fell open, revealing an expanse of white shirt and red silk tie.

"It depends on what?" she asked, scooting to the edge of the chair.

"On whether or not the child you're carrying is mine." He made the statement as calmly as if he'd said the sky is blue.

Paige's face paled. Her eyes widened into huge brown globes. She opened her mouth on a silent gasp. He knew! He knew she was pregnant. But how? No one knew except her parents and Kay.

"How do you know I'm pregnant?" she asked.

"I came back to the office while you and Kay were having lunch in the employees' lounge." He watched Paige closely, keeping his gaze riveted to her face, duly noting her worried expression. "I overheard a couple of sentences of your conversation. Enough to learn that you're four months pregnant and that Kay thinks you should tell the father."

"You were eavesdropping. You had no business listening to our private conversation."

"If the child is mine, then your conversation was very much my business."

"What makes you think the child is yours?" Slipping the fingers of both hands together, Paige repeatedly rubbed her right thumb across her left palm.

"Don't play games with me, honey." Removing his hands from his pockets, he balled them into tight fists and leaned forward. "You're four months pregnant, and we had sex four months ago. Unprotected sex." He rested his fists on top of his knees.

Ever since the moment the doctor had confirmed her pregnancy, Paige had wondered just what she'd say to Jared at this precise moment. She had played through several different scenarios in her mind, but knew it all boiled down to one very important fact. Jared deserved to know the truth. She counted slowly to ten.

"I am four months pregnant," she said. "And you're the only man I've had sex with in the past three years."

"Then there's no question that the child is mine."

"No question at all. You're my baby's father."

"I see."

"Not what you wanted to hear, was it? I'm sorry." She sucked in her cheeks, then breathed deeply. "I did consider inventing an imaginary *other man* and telling you he was the father, but I thought you deserved to know the truth. And so does my child."

"You're right," he said. "I'm glad you didn't try to lie to me."

"Look, I don't blame you for the situation. I blame myself. I'm a big girl who should have known better. All I ask of you is to allow me to continue working at Montgomery's. The insurance will take care of most of my doctor and hospital bills, and I can get by just fine on my salary."

"You don't expect me to take care of all your maternity bills? You don't want some sort of settlement or some form of child support?"

"No. No, I don't want or expect anything from you," she assured him. "But I would like to keep my job, at least until after the baby is born. So the insurance will cover everything. Then you can give me a good reference and I can find another job."

Was Paige for real? Jared wondered. Or was this some sort of game she was playing? Had his fears that she'd deliberately trapped him been groundless? Or was she just a very good actress?

"Are you saying that you don't plan to tell anyone I'm the father?"

"No, of course not. But someday, I do plan to tell my child about you."

Jared shot up off the sofa like a cannon blast. "Dammit!" Tightening and loosening his fists repeatedly, he glared at Paige, who sat ramrod straight on the edge of the big easy chair. He didn't know what to think, didn't know if he dared to take Paige at her word. Past experience had taught him not to trust anyone. Would he be a fool to trust Paige Summers? "I could use a drink."

"Oh. Yes. I suppose you could." Paige nodded, then quickly stood up and rushed into the kitchen. "I'm afraid all I have is some white wine. Will that do?"

"Nothing stronger?" He needed a good stiff belt of something at least a hundred proof.

"No, I'm afraid— Oh, wait a minute," she called out from the kitchen. "I may have some whisky left over from last winter, when Mama brought a bottle over and fixed me a honey-and-whisky toddy. I had a horrible cold."

She opened doors and slammed them shut, searching for the whisky. Finally she saw it on a top shelf, far out of her reach. "I found it," she told him. "It'll take me a minute. I'll have to get a chair to reach it."

She pulled a chair from the table, pushed it over to the counter and climbed up on the seat. Just as she reached out for the whisky bottle, Jared stormed into the kitchen and grabbed her around the waist. She plucked the nearly full bottle of Johnny Walker off the shelf seconds before Jared lifted her into his arms.

"What are you doing?" She stared at him, breathless and flushed, her heart beating ninety to nothing.

"You shouldn't be climbing up on chairs. You could fall and hurt yourself. Hurt the baby."

"Oh."

She clung to the whisky bottle as if it were a golden

prize, all the while staring at him with hungry eyes that reflected his own deep, devouring need.

"Paige?" He wanted to carry her to bed and make slow, sweet love to her all night long, if only she'd let him.

"Please, put me down, Jared, and I'll pour you a drink."

He didn't want to put her down, but he did. Easing his hand across the back of her legs, he slid her over the front of his body, slowly, intimately, allowing her to feel his arousal.

"Every time I get near you, honey, I get hard." He took the whisky bottle from her with one hand while he gripped the back of her neck with the other. "But you know that, don't you?"

She stared him straight in the eye, unflinching. Her chest rose and fell rapidly with the force of her accelerated breathing. "Please, don't do this to me. Don't take advantage of the way you make me feel."

"How do I make you feel?" He brushed her lips with his and smiled when she gasped. "All hot and damp and needy?"

She squirmed, trying to free herself from his hold. He set the whisky bottle down on the table behind him and clutched her hip, drawing her even closer against his body.

"What do you want me to say?" She looked at him, a fine mist of unshed tears in her eyes. "You make me want you. Want you enough to ignore my common sense. I did that once, the first time we met, and look what happened."

"Yeah, honey, I guess you're right." He loosened his hold around her neck but didn't release her. Lowering his head, he nuzzled her throat and breathed in her sweet, flowery, feminine scent. The purely male instinct part of him wanted to tell her that the damage had already been done, so what would be the harm of giving in to their desire now? But the sane, sensible part of his brain warned him that Paige wouldn't see it quite that way.

Raising his head, he stared into her moist eyes and smiled sadly, then tenderly caressed her cheek. He released his hold on her and took a step backward, away from temptation. Paige sighed deeply but didn't move.

"I could use that drink now, honey," he said.

"Certainly." Turning around, she opened a cupboard door, retrieved two small juice glasses and handed them to him. "I could use a drink myself."

Jared placed the glasses on the round wooden table, then opened the whisky bottle, poured his glass half full and gulped down a large swallow. He blew out a breath as the liquor burned a trail down his throat and landed like a ton of hot bricks in his belly. "Want me to fix one for you?" Glancing around, he noticed her opening the refrigerator door. "Good idea. Get some ice. We'll have our drinks on the rocks."

Turning to face him, Paige held a milk carton in her hand. "I'm pregnant. Remember? I'm not supposed to have any liquor. This—" she hoisted the carton of skim milk in the air "—is my drink of choice for the next few months."

"Pregnant women can't drink liquor, huh?" He shook his head as if sympathizing with her. "Bad for you?"

"Bad for the baby." Paige set the carton on the table, then opened the freezer compartment in her refrigerator and lifted out a small plastic container filled with ice cubes. "Here's your ice."

Reaching across the table, Jared grabbed the bowl, transferred a couple of ice cubes into his glass and placed the bowl on the table. He filled the glass to the rim with the Johnny Walker, then pulled out a chair and sat down.

"Sit down, Paige. We need to talk."

She hesitated for a split second, then nodded agreement and sat. Jared sipped on his drink, all the while watching Paige, waiting for her to say something. She didn't say a word, just poured herself a glass of milk and drank it very slowly.

"So, all you want is to keep your job?" Jared asked. Some men would be grateful to think that they could get off so easily. Some men could walk away from a situation like this and never look back. Some men could forget a one-night stand with a stranger. Some men could deny their own child and not give a damn. Some men. But not Lawrence Jared Montgomery!

What sort of heartless bastard did she think he was? He might not like the idea of having to marry her and take on the responsibility of a child he hadn't planned to father, but he wasn't the type of man who could walk away and never look back. He was responsible for getting her pregnant. If he had been thinking with his head instead of his— But that had been the problem; he hadn't been thinking at all. Regardless of the circumstances of the baby's conception, the child was his. His, dammit, and no child of his was going to come into this world illegitimate.

"I've already told you what I want," she said, then finished off her glass of milk and poured herself another. "Maybe it's time for you to tell me what you want."

"I want to marry you." He emptied his glass and refilled it quickly, adding more ice cubes.

The music from the CD player permeated the uneasy silence. An ice cube in Jared's glass cracked. Paige wiped her mouth with her index finger and thumb, then crossed her arms over her waist and stared at him.

"Why?" she asked.

"Because you're pregnant with my child."

Sweet, warm relief spread through Paige's stomach. She sighed. He wanted to do the right thing. She'd been so afraid he might not even believe the child was his, and now here he was offering her an almost perfect solution. Of course, he hadn't said anything about love. But he did want her. He'd made that perfectly clear. And love could grow out of need, couldn't it? If a man wanted a woman as much as Jared said he wanted her, then there was every chance that he might love her and just not know it yet.

"I don't know what to say," she told him. "I didn't expect this. I had no idea you'd want to marry me." Hoped you would. Prayed you would. Dreamed you would. But never thought you would.

Jared poured himself another drink. He didn't usually drink much, certainly not the quantity he'd consumed today. But then it wasn't every day that a man found out that he'd gotten a woman he barely knew pregnant, and he was going to be a father.

"Well, I can't think of a better solution," he said. "Of course, getting married now wasn't a part of my plan. But then getting you or anyone else pregnant right now wasn't a part of my five-year plan, either."

"Your five-year plan?"

"Yeah, I'm the kind of man who makes plans. I had my life all mapped out, until I met you."

"And I messed up your plan."

Jared nodded, then took another gulp of whisky. "If my calculations are correct, Montgomery Real Estate and Land Development will fulfill all my expectations within the next five years. That's when I had planned to find the perfect wife, get married and have a son."

She had enacted this scene once before. With Kevin. He had told her that he wanted her, even that he loved her, but she hadn't been quite what he needed in a wife. He had wanted to change her into his idea of the perfect woman, and for a while, she'd tried to be that woman. But in the end, he'd found his Ms. Perfect when he'd moved to L.A. and Paige had been left with a broken heart. And a determination never to try to remake herself into someone she wasn't. Not for anyone. "A perfect wife, huh? I guess I'm not quite what you had in mind, am I?"

"No, honey, I'm afraid you're not." Jared's speech was beginning to slur just a fraction. "You're beautiful. And you have the most fabulous body. And just looking at you drives me crazy."

He smiled at her. That damned killer smile that made her insides quiver. She didn't like the way this conversation was going, but she had no intention of putting an end to it. While he was teetering on the verge of drunkenness, he was more likely to be completely honest with her. And that's what she needed—honesty. Her future and the future of her child depended upon the decisions she made now. Without complete honesty between Jared and her, she might make the wrong decision and regret it the rest of her life.

He drained the last drops from his glass and reached for the bottle. "I'll bet you didn't know that in the last four months every time I heard your voice over the phone, I got hard." He leered at her, his gaze filled with lust. "You put the hoodoo on me, honey. I don't want anybody else but you."

She knew the feeling. She didn't want anyone else but him. Unfortunately, their wanting each other so desperately had gotten them into this situation. But only love could get them out of it, and Paige was afraid that for Jared, love didn't enter into the picture. Responsibility, duty, maybe even an old-fashioned sense of honor. But not love.

"Don't you think you've had enough?" She placed her hand over his where he held the whisky bottle.

"Too much, actually," he admitted, releasing his hold on the bottle. "We need to make new plans. Figure out all the details."

"We don't have to do that tonight," she said. "Tomorrow will be soon enough, when you're completely sober.''

''I'm not drunk, just a little fuzzy.'' He grinned, the corners of his mouth curving up in a lopsided, close-mouthed smile. ''Besides, I came here to get everything settled. Tonight.''

''It can wait another day.'' When she started to rise from her chair, he reached across the table and grabbed her wrist. Looking at him, she saw that his smile had vanished. He stared at her with a hard, uncompromising glare.

''Sit down, honey.''

She eased back down onto the chair. He released her wrist.

''I'm going to have to alter my plans to accommodate this accident.''

Accident! She wanted to scream but didn't. Instead she gritted her teeth and counted to ten.

''I guess we both know there's a good chance the marriage won't last, but for the sake of the child, I think we should get married as soon as possible,'' he said. ''Next week, unless you'd prefer to plan something more elaborate than a brief ceremony in the judge's chambers.'' He paused; she didn't respond, only stared at him. ''Whatever you want. Money is no object.''

''No, it wouldn't be with you, would it?''

He missed the sarcasm in her voice. ''Of course, I'll expect you to sign a prenuptial agreement, but while we're married, I'll buy you whatever your heart desires.''

Paige didn't doubt for a minute that Jared could buy her just about anything. But he couldn't buy her the one thing she wanted most. His love. And without his love, or at least the hope that he would grow to love her, she would never marry him.

''Signing a prenuptial would be no problem...if I agreed to marry you. Your money isn't what I want.''

"Good. Then that's settled, isn't it? We'll live in the new house I just bought up in the mountains toward Squaw Creek," he told her. "I'll even deed the house over to you as a little wedding present. And after the baby's born, I'll want us to move back to Texas. That's my home base. We can visit Grand Springs fairly often as I'll need to keep check on the branch office here."

"You've given this a lot of thought, haven't you."

"Yes, I have. Despite the fact that this baby of ours—" he looked meaningfully at her slightly rounded tummy "—wasn't a part of my plans, he's a reality neither of us can escape. I take full responsibility for my mistakes. This whole thing is my fault. If I'd used a condom—"

Paige jumped up, knocking over her chair in the process. "Why you arrogant, egotistical, macho jerk, I wouldn't marry you if you were the last man on earth!"

Leaving the chair overturned on the floor, she whirled around and stomped out of the kitchen. Jared sat there for several seconds, not quite sure what had hit him, then he realized that Paige was angry. Very angry. Very, very, very angry—with him!

Damn, what had he said that upset her so much? Hadn't he taken full responsibility for the mess they were in? Hadn't he told her that he'd marry her? Hadn't he promised to buy her whatever her little heart desired?

Scooting back his chair, Jared stood. The room spun around and around, then suddenly righted itself. Whoa, boy. You've had a little too much of the good stuff. It's dulled your senses. Maybe that's why she's upset. Could be she doesn't like a drinking man. But I'm not a drinking man, he told himself. Not usually. Just a rusty nail occasionally.

Steady on his feet, he made his way into the living room without any trouble. He couldn't be all that drunk. He wasn't staggering, but he certainly was in no shape to drive up the mountain tonight.

She sat on the sofa, her arms crossed over her chest and her feet tapping nervously against the wooden floor. She glared daggers at him. If looks could kill, he'd be a dead man.

"Paige?" He walked farther into the room. "Honey?"

"Leave me alone, Jared Montgomery!"

He maneuvered his way across the living room at a snail's pace, not wanting to say or do anything to set her off again. When he reached the sofa, he glanced down at her and smiled. Ignoring him, she tilted her chin and looked up at the ceiling. He sat down beside her; she scooted to the opposite end of the sofa.

"Whatever I said to offend you, I apologize," he said. "I didn't come here to upset you. I came here to tell you that I'd marry you. That I'd make everything all right."

Tears gathered in the corners of her eyes. She gritted her teeth and swallowed hard. "You can't make everything all right."

He slid across the sofa and put his arm around her stiff shoulders. "Of course I can. I'm L. J. Montgomery. I'm stinking rich. I can—"

"You're stinking, all right." She tried to shrug his arm off her shoulders. He gripped her upper arm. "How many drinks did you have before you came here tonight?"

"I don't remember," he said.

"Needed a little false courage?"

"All I need…all you need…to settle this whole affair and make things right is for us to get married."

"I can't marry you."

"Of course you can. You're going to have my baby. Who else would you marry?"

"We aren't going to settle this tonight, not with your

senses dulled by so much whisky. Go home. Sleep it off
and we'll talk tomorrow.''

"It's already settled,'' he told her. "You'll sign the prenuptial agreement and we'll get married next week.'' He
tried to stand but swayed on his feet, then slipped back
down on the sofa and rested his head on the cushioned
arm.

Paige tried to help him stand again, but he wouldn't
cooperate, and he was far too big for her to force him.
"Come on, Jared. Get up. I want you to leave."

"I can't."

"What do you mean, you can't?"

"I shouldn't drive in my condition."

Damn, he was right. She couldn't let him drive. "I'll
call a taxi and have the driver take you to a motel for the
night."

"Why can't I stay right here?" He lifted his feet up on
the sofa and bent his knees, curling up like a drowsy lion.

"Because I don't want you here." She grabbed his legs
and swung them off the sofa. He groaned but didn't open
his eyes. She punched him on the arm. "Get up, dammit.
Jared? You cannot stay here all night." He didn't respond.

She got up off the sofa, placed her hands on her hips
and stood over him, glaring. He stretched out his legs as
far as he could, rolled over onto his back and snorted. He
was asleep! Now what was she going to do? She'd have
to let him stay the night.

Resigned to the situation, she went into the hall, opened
the linen closet and removed a blanket and pillow. When
she returned to the living room, Jared was snoring. She
bent down on her knees in front of the sofa, lifted his head
and slipped a pillow under it. She removed his tie, laid it
on the coffee table, and then did the same with his shoes
and socks. After unbuttoning the first two buttons of his
shirt, she jerked her hand away. Despite everything that

was wrong between them, it was all she could do not to caress him, not to lean over and kiss him.

Damn him! Damn his arrogant, egotistical, macho hide! How dare he think she wanted his money! How dare he think he was doing her such a big favor by marrying her! Who the hell did he think he was, anyway? Oh, she knew who he was, all right. He was L. J. Montgomery. He had more money than God! What he didn't have was a heart. And a man without a heart couldn't love anyone. Not her. Not her baby.

Paige unfolded the blanket and spread it out over Jared's long, lean body, tugging it snugly around his broad shoulders. Of all the men in the world, why was he the one she wanted?

Standing, she looked down at the man sleeping on her sofa and wondered how on earth she was going to deal with him in the morning.

Four

Jared couldn't remember the last time he'd awakened with a hangover. The best he could figure, it had been fifteen years ago, the night after Grandpa Monty's funeral. At the time, he'd had two choices, either cry or get drunk. He'd gotten drunk first, and then he'd cried. He hadn't done either since, not even when he lost his father three years ago.

He opened his eyes, then shut them quickly. Bright morning sunshine flooded the room. He tried to lift his head off the pillow, but pain shot through his temples. Groaning, he massaged his forehead.

"Good morning," Paige said. "Want some coffee?"

Jared's eyes flew open. He gazed up at Paige, who stood behind the sofa. She held a mug in her hand.

"Is that coffee you've got there?" he asked.

"It's hot chocolate," she said. "Caffeine is off-limits to me for the duration of my pregnancy, and I can't stand the low-octane stuff. But there's a pot of regular coffee brewing in the kitchen."

"Thanks." He forced his head up off the pillow. Now he remembered why he didn't get drunk. The morning after was hell.

"Need some help?" she asked.

"I think I can make it." He kicked off the blanket from where it had twisted around his feet, then sat up sluggishly and leaned his head back on the sofa. Glancing down at his slacks, he suddenly realized that he had slept in his clothes. He wriggled his toes. His feet were bare. Someone had removed his shoes and socks. He rubbed his neck. And that same someone had taken off his tie and unbuttoned his shirt.

The missing articles of clothing lay neatly arranged on the nearby coffee table. "Sorry about last night," he said, venturing a glance her way. "I'm afraid I didn't handle things very well." When she didn't reply and sipped her cocoa as if he hadn't spoken, he cleared his throat loudly. She continued ignoring him. "My only excuse is that the news about your pregnancy kind of threw me."

"Yes, I suppose it would," she said. "It kind of *threw me,* too, at first."

"Do you think I could have that coffee now?" he asked.

"Sure. Can you make it to the kitchen or do you want me to bring you a cup in here?"

"Would you mind bringing me a cup in here? After a shot of caffeine, I might be able to stand up."

While she was in the kitchen pouring the coffee, Jared tried to clear his head and remember exactly what had transpired the evening before. The last thing he remembered clearly was Paige calling him an arrogant, egotistical, macho bastard. God, what had he said to prompt such an outburst from her?

He had told her that he would marry her. He had told her that he would put the deed to the mountain house in her name. He'd told her that he was rich enough to buy her anything she wanted. Those statements should have made her happy, not angry. Any other woman in her position would have been thrilled by such a generous offer.

Oh, no! He'd told her about his five-year plan, hadn't he? He'd told her that she wasn't quite what he'd had in mind for the perfect wife. Jerk! How could he have said something so stupid? And he'd called the baby an accident that had messed up his plans!

And don't forget that you told her you expected her to sign a prenuptial agreement, he reminded himself. Hell, no wonder she'd lit into him the way she had. He was just surprised that she hadn't called him a lot worse than an arrogant, egotistical, macho bastard. Undoubtedly, her vocabulary of gutter words wasn't all that extensive.

"Here's your coffee." Paige handed him a white ceramic mug.

"Smells great. Thanks."

"Be careful. It's hot."

He sipped the steaming brew slowly, eyeing Paige over the rim of the cup. Obviously she had already showered and dressed for the day. She looked immaculate in her brown corduroy skirt, crisp beige cotton blouse and dark gold jacket. She had plaited her long, glorious hair in a neat French braid. A pair of small gold hoops dangled from her ears. How could she look so good so early in the morning?

"What time is it?" Jared asked.

"Nine-fifty," she said.

"Damn, why did you let me sleep so late? I've got that meeting with Saunders at eleven and I haven't even gone over my notes." Jared gulped a mouthful of hot coffee. Yelping when it burned his tongue, he slammed the mug down on the end table and reached for his shoes and socks.

"I've already called Kay and told her to reschedule your meeting with Mr. Saunders for one-thirty this afternoon."

"You did?" He slipped on his socks, then his shoes. "How did you explain about our not coming into the office this morning?"

"I told her that you got drunk last night, passed out and had to sleep it off on my sofa." Paige grinned mischievously.

"You what!"

"Relax, Mr. Montgomery."

When he tried to stand, Paige shoved him back down on the sofa. "I told Kay that you knew I was pregnant with your child and that we were both taking the morning off to discuss our options. And I cautioned her not to tell anyone about my being pregnant or your being the father, so you'll have to think up a reasonable explanation for Mr. Addison."

"You're a regular Miss Bossy-butt, aren't you." Jared suddenly realized how very little he knew about Paige Summers, the mother of his child.

"I can be," she said. "When it's necessary."

Jared glided his tongue over his teeth. His mouth felt downright rancid. Cradling his chin in his hand, he ran his thumb over his heavy beard stubble. "Guess I look like hell, don't I. I need a shower, a shave and some clean clothes, and I hardly have time for us to settle things between us, then drive all the way out to my house and get back in time for my meeting with Jim Saunders."

"There's a one-hour laundry and cleaners in a minimall about a mile from here," Paige said. "So, while you shower, shave and have some more coffee, I'll take care of your clothes and bring us back some lunch."

"I knew you had everything at the office organized to perfection, so I guess it should come as no great surprise to me that you're able to reorganize our morning so competently." Jared removed his shoes and socks. "I'm surprised you didn't have a plan for your life, too, the way I had, considering—"

"I did have a plan," she told him. "As a matter of fact, having a baby doesn't change my plan. It just alters it a little and delays things by a few years."

He wanted to believe her. His heart told him that he could. But his mind warned him to be careful. Maybe snagging a rich husband by getting herself pregnant had been a part of her plan all along.

"Look, Paige, what I said last night about the baby being an accident and your not being quite what I wanted in a wife, well—"

"We'll discuss all that later, after we eat lunch. For now, go in the bathroom and strip, then toss your clothes out into the hall."

Jared wanted to suggest that he'd enjoy his shower a lot more if she shared it with him, but he knew better than to even hint at the possibility. It was apparent that she had made their plans for the morning. As much as he admired strong, aggressive, take-charge women in the business world, he wasn't sure those were qualities he wanted in a wife. He had assumed that a young working girl such as Paige would be more pliable, more easily influenced by his likes and dislikes. Perhaps she would even eagerly look to him for guidance.

How wrong could a guy be? Apparently, Paige intended to be the one in charge. Did she think that by denying him sexually, she could bend him to her will more easily?

"Hurry up," Paige said. "We have a lot to do before your one-thirty meeting with Mr. Saunders."

"Yes, ma'am."

Jared followed her orders to the letter. He stripped off in the bathroom, tossed his clothes out into the hall and turned on the shower. The front door slammed shut. He grinned as he reached for the soap. His little redheaded drill sergeant was going to be hard to handle, but she'd met her match in him. If she thought she was going to run this show, then she'd better think again. He would let her have her way—up to a point—then he'd let her know who was boss. The last time a woman had him wrapped around her little finger, he'd been a horny young fool of twenty. But no woman, no matter how much he wanted her, would ever make a fool of him again.

* * *

"How dare you pilfer through my things!" Paige threw his neatly laundered and dry-cleaned clothes at him and dropped the brown paper sack she held.

Jared stood there with a large blue towel draped around his waist, his long, hairy legs and broad hairy chest naked, and shook the appointment card in her face. "You weren't going to tell me, were you."

"No, I wasn't going to tell you!"

"This is the reason you let me sleep so late this morning. The reason you rescheduled my meeting with Jim Saunders for exactly one-thirty."

"That's right. You can't be in two places at one time, and I was afraid that if I told you about my appointment, you'd want to go with me."

"I'll cancel with Saunders," Jared said.

"Mr. Saunders won't like it if you don't show up after canceling on him this morning."

"Tough."

"I don't want you to go with me," she told him. "I don't need anything from you except my job until after the baby's born."

"Tough."

"You need to broaden your vocabulary a little."

"Tough sh—"

"You're not going with me to see Dr. Petrocelli and that's final!"

Ignoring the clothing lying at his feet, Jared placed his hand over Paige's belly. "I'm the father of this baby and I have every right to be present when you have a sonogram." He pointed the card in her face. "That's what this says, doesn't it? 'Paige Summers. One-thirty. Sonogram.'"

Paige grabbed his hand and flung it off her stomach. "I don't want you there. Can't you understand plain English?"

Jared willed himself to get under control. Maybe he had overreacted just a little when he'd accidently noticed her appointment card attached to the side of the refrigerator with a plastic magnet. His gut reaction had been a feeling of betrayal. Here he was offering Paige *everything* on a damn silver platter, and her thanks to him was to deny him his paternal rights. What sort of game was the woman playing? Did she think playing hard to get would up the ante? Did she think he'd want her enough to give her absolutely anything if she held out long enough?

"I don't understand why you're so damned and determined to keep me from going with you. I'm the father, dammit. I'm practically your husband. We're getting married next week. You're moving into my home."

"Get dressed, Jared." She glanced down at his clothes. "We need to talk. I promise to stay calm and explain exactly how I want to handle everything."

Not only didn't he like what she'd said, he didn't like the way she'd said it. What did she mean, *she* would explain how *she* wanted to handle things? Just who did she think she was, dictating the rules to him?

Jared grabbed her arm and drew her up against him. Paige huffed loudly, but didn't try to pull away. He lowered his face so that their noses almost touched. "Go ahead, honey. Explain how you want to handle things."

"I'd prefer to talk after you're dressed." She met his piercing glare defiantly, narrowing her eyes as she returned his stern look.

"And I'd prefer we talk right now."

"All right, if you insist."

"I insist."

Jared dragged her over to the sofa, sat down and pulled her onto his lap. She struggled to get up, but he held her in place.

"Keep wriggling around like that and you're going to wriggle this towel right off me. Is that what you want?"

She sat perfectly still, her back straight as a board, but she refused to look at him, gazing instead at her lap where she'd folded her hands together.

"There, that's better," he said as he slipped his arm around her waist. She didn't move a muscle. "I'll go first. It won't take me long, and then you can have your say. Is that all right with you?"

She nodded agreement.

"I'll take care of you and our child. We can be married as soon as possible. All I ask is that you sign a prenuptial agreement. I'm not the kind of man who can walk away from my own child, so I'm willing to adjust my plans to include you and our baby." He surveyed her from head to toe. "So what do you say, Paige? Marry me and I can turn Cinderella into a princess."

She didn't respond immediately. Her body trembled slightly. She counted to ten. Turn Cinderella into a princess, indeed! "You don't love me, do you?"

"What?"

"You don't love me, do you?" she repeated.

"No, I don't love you. I hardly know you. What's that got to do with our getting married?"

"Nothing to you, I suppose, since you never planned to marry for love, anyway, did you? But I did, and that's the problem. When I marry, it will be for love. And the man who really loves me will love me for exactly who I am." *He won't think he needs to change me, to turn me into a princess. He'll think I'm already a princess!*

"Love is just a romantic notion that keeps songwriters and romance novelists in business," he said. "You and I share something far more real, honey. We may not love each other, but we sure as hell want each other."

"I need love, not just lust."

"You're being unreasonable."

"I think it's my turn," Paige told him. "I will not marry you. Let's get that straight right now. All I want from you is my job until the baby's born, so I can keep my insurance. I won't tell anyone else that you're the father, but if you choose to be a part of our child's life, I'll allow you visitation rights. But this is my body." Opening her palms, she spread them over her abdomen. "And this is my baby. I make all the decisions. The only rights you have are the ones I grant you." She paused long enough to take a deep breath. "And I do not want to be turned into a princess, thank you very much!"

At that precise moment, Jared wanted to throttle her. She was being totally unreasonable. Thinking like an irrational woman. But then, he supposed her hormones were raging now that she was pregnant and that might account for her ridiculous attitude. The last thing he wanted to do was upset her and possibly harm her and their child. His wisest course of action, he decided, probably was to go along with whatever she wanted. At least for the time being. Sooner or later, he'd wear her down and convince her to marry him. He just hoped he could do it sometime in the next five months. In time to save his son and heir from illegitimacy.

Jared draped her body with both arms, sliding his hands over hers across her stomach. "This is *our* baby. But however you need to handle the situation is the way we'll deal with it. Just don't shut me out. Please, let me take care of you and the baby."

More than anything, Paige wanted to curl up in his arms, rest her head on his shoulder and surrender completely to him. But she couldn't. She didn't dare. If she gave him an inch, he'd take a mile. L. J. Montgomery was just the type. If she wasn't very careful, she'd find herself agreeing to marry him and then spend the rest of her life regretting it.

She couldn't endure the thought of a loveless marriage, and that's the only kind Jared would ever have. The man simply wasn't capable of love. He wanted to own her, to rule her, to guide her!

She pulled out of his arms. "If you meant what you just said, get dressed, and then we'll eat lunch. Afterward, you can go into the office for your meeting with Mr. Saunders while I keep my appointment with Dr. Petrocelli for the sonogram."

As much as Jared wanted to protest, he didn't. "All right. Then tonight, I'll take you out to dinner and you can tell me about the sonogram and what the doctor said and—"

"I'm having dinner with my family tonight. I've already promised my mother."

It took every ounce of control he could muster not to blow sky-high, but he reined in his anger and frustration enough to say, "Whatever you want, honey."

He'd let her think she'd won this round, that she was getting things her way, but by day's end he'd figure out a way to get what he wanted. If Paige actually thought she could keep him at arm's length for the next five months, then she'd definitely better think again.

Paige couldn't wait to get to her parents' home on Juniper Lane, a neat two-story frame they'd bought shortly after her father's retirement. She'd show her mother the sonogram pictures before dinner, and then afterward, they'd watch the video. Accepting the fact that his unmarried daughter was pregnant was difficult for her father, but he loved her and she knew she could count on his support during the months and years ahead. She didn't think she'd ever be able to bring herself to tell him that she'd gotten pregnant by a stranger the night she'd been trapped in the Wellman Building elevator. Walt Summers was far too old-fashioned. If he had any idea about the identity of the man who had fathered Paige's child, he'd go after the guy with a shotgun.

Paige giggled when she pictured her father holding a shotgun on L. J. Montgomery and demanding the man marry his daughter. But the image of her walking down the aisle with Jared quickly wiped the smile off her face. Nothing short of a wedding would satisfy her father or Jared.

If circumstances were different, if Paige thought there was a chance Jared might learn to love her and accept her for the woman she was, she'd willingly marry her baby's father. If they loved each other, they could find a way to overcome their many differences. But any man who could map out his personal life the way he planned his business ventures wasn't capable of real love. If Jared loved her, he wouldn't be so concerned about her being such an unsuitable mate.

And even if she loved Jared—and that was a big if— her romantic heart would wither and die without having her love returned in full measure. Her soul needed a soul mate. Although she couldn't deny that she was physically attracted to Jared, that she found him downright irresistible, she wasn't sure whether what she felt for him was just infatuation or real love.

Perhaps she had been trying to convince herself that she'd fallen in love with Jared at first sight because loving him would justify her pregnancy. After all, what woman would want to admit that she'd done something so monumentally foolish for any other reason than love?

Maybe she *had* fallen for the cowboy stranger she'd made love with in the elevator, but L. J. Montgomery was a different man. How could she possibly love someone so domineering and arrogant?

She turned her white Grand Am into her parents' drive,

directly behind her brother Austen's mud-splattered Chevy pickup. The front porch light shone brightly, casting a creamy glow over the wide front yard filled with neatly trimmed shrubs and barren flower beds. Paige dropped her keys into her shoulder bag, double-checked the zippered side pouch to make sure the sonogram pictures and video were still there and got out of the car.

The moment she opened the door, the cool October wind chilled her to the bone. Adjusting her shoulder bag, Paige buttoned her wool jacket before she hurried up the drive and onto the porch.

Apparently her mother had been watching for her. Dora Summers flung open the front door, reached out and pulled Paige inside, then closed the door quietly.

"Mama—"

"Shh!" Dora put a finger to her lips, then yanked Paige into a corner of the foyer. "He's here!"

"Who's here?" Paige asked.

"Him."

"Mama, I have no idea what you're talking about. Who's here?"

"Your fiancé, of course."

"My what?"

"L. J. Montgomery," Dora replied, her brown eyes huge as saucers. "Your daddy was fit to be tied when he told us that he was your baby's father—"

"He did what?"

"But it's all right now. The minute he showed us the diamond ring he's going to give you and told your daddy that he wanted to ask his permission before y'all made it official, Walt's attitude changed completely. Land sakes, they're in the den now with Austen, the three of them talking about football and skiing and the army. You know, all that man stuff."

Paige had noticed over the years that whenever her

mother got excited, her Mississippi accent became more pronounced. And Dora was quite excited now. Happily excited. But why shouldn't she be? Why shouldn't her entire family be delighted? After all, they'd been told that their unmarried, pregnant daughter was engaged to one of the wealthiest men in the Southwest.

She should have known that Jared wouldn't abide by their agreement and let her handle their *situation*. He was too accustomed to being in charge, to issuing orders and having them instantly obeyed. He planned and arranged every element of his life to his liking. He didn't leave any room for other people's feelings, other people's hopes and dreams.

He had screwed up his precisely made plans for the future, but he was adapting quickly, altering his plans to include a wife and child, neither of whom he loved or wanted. He was so determined to have his own way that he didn't care what she wanted. And he was in the den with her father and brother right now, cleaning up the mess he'd created four months ago.

Paige hung her bag on the pine coat tree, then removed her jacket and hung it over her purse. "He's not going to get away with this," she murmured.

"What did you say?" her mother asked.

"Nothing, Mama. Just muttering to myself." Paige wrapped her arm around her mother's shoulders. "How long has Jared been here?"

"About an hour, dear. A taxi brought him. And Mr. Montgomery…I mean Jared…he told us to call him Jared. Well, anyway, he brought flowers and wine and told us who he was and that you had invited him to join us for dinner." Dora slipped her arm around Paige's waist. "Why on earth didn't you tell us about Jared, that the two of you were planning to get married?"

"Because I haven't agreed to marry him."

"Why on earth not?"

"Because he doesn't love me, Mama. He just wants to marry me because of the baby."

"Well, in my day, that was a darn good reason."

Paige had never heard her sweet, gentle mother say a curse word, no matter how angry or upset she became. Dora Elkins Summers was a sparkling ember from the dying fire of Southern gentility.

"Mama, please. I'm going to need you to be on my side." Paige grasped her mother's hands. "I know Daddy will want me to marry Jared, no matter what. But I can't."

"Don't you love him, Paige?"

She looked into her mother's dear, worried face and accepted defeat. Temporary defeat. After this little family dinner party ended, she was going to get Mr. Wonderful Future Son-in-law alone and give him a piece of her mind. When she got through with him, he would be sorry he'd ever tried to get the best of her.

"Jared Montgomery wouldn't be an easy man to love. You can't imagine how infuriating he can be. Half the time he acts like an infuriating jerk."

"Oh, sweetie, he's a man. Most of them are like that. Being infuriating is a male trait." Clasping Paige's hand, Dora tugged gently, urging her daughter to follow her. "Let's go on in. We all heard your car drive up, but I told them I needed a few minutes alone with you for mother-daughter time."

"Thanks, Mama." Paige plastered a phony smile on her face, tilted her chin high, squeezed her mother's hand, and together they paraded into the den.

"There you are, sweetheart." Walt Summers held his arms open.

Paige caught a glimpse of Jared standing near the rock fireplace beside Austen, but she didn't glance his way. Instead she rushed into her father's arms.

"We've been getting to know your Jared." Walt gave Paige a bear hug, then released her.

"So Mama told me," she said.

Paige's heart sank when she saw her father's broad smile. Dammit! He liked Jared. It wasn't supposed to be this way. Jared wasn't supposed to be here.

Without any warning, Jared slid his arm around Paige's waist and drew her to his side. He nuzzled her ear. She shivered. "Honey, I hope you aren't upset with me for showing your folks your engagement ring and springing our good news on them before you got home."

Smiling politely, her jaws aching from the effort, she patted Jared's cheek, barely refraining herself from slapping him. "Why, no, darling, how could I ever be upset with you when your every thought is of what's best for me."

"I knew you'd understand why I decided that I should be the one to introduce myself and assure your parents that I'm going to take very good care of their little girl."

"Isn't this just too wonderful for words?" Dora wiped the tears from her eyes with the edge of her gingham apron. "And to think how worried we've all been."

"Now, now, all's well that ends well." Walt cleared his throat. "Mama, why don't you and Austen and I go on out in the kitchen and leave these two lovebirds alone? I'm sure Paige is dying to get a look at that ring."

"No!" Paige cried out. "Don't go." When everyone stared at her, their eyes questioning her plea, she took a deep breath. "I mean, why don't we go ahead and have dinner. Jared and I plan to go back to my apartment later and discuss our future."

Short, stocky, seventeen-year-old Austen slapped Jared on the back. "Hey, man, if she had any idea of the size of that rock, she'd want it on her finger right this minute. Why don't you show it to her?"

"Good idea." Jared pulled a velvet box out of his coat pocket, flipped open the lid and held it up in front of Paige. "The moment I saw it, I knew it was meant for my future wife."

Paige gasped. Oh, my God! He had to be kidding? The emerald-cut diamond sparkled like a star. A large star. Maybe this ring was meant for his future wife, but not for her. He hadn't been thinking of her when he'd chosen the diamond; he'd been thinking of what was suitable for L. J. Montgomery's fiancée.

"She's speechless," Austen said. "See, what'd I tell you? Hey, sis, I bet you never thought you'd ever be wearing a perfect six-carat diamond, did you?"

Paige swallowed. "No. Not ever." If Jared's intention had been to dazzle her, he had succeeded. Indeed, he seemed to have dazzled her whole family. But if his intention had been to please her, he had failed miserably.

While she stared at the diamond, totally mesmerized, Jared removed it from its velvet bed. "Let's make it official, honey." He lifted her hand, slipped the ring on the third finger of her left hand and brought her hand to his lips.

Paige tugged on her hand, trying to remove it from his grasp. He tightened his hold, then kissed the knuckle on her ring finger. She bit down on her bottom lip, whether in an effort not to cry or not to spit in his eye, she wasn't sure.

"Let's open that bottle of wine Jared brought and make a toast to the happy couple," Walt said.

Three-and-a-half hours later, Paige unlocked her apartment, opened the door and flipped on the light switch. She wasn't sure how she had managed to spend the entire evening at her parents' home and endure the drive back into town alone with Jared, without strangling the man. She had counted to ten a least a dozen times.

God, he was such a manipulator. She could hear him now.

"Austen, whenever you or Bryant want to take a few friends to Aspen, you're welcome to use my condo."

"Wow, man, thanks!" Austen had been duly impressed.

"And, Walt, I'd really appreciate your including me in your plans the next time you and your boys go hunting," Jared had said.

After dinner he'd raved to her mother. "Mrs. Summers, that was the best fried chicken I've ever eaten. And the peach cobbler was delicious."

The minute they'd gotten into her car, she'd warned him not to say one word to her. "I can't drive and chew your ass out at the same time."

"Tsk-tsk, honey," he'd said. "Your mother wouldn't approve of your being mean to me, would she?"

Paige had given him an evil glare. He'd grinned, but he had shut up and remained silent all the way into Grand Springs.

Jared walked into Paige's apartment behind her, closed the door and casually crossed his arms over his chest. "I like your family," he said. "They're good people."

"Yes, you're right, they are good people. And I don't appreciate the way you manipulated them tonight."

"And just exactly how did I manipulate them?"

"You know damn well how." Paige laid her shoulder bag on the coffee table. "You invited yourself to dinner when you knew I didn't want you there. You told my parents that you're the father of my child and that we're going to get married."

"I am the father of your child. And sooner or later, you *are* going to marry me."

Crinkling her face into a disgusted frown, Paige threw

up her hands and screeched. "I am not going to marry you. I thought I made that perfectly clear this morning. And I thought you agreed." Paige removed her jacket and flung it on a nearby chair.

"What you made perfectly clear this morning was that I had to take some drastic measures to persuade you that marrying me is the best thing for you and our child."

"It isn't going to work, you know." She kicked off her heels and slumped down onto the sofa. "Just because you charmed my family and put this—" she held up her right hand "—expensive ring on my finger, does not mean you've won." She jerked off the ring and held it out to him. "Here, take this thing to the jeweler's and get your money back. A ring like this isn't my style, anyway."

Glancing down at the ring lying in her palm, Jared shrugged. "Well, that ring—" he nodded to the perfect six-carat diamond "—*is* my style, and it's exactly what my fiancée would wear. So, you're going to keep it. Besides, if you don't keep the ring, you're going to find it difficult to explain to your parents why you gave it back to me. After all, I'm their grandchild's father, and I'm more than willing to make an honest woman of you."

"I understand now why you're so successful." Paige glared at him. He grinned. Damn the man! Damn him for making her stomach do evil flip-flops every time he smiled at her. "You're manipulative and underhanded and conniving and deceitful and ruthless." She laid the ring on a brass coaster on the end table.

Uncrossing his arms, Jared strolled across the room toward the sofa. "You forgot to mention 'determined.' I never give up until I get what I want." He sat down beside her, trapping her between him and the sofa arm.

She tried to get up; he held her down. "You can't force me to marry you," she said.

He pulled her into his arms. "No, but I think I can

persuade you." When he tried to kiss her, she thrashed around, twisting her head from side to side.

Laughing, Jared released her and leaned his head back against the sofa. "You don't want to disappoint your parents, Paige. They're the kind of people who expect their daughter to be married when she has a child."

"I know what my parents expect," she said. "But they wouldn't think I was going to marry you if you hadn't lied to them."

"Look, I like your parents. I wouldn't intentionally hurt them. They're warm, loving people and I envy you the life you must have had growing up in such a caring, supportive environment."

"I'm very lucky."

"Yes, you are. My parents were always too busy for me when I was a kid. My father didn't have time for anything except working and chasing women. And my mother didn't have time for anything except her social obligations."

"I'm sorry, Jared, you must have been a lonely little boy. Were you an only child?"

"Yep, I was the only heir to the throne. But don't feel sorry for me. I had everything money could buy."

Paige glanced over at her purse lying on the coffee table and thought about the sonogram pictures and video. Her family had been so excited about her "engagement," she'd never had a chance to bring out the sonogram results. How would he feel if she told him about his child? If she did, maybe he wouldn't be so eager to marry her. "You want a son, don't you? An heir for all your millions."

"Of course that's what I want. It's what every man wants."

"You won't get what you want if you marry me. I'm totally unsuitable to be L. J. Montgomery's wife. You said so yourself. You need to follow through with your five-year plan and find another woman to give you a son. You see—'' she looked him straight in the eye ''—the baby I'm carrying is a girl.''

''A girl?'' he asked. ''Are you sure?''

''Yes. I had the sonogram today. Remember? I'm going to have a daughter, not a son.''

''Well, I'll be damned.''

Jared had never for one minute considered the possibility that he might have fathered a girl. Hell, he'd never even thought about having a daughter. He had planned for a son. He had also planned to wait another five years to marry and produce an heir. But Paige Summers had changed his plan. He was going to marry now, instead of in five years. He was going to have to mold Paige into the kind of wife he wanted and needed, instead of choosing someone already suitable. And he was going to have a daughter and not a son.

''Well, I suppose things have a way of working out, don't they? You want a son,'' Paige said. ''I'm having a daughter. So, I'll have my little girl and one day you'll marry someone else and she'll give you a boy.

''I'll explain to my parents that we reconsidered marrying just for the sake of the baby and decided not to trap ourselves in a loveless marriage. I know my father will be disappointed, but in time, he'll understand. And my mother will—''

Jared grabbed her shoulders and kissed her soundly. She was too startled at first to resist, and by the time she realized what he was doing, he ended the kiss and stared at her, a self-satisfied smile on his face.

''Little girls adore their fathers, don't they,'' Jared said, a dreamy look in his eyes. ''You adore yours. I could tell tonight that you've got him wrapped around your little finger.''

"Yes, I adore my father," she agreed. "But what does that fact have to do with anything?"

"I was just wondering if my little girl will adore me." He had sworn that no woman would wrap him around her little finger, not ever again. But a man's daughter—his own child—was something entirely different. He sort of liked the idea of doting on his child.

"You don't want a little girl. Remember? You want a son. Someone to fill your shoes when you're gone." Paige didn't like the way Jared was smiling, all goofy and soft and silly, as if he'd been hit in the head.

"The more I think about having a daughter, the better I like the idea." Yes, sir, he couldn't think of anything nicer than having a little redheaded toddler in a frilly dress put her arms around his neck and call him Daddy. There wasn't anything in this whole wide world he wouldn't do for his little angel. He'd give her the world. Hell, he'd buy her the moon and the stars!

"But—but you said you wanted a son, that you'd planned for a son!" Dammit, she was not going to let him do an about-face on this issue. How could a man, who had his whole life mapped out in detail, adapt to so many changes so quickly?

"Maybe we'll have a boy next time." Jared ran his hand down her arm, over her waist and across her stomach. He caressed the tiny bulge. "Let's name her Angel."

"What?" Paige grabbed his hand and tried to lift it off her stomach.

Clasping her hand, he draped her arm around his neck. "Well, if you don't like Angel, I suppose we could name her Angelica or Angela or—"

"What do mean we'll have a boy next time?"

"You don't want our Angel to be an only child, do you?" Jared lifted Paige's other arm and draped it over his shoulder so that her hands overlapped across his neck.

"If this marriage thing between us works out, I'm sure we'll both want more children."

If this marriage thing works out! "There isn't going to be any marriage thing between us. We aren't in love. No love. No marriage. We can't give a child the kind of family life I had because we don't love each other the way my parents do. And that's what I want. I'm not going to settle for anything less!"

"Why are you being so stubborn, honey?" Jared drew her into his arms. "You're just making things more difficult for yourself. I'm not going to give up. And in the end, I'll get what I want."

He was too close, far too close for comfort. Her heartbeat roared in her ears. Her stomach churned. Her nipples tightened. "I'm not what you want. Remember your five-year plan? I'm the woman who messed up everything for you. You want a suitable wife and a son, not me and my baby girl."

He nuzzled her neck. Paige moaned. He ran the back of his thumb across her lower lip. She sighed.

"But I do want you and our little girl. We can have a son later. And as far as your not being suitable, we can work on that. You're young and bright and lovely. With the proper tutor, you can learn how to be the perfect wife for me."

Before she could utter a word of protest, Jared covered her lips with his. Her mind warned her to fight, but her body melted against his and she returned his kiss with equal fervor. Every time he touched her, she fell to pieces. It just wasn't fair that she had no control over her response to him. This wild, crazy passion between them was what had gotten her into trouble in the first place.

Breaking away, she shoved against his chest. "No! I can't do this. I can't let you seduce me into agreeing to marry you."

Paige jumped up off the sofa. "Go home, Jared. Please. Go home and leave me alone. I can't think straight when you're around. Every time you get near me I either get so angry I want to strangle you or I get so…so—"

"Aroused?" he offered her a suitable word.

"Yes, all right, damn you. I get so aroused that I'm tempted to…to do what we did in the elevator."

"Make love?"

"Have sex."

Jared stood, picked up the diamond from the end table and reached out for Paige's hand. She tried to avoid his touch, but he grabbed her hand, slid the ring on quickly and folded her fingers over into a loose fist.

"Marriages have succeeded on a lot less than fantastic sex. Just think about what it could be like for us, honey. Sleeping in the same bed every night. Setting the sheets on fire every time we make love."

Paige stood in the middle of her living room and watched Jared open the door and walk out. He didn't look back or even say goodbye. When he disappeared from sight, she rushed over and slammed the door closed, then locked it.

She shook from head to toe. Why did she let him get to her that way? *Because you're probably in love with him and you don't want to be.*

Paige held out her hand. Jared's big diamond twinkled brightly, as if it were winking at her. She dragged the ring to the tip of her finger, then stopped and slid it back into place. She'd wear it, just for tonight. It *was* beautiful. And it fit her finger perfectly. If only it were a symbol of Jared's love, instead of an emblem of his victory. If only he had chosen it specifically for her and not for the future Mrs. L. J. Montgomery.

Tomorrow, she promised herself, she'd give the ring back to him.

Five

Paige arrived at work early, put on a fresh pot of coffee in the employees' lounge and began her daily routine. She had gone over what she wanted to say to Jared at least a dozen times, determined to get through to him this time and make him understand her point of view. But the very thought of another confrontation with him twisted her stomach into knots. To be totally honest, the very thought of being alone with him in his office unnerved her. Every time they were alone, sparks flew. The same highly charged, sexual sparks that had ignited a forest fire between them four months ago in the elevator threatened to set them afire again.

Paige had to admit that she was tempted to accept Jared's proposal. Marrying him definitely would solve all her immediate problems. And he'd been right about the fantastic sex. Every time he touched her, it took all her willpower not to crawl all over him. And he certainly never tried to hide the fact that he wanted her. He'd even said that just hearing her voice over the phone aroused him. But Paige knew herself too well. Great sex might be enough to hold their marriage together for a while, but sooner or later, she'd want more. If Jared couldn't give her the love and unconditional acceptance she needed, she could never be happy with him. And when Jared realized that he couldn't transform her into the *perfect* wife, he'd know what a mistake their marriage had been.

No, she couldn't marry him. It wouldn't be fair to either

of them and certainly not to their little girl. Angel, he'd called her. Or Angelica or Angela. Damn him for acting as if he were enchanted with the thought of having a daughter. *Little girls adore their fathers, don't they?*

Paige shook her head, trying to dislodge the image of a little redheaded girl sitting in Jared's lap, looking up at him with green eyes identical to his and saying, "Daddy, please. I really, really want a puppy."

"Good morning. You're here bright and early." Kay Thompson stood in the open doorway of Paige's office.

Glancing up from her desk, Paige smiled at her friend. "You're here early yourself. It's barely eight-thirty."

"I called your apartment and got your answering machine, so I assumed I'd find you here." Kay walked in and sat down in a leather chair across from Paige's desk. "Let's see it."

"See what?"

"The diamond L.J. gave you last night."

"How did you know? Who told you?"

"The boss man himself called me last night, after he left your apartment," Kay said.

"He called you? Why? What did he say?"

"He said that since you and I were friends, he needed my help in persuading you to marry him."

"I cannot believe he tried to enlist your help." But she could believe it. She could believe he was capable of doing just about anything in order to get his own way. Jared was arrogant, self-centered and demanding. But he also had an old-fashioned sense of honor that dictated his actions.

"Show me the ring," Kay said, repeating her request. "You are wearing it, aren't you?"

Paige laid her left hand on the desk. "I'm giving it back to him as soon as he comes in this morning. I tried to give it back to him last night, but he wouldn't take it. He's very forceful and very persuasive."

"So I've heard. Greg has told me that L.J. never loses. He's so single-minded and determined that he won't give up when he wants something." Rising out of the chair, Kay leaned over and looked at Paige's engagement ring. She let out a long, low whistle. "That's the reason he was able to start his own business, straight out of college, and in fifteen years' time become a multimillionaire in his own right."

"I'm not going to marry him." Closing her fingers over her palm, Paige swept her hand off the desk and onto her lap.

"Why ever not? He's gorgeous, rich, charming and obviously wild about you." Kay glanced meaningfully at Paige's tummy. "And you are pregnant with his child."

"He doesn't love me." Paige lifted a pencil off a stack of file folders and repeatedly tapped the edge of her desk.

"What makes you think he doesn't love you?"

"He told me he didn't." Gripping the pencil in her hand, Paige rubbed her thumb up and down the smooth wood surface. "L. J. Montgomery doesn't believe in love. He never planned to marry for love. Besides, if he loved me, he wouldn't want to change me into his idea of a perfect wife. He'd accept me for exactly who I am. I tried to change myself for Keith and he dumped me for someone else. Someone more suitable. Believe me, I learned my lesson. I'll never try to be someone I'm not."

"Oh, Paige. You poor little romantic fool." Kay sighed dramatically. "Millions of people marry for love, and what does it get them? Half those love matches end in divorce, like mine did. L.J. is offering you something better than love. He's offering you a lifetime of security. For you and your baby."

"It's not enough. Call me a romantic fool if you want to. Maybe I am. But I grew up with two parents who, after nearly thirty years of marriage, are still deeply in love.

That kind of relationship is what I've wanted all my life. Jared sees me and this baby—'' Paige circled her palm over her tummy ''—as a mistake he has to correct. He wants to marry me for the baby's sake and then make me over to suit his idea of a perfect wife.''

''So, you've made up your mind not to marry him?''

''I have. Now all I have to do is convince Jared that I mean what I say.'' Paige snapped the pencil in two, then threw the halves into the wastebasket.

''You may be fighting a losing battle.'' Kay gazed sympathetically at Paige. ''After all, let's face it—what woman could resist L. J. Montgomery indefinitely? Especially a woman who's already halfway in love with him. And you are, aren't you?''

Before Paige could reply, someone knocked loudly on the door. Paige jumped. Gasping, Kay jerked around in her chair.

'''Morning, ladies.'' A clean-cut young man stood in the doorway holding a vase filled with a large number of red roses. ''I'm looking for a Paige Summers. These are for her.''

''Bring them in here, sonny,'' Kay said. ''This—'' she pointed at Paige ''—is Ms. Summers.''

''Where do you want them, ma'am?'' he asked.

''Just put them here on my desk,'' Paige said.

The minute the deliveryman left, Kay snatched up the attached card, opened it and handed it to Paige. ''So, what does it say?''

Paige read aloud. ''Marry me.''

Fingering the petals on the long-stemmed beauties as she silently counted them, Kay sighed. ''You've got to give Jared credit. The man knows all the tricks. What woman doesn't love red roses. And two dozen!''

''This is a perfect example of how little Jared knows me,'' Paige said. ''He chose red roses for his ideal fiancée, but I prefer white roses. If he cared about me, truly cared, he'd bother to find out who I am and what I like."

Greg Addison marched into Paige's office, followed by a young woman wearing brown slacks and matching shirt, the emblem of a local delivery service stitched on her shirt pocket. She carried two boxes wrapped in pink paper and tied with white ribbon.

"So the campaign begins." Greg eyed the roses, then pointed to Paige. "There she is. The beautiful redhead behind the desk is Ms. Summers."

The deliverywoman asked Paige to sign for the two items, then as soon as that requirement was out of the way, she handed the gifts to Paige and left.

Paige stared at the boxes, knowing that Jared had sent them. Flowers. Gifts. What next? she wondered.

"Go ahead and open them," Greg said. "I'm eager to see what the father-to-be has sent the mother-to-be."

Paige glared at Greg. "How did you know? No, no, don't tell me. Jared shared the news about our blessed event with you, too, didn't he."

"Yep. He came by my apartment last night and confessed all." Shaking his head, Greg clicked his tongue. "My, my, Ms. Summers, you amaze me. You, a lowly working girl, have accomplished what every wealthy debutante and society maid in two dozen states have failed to accomplish. You've brought the great man to his knees."

"Quit being such a jerk," Kay said. "She didn't get pregnant by herself, you know."

Paige gasped, amazed that Kay would speak to her boss in such a way.

"The woman knows I won't fire her," Greg said. "I can't get along without her. She knows more about Montgomery Real Estate and Land Development than I do. And I'm sorry, Paige, if what I said offended you. I didn't mean it that way. You'll have to pardon me if I find this whole situation rather amusing and if I milk it for all it's worth.''

"I'm afraid I fail to find the humor in all this, Mr. Addison," Paige said.

"Greg has a rather warped sense of humor." Kay stood, slipped her arm through Greg's and nodded toward the open door. "Why don't we leave Paige alone and let her open her gifts?"

"Is it true that you turned down his marriage proposal?" Greg asked.

"Yes." Paige wondered who else Jared had shared their little secret with. Had he taken out an ad in the paper?

"Then be prepared," Greg told her. "He's mounting a full-fledged attack. L.J. is a man with a mission, and you, little lady, have no idea what you're in for. I've seen him in action before. He always gets what he wants, and he wants you."

"Come on, doomsayer. Paige needs time to open her gifts and collect her thoughts before the man in question arrives." Kay led Greg toward the door. "She's giving him his ring back as soon as he comes in."

"I'd give a month's salary to see that," Greg said.

Kay closed the door on her way out, leaving Paige alone, staring at the two pink boxes. Go ahead and get it over with, she told herself. They're gifts, not bombs. Maybe she shouldn't open them. Maybe she should just return them to him still prettily wrapped when she gave him back his ring.

Reaching out hesitantly, she ran her finger over the satin ribbon on the larger box. What sort of presents had Jared sent? Paige untied the ribbon, ripped off the paper and removed the lid. Beneath the pink tissue paper lay a white leather photo album. A handwritten note had been placed on top.

With trembling fingers, Paige picked up the note. *For*

all the pictures we're going to take of our little girl. Tears welled up in her eyes. She already had the first pictures of their baby—the sonogram pictures—and she hadn't shared them with Jared.

Wiping her tears, Paige opened the second gift. Inside, a tiny silver spoon nestled against another note. After picking up the spoon, she saw the letter *A* engraved on the handle. She lifted the note. *I've decided I like the name Angela. Do you?*

What was she going to do with Jared Montgomery? How was she going to fight a man so determined to marry her, especially when she would not only be fighting Jared, but her own desires, too?

Smiling and self-confident, Jared breezed into Paige's office at ten o'clock. "Good morning, honey." He glanced at the roses on her desk. "It's a beautiful day, isn't it? Bright sunshine, crisp autumn air, red roses for my favorite redhead and—"

"Jared, may I see you in your office right now?" Paige scooted back her chair, stood and walked around her desk.

"Did you get the gifts?" he asked.

"Yes, thank you. They're both very nice. You must have gone to a lot of trouble to buy the roses and the gifts and have them delivered before business hours." She nodded toward his closed office door.

"Money has its privileges." Jared opened the door, stood back and waited for her to enter first. The minute she was inside his office, he closed and locked the door. "I assume you want our conversation to be private."

"Yes. Although I don't know why. We don't seem to have any secrets from Kay and Greg. For all I know everyone else at Montgomery's knows that I'm pregnant with your child."

"I didn't tell anyone else. Did you?" Slipping his arm

around her waist, he drew her close, lowered his head and covered her mouth with his.

She wanted to lose herself in the kiss, wanted to forget the reason she'd asked for this private audience with Jared. For one brief instant, she allowed herself to enjoy the kiss. She even responded. But as quickly as she'd succumbed to the temptation, she fought it, pulling back and shoving forcefully against his chest.

"We cannot solve all our problems this way," she said breathlessly. "I know what you're trying to do, and it won't work. I will not allow you to cloud my mind with passion."

His killer smile aimed directly at her, Jared shrugged, walked around his desk and sat down in the big, oxblood leather swivel chair.

Paige slid the six-carat diamond off her finger and laid it directly in front of him on his desk. "I'm not going to marry you. I can't keep the ring. And you're not going to change my mind."

"I've made reservations for us for lunch today," he said, speaking as if he hadn't heard a word of her adamant declaration. "I plan to make sure you have a proper meal at noon every day."

"Fine. No problem. I'll have lunch with you today and every day until the baby is born, but I am not going to marry you."

"I've arranged for Menderson's Office Supply to deliver a new chair for your desk. Something larger, more plush, with a good back support."

"Thank you," she said through clenched teeth. "I appreciate your concern for my comfort, but—"

"Of course, I'd prefer that you didn't work, but since you've made it abundantly clear that you want to continue working until after Angela is born, I intend to do everything I can to make things as easy as possible for you."

"Jared, you don't really want to marry me."

"I don't?"

She wished he'd stop smiling, stop acting as if they were playing some sort of game. She was deadly serious and he was treating the whole situation as if he found it highly amusing.

"No, you don't," she told him. "You've gotten so wrapped up in getting your own way—in making me marry you—that you haven't thought things through. You want and need a chic, sophisticated woman who's been bred to be a millionaire businessman's wife. I'm just an ordinary working girl, with a middle-class mentality. All I want is to buy my own small doll shop, marry an accountant or a teacher, have a little house with a white picket fence and live happily ever after. Can't you see that I'm the wrong girl for you?"

"Maybe you're right," he said, still smiling.

"What?" He was agreeing with her? Was it going to be this simple to change his mind?

"I'm willing to try to see things your way, to admit that you might be right about us." Leaning back in his swivel chair, he crossed his arms behind his head. "But I'll expect the same from you."

"What do you mean?" She had a sinking feeling in her stomach.

"I mean that I think we should both keep an open mind about marriage. Right now, I still think it's the best solution to our problem. Obviously, you don't. So, let's say for the next month we agree not to make a decision. You'll allow me to try to bring you around to my way of thinking and I'll allow you to try to convince me that you're right about what a disaster it would be for us to marry."

"I—I think that's a very reasonable suggestion." A cautious little voice in the back of her mind warned her not to trust him. She disregarded the warning.

*   *   *

By the time a week had passed, she regretted not listening to that foreboding little voice. Greg Addison had warned her. Her own instincts had warned her. But she'd been too stupid to listen!

"For a solid week, he's been driving me stark, raving mad with endless attention," Paige complained to Kay.

"I think it's kind of sweet the way he checks on you constantly during the day to make sure you aren't overdoing it, and the way he's always asking if you need anything."

"You think it's kind of sweet, do you? Well, you try being the object of his constant attention and see how you like it." Paige groaned. "Lunch has become a daily ordeal. Jared has all the chefs at the local restaurants busy preparing nourishing meals for me."

"He's just concerned about you and the baby."

"He's trying to run my life. That's what he's doing. He treats me as if I don't have enough sense to make even the simplest decision without his input. And even though I'm barely showing, I'm pretty sure that everyone in Grand Springs and perhaps even as far away as Denver knows that I'm pregnant with L. J. Montgomery's baby."

"So you're sick and tired of the daily delivery of red roses and all the gifts he's sent to your apartment for you and the baby, huh?"

"I like white roses!"

"So tell him."

"The point isn't the color of the roses. Not really. And it's not even the fact that my apartment is beginning to look like Babyland at the department store."

"Then what is the point?" Kay asked.

"The point is that I've had just about all the smothering attention I can stand. I'm tired of Jared trying to control me, of trying to change my life and—"

"So tell him."

"I'm going to. Today." Paige squared her shoulders. "I'm going to tell him that he's taken advantage of the terms of our truce agreement and I want him to stop his overbearing actions immediately!"

"If necessary, you can even tell him about your dinner date for tonight." Kay grinned wickedly.

When Kay had introduced her to Martin Smith, the most mysterious man in Grand Springs, and Martin had asked her out, Paige had declined his offer at first. But after Kay pointed out to her that by dating someone else, she might convince Jared that she was serious about her refusal to marry him, Paige had agreed to have dinner with Martin. Also, she felt a bit sorry for him. The night of the Grand Springs blackout, he'd entered Vanderbilt Memorial with no idea who he was. His amnesia continued to this day.

Kay had also pointed out that it certainly wouldn't be a hardship to spend an evening with a handsome and incredibly fascinating guy. Someone even L. J. Montgomery would consider a worthy opponent.

"If Jared won't listen to what I have to say, then maybe I will tell him about Martin." Paige admitted to herself that, if the circumstances of her personal life were different, she might find Martin Smith irresistible. Big, blond and sexy as all get out, he was more than a match for Jared.

"There's no time like the present, is there?" Kay's mischievous smile broadened.

"You're right. I've put this off long enough." Despite the queasy unease in her stomach, Paige stood, smiled half-heartedly at Kay and walked toward Jared's office.

She swung open the door, marched into his office and stood in front of his desk. She planted her hands on her hips. "We have to talk."

"Is something wrong? Are you sick? Are you in pain?" Jared rounded his desk in two seconds flat and grabbed

Paige by the shoulders. "Is Angela all right?" He placed one hand on Paige's tummy.

"I'm fine. Angela— The baby's fine."

He guided Paige to the leather sofa in his office. "Sit down, honey, and tell me what's wrong. Whatever it is, I'll fix it for you."

She allowed him to assist her, and when he was seated beside her, she turned to him and laid her hand on his arm. "Thank you, Jared. You're the only one who *can* fix things, because *you* are my problem."

Lifting her hand in his, he gazed into her eyes, his face etched with amusement. "I know that I caused your problems, Paige, but I've been doing everything I can to convince you that I have the solution to those problems."

"Your campaign to convince me has *become* the problem." She pulled her hand out of his grasp. "You're smothering me. You've tried to take over my life. You even set up an appointment with Dr. Petrocelli to discuss my pregnancy."

"He refused to tell me anything, except that mother and baby are fine," Jared said. "He sympathized with my predicament, but ethics prevented him from revealing more specific data on you and Angela."

"That's another thing. Stop calling my baby Angela. I haven't decided what to name her yet." Glancing down at her tummy, Paige laid a protective hand over her unborn child. "Besides, if we give her a name now...and start calling her by that name...and something happens...It would be easier if she wasn't already a real person, with a real name and—"

Jared placed his index finger over Paige's lips, silencing her. "Our little girl is already very real to me, and I suspect she's just as real to you."

Sitting up straight and squaring her shoulders, Paige

looked directly at him. "We've gotten sidetracked from what we need to discuss."

"Which is?"

"I want you to cease and desist. Immediately. Today."

"Too many roses? Too many little gifts?"

"Too many and too much. Of everything," she said. "I've accepted the fact that as my child's father, you have certain rights, but—"

"That's good of you."

Jared grinned. Paige groaned.

"I promise to keep you posted on my physical condition, and if I need anything, I'll let you know. But no more lunches. No more red roses. And no more gifts! And most important..." She paused for effect. "I want you to live your life the way you did before we met, and I'll live mine."

"Exactly what do you mean by that?"

"I mean, stop hovering over me all the time. Stop sending Greg on business trips you should make. Start dating again."

"Start dating again?" Narrowing his eyes, he glowered at her. "Are you planning on dating someone else?"

"As a matter of fact, I am."

"You can't date someone else. You're four-and-a-half months pregnant with my baby."

"So? I'm not showing. Much. Other men still find me attractive."

"I'll just bet they do. I'll bet they find you very attractive." Jared's nostrils flared, and his jaw tightened. "You are not going to date anyone else. I forbid you."

He reached for her as she shot up off the sofa. "You forbid me? You forbid me?"

When Jared rose to his feet, Paige punched him in the center of his chest with her index finger.

"You're mine," he told her. "And that's mine." He pointed toward her tummy.

"Wrong," she said. "I do not *belong* to you. And you may be the father of my baby, but she doesn't *belong* to you, either. And for your information, Martin Smith is taking me to dinner at Josephina's tonight, whether you like it or not."

"Martin Smith? Who the hell is Martin Smith? And how did you meet him?"

"Kay introduced us. He's—"

"Hell, he's not that guy Greg told me about, is he? The mystery man nobody knows anything about?"

"I know that he's good-looking, charming and—"

"The man could be a criminal or an escapee from a mental institution or a bigamist or—"

"Well, whatever he is, tonight he's my dinner date."

Paige turned to leave, but before she could take a step, Jared grabbed her shoulder and whirled her around to face him.

"Don't do this, Paige."

"From now on, I'm going to do whatever I want to do. Date whomever I want to date. Live my life on my own terms. I suggest you do the same."

He wasn't jealous. He couldn't be! Jealousy implied a certain lack of self-confidence. The very thought that Lawrence Jared Montgomery lacked self-confidence was ludicrous. And in order to be jealous, he'd have to be afraid of losing something he cared for deeply, even loved. And that wasn't the case at all. Yes, he liked Paige. And hell yes, he desired her greatly. But *love* wasn't a word in his vocabulary. He didn't know what love was—that all-consuming, romantic passion Paige claimed she prized above everything else. Even if love existed, he doubted he was capable of the emotion, of truly loving a woman, or completely trusting one, for that matter.

He'd been fond of his parents, as they had been fond of him, but he'd never felt that they loved him. He had been their son, their possession, the heir to the family millions. The only person Jared had ever cared for deeply had been Grandpa Monty. He supposed some people might call what he'd felt for the old man *love*. But the word hadn't been one either of them had used.

No, it wasn't jealousy that had driven him to take such drastic actions. There was a simpler explanation for why Jared had commandeered a rather reluctant Kay Thompson into accompanying him to dinner tonight at Josephina's. He was concerned about Paige. That was all there was to it. Plain and simple concern for the well-being of his child's mother. After all, no one seemed to know anything about Paige's date, this Martin Smith. The man could be dangerous. It was Jared's duty to keep an eye on her and make sure she was safe.

And he had to admit that in a dark corner of his mind, he suspected Paige was using this Martin Smith to manipulate him in some way. He didn't want to distrust Paige, didn't want to question her motives. He wanted her to be just what she seemed—an independent, stubborn, honest, young working girl. But no matter how hard he tried, he couldn't shake the notion that maybe Paige had deliberately trapped him. That she'd known who he was that night in the elevator.

Kay sipped her chardonnay, then set the flute down on the table. "I think you're making a big mistake coming here like this. When Paige sees you, she's going to be furious."

Jared swirled the wine around in his glass. "I didn't ask for your opinion, did I, Ms. Thompson?"

"No, sir, you didn't," Kay said. "All you did was order me to come to dinner with you tonight."

Ignoring Kay's comment, Jared glanced across the room where Paige and Martin Smith were enjoying their meal and obviously enjoying each other's company even more. Jared didn't like the way Paige kept smiling at her dinner companion, and he hated the way she occasionally laughed at something the guy said. But more than anything, he despised the way the big blond man was looking at Paige, as if she were tonight's dessert.

"How naive can Paige be?" Jared slammed his glass down on the table. Wine sloshed over the side of the flute. "Smith is practically drooling all over her. Doesn't she know what that guy's after? Or doesn't she care?" Despite what Paige had told him, Jared really didn't know how many men there had been in her life before he met her.

"I assume you think he's after the same thing you were after the first time you met Paige." Kay picked up her fork and speared a piece of lettuce from her salad plate. "A woman who looks like Paige has that effect on men, doesn't she. Well, at least Martin's buying her dinner first."

"What the hell do you mean by that?" Jared glared at Kay. "You don't actually think Paige would...I mean she wouldn't... Dammit, she can't. She's pregnant."

"I didn't say that Paige is going to do anything. You're the one who assumes that Martin is out to seduce her...or vice versa." Kay crunched on the lettuce, then speared a tomato slice. "But if you think being pregnant prevents a woman from having sex, then it's obvious you don't know the first thing about pregnancy. There usually aren't any restrictions on sexual activity until the last few weeks. Besides, I understand that some women get very horny while they're pregnant."

Raging anger suffused Jared, heating his body. "Dammit all!'' If Paige was going to have sex with anyone while she was pregnant, she'd have it with him. Not some muscle-bound blonde. ''Why did you introduce her to him anyway?''

''I thought they'd make a nice-looking couple,'' Kay said. ''And since Paige has made it perfectly clear that she isn't going to marry you, I thought—''

''You're damn lucky I don't fire you!''

''You can't fire me. I'm an essential member of your organization.'' Kay twirled an onion curl around on her fork. ''Besides, I'm simply telling you the truth. It's not my fault if you don't like to hear it. Sooner or later, Paige is going to meet Mr. Right. He's going to adore her for the person she is and not want to change her. And then they're going to fall madly in love and get married.''

Paige married to someone else? No way. Another man raising his daughter? Never!

Paige was his. Angela was his. His, by God, and he'd kill any man who tried to take them away from him.

Ignoring Jared's heated glare, Paige hoped Martin didn't notice that someone was staring daggers at him. She supposed she shouldn't be surprised that Jared had followed her to Josephina's. The man was capable of anything.

''Is something wrong?'' Martin asked. ''Is your prime rib—''

''Oh, no, the prime rib is delicious.'' Reaching across the table, she covered his hand with hers. ''I'm sorry. I'm afraid I let my mind wander. I was thinking of something unpleasant.''

''I see.'' Martin clasped Paige's hand. ''Was your mind wandering several tables over to the left? And was the unpleasant thing you were thinking about the scowling man sitting with Kay? The man who looks as if he'd like to kill me with his bare hands?''

''Oh, Martin. I am so very sorry.'' Paige squeezed his

hand. "I had hoped you wouldn't notice Jared. He has no right to follow me around and try to intimidate my date."

"What's with him, anyway?" Martin asked. "Are you two involved?"

"We were," Paige admitted. "And to be honest, we still are. In a way. He's asked me to marry him and I've said no, but he refuses to take no for an answer."

"Ah, a man in love. What's the problem? You don't feel the same way about him?"

"He's not in love with me. He just wants me."

"Well, I can't say I blame him for wanting you," Martin said. "But there must be more to it than that. I know a jealous, possessive man when I see one. Your Jared obviously thinks he has a claim on you."

"He's not *my* Jared. Oh, no, he's coming over this way." Paige groaned. "Please, Martin, ignore anything he says or does. And whatever you do, don't let him goad you into doing something stupid."

Leaning forward, Martin brought Paige's hand to his lips and kissed it. "I won't strike the first blow, I promise."

Pausing beside the table, Jared bestowed his devastating smile on Paige, then, still smiling, he gave Martin a deadly stare before returning his attention to her. She eased her hand out of Martin's.

"Hello, Paige. I hope you're having a pleasant evening," Jared said.

"It was very pleasant. Until now," Paige told him.

Kay slipped up behind Jared. Looking directly at Paige, she nodded her head and shrugged apologetically.

"You aren't drinking wine, are you?" Jared surveyed the table. "You know that in your condition, you aren't supposed to drink any alcohol."

Martin gave Paige a quizzical look. Her face flushed. Kay punched Jared in the ribs.

"I'm drinking water." Paige lifted the glass. "Would you care to do a taste test?"

"Of course not, honey. I trust you." Jared turned to Martin. "Aren't you going to introduce me to your date?"

"Sure. Martin Smith—" she extended her open palm toward her date in an introductory manner, then pivoted it toward Jared "—L. J. Montgomery."

The two men nodded, each eyeing the other. Jared glared at Martin and Martin glared right back, not giving an inch. Paige sighed.

"Make sure you don't keep Paige out too late, Mr. Smith," Jared said. "Pregnant women need their rest."

"Pregnant?" Martin's gaze jumped from Jared's self-satisfied smile to Paige's startled brown eyes.

Jared patted Paige affectionately on the shoulder. "You know I don't mind your going out and having a good time, as long as you remember to take good care of my baby."

"Baby?" Martin asked. "Paige, is this guy for real? You're pregnant?"

Paige nodded affirmatively.

"With his baby?"

Flinging her napkin down on top of her dinner plate, Paige shoved back her chair, stood and ran away from the table.

"Now look what you've gone and done," Kay said.

"Paige, honey, wait!" Jared called after her as she rushed past the curious customers staring at her.

Kay grabbed Jared's arm, halting him before he could chase Paige. "You've done enough for one night, Mr. Montgomery. I don't think Paige is in the mood to listen to anything you have to say."

"Maybe I should go after her," Martin said. "I can take her home and—"

"If anyone is taking Paige home, I am." Jared's harsh glare dared Martin to disagree.

"Neither of you are taking Paige anywhere," Kay said. "I'll make sure she gets home. You—" she pointed an accusatory finger at Jared "—stay away from her tonight." Kay ran, catching up with Paige just as she walked outside.

Jared realized that everyone in Josephina's was staring at Martin Smith and him. He'd made a complete fool of himself in public, but he had accomplished his goal. He had ruined Paige's date. But at what cost? He had also antagonized her. He wondered if she'd ever forgive him.

"If you don't marry that woman, you're a fool," Martin said. "It's plain to see that she's one in a million."

"You don't have to tell me she's one in a million. No one knows better than I do how special Paige is."

Jared's declaration startled him. Did he truly believe what he'd said? Was Paige really special to him? Yes, dammit, she was. Somehow that little earthy redhead had gotten under his skin. She'd caught him in a trap from which he didn't really want to escape.

Either she was the most naive innocent he'd ever known or the shrewdest, most conniving, calculating female he'd ever met. His gut instincts told him that Paige Summers was exactly what she appeared to be. But his male ego warned him to be cautious.

Six

No roses had been delivered to her office on Friday nor any gifts sent to her home during the weekend. Jared hadn't taken her out to lunch on Friday because Jared hadn't come into the office. He had left a message for Greg Addison, telling his partner that in case of an emergency he could be reached at his Texas ranch.

Paige had been prepared to confront Jared and rake him over the coals for the idiotic, macho, jealous scene he had created at Josephina's on Thursday night. But with his conspicuous absence, he had given her time to cool off and to wonder just what he was up to now. Kay thought he might have gone away to regroup, to reorganize his strategy, since his first plan of action had failed so miserably.

Paige didn't care why he'd chosen to fly off to Texas, she was just glad that he had. She'd never been as angry with anyone as she'd been with Jared. If for one minute she thought that his foolish actions had been prompted by love, she could forgive him his jealousy. But the only thing that had prompted Jared was a fear that he might lose something he considered his personal possession. He didn't love her; he wanted to own her. He thought that she and their baby belonged to him.

Kay laid two sandwiches, a couple of bananas and a carton of milk on the table in the employees' lounge. "No sign of the boss man again today. It could be he's too ashamed to show his face after his performance at Josephina's. People here in Grand Springs will be discussing that little fiasco for weeks to come.''

"I doubt he's ashamed of what he did," Paige said. "He accomplished what he set out to do. Embarrass me in front of Martin, ruin my date and warn off anyone else who might show an interest in me. All Jared cares about is getting his own way, and he doesn't care who he hurts.''

"I admit you have good reason to be upset with him." Kay poured a cup of coffee and placed it beside her lunch. "But don't you think you're being a little too hard on him? I was with the guy, and I can tell you that he was in agony seeing you with Martin.''

"He wasn't in enough agony to suit me." Paige unwrapped the club sandwich, separated the two halves and lifted a piece to her mouth.

"You know I understand your side of this situation." Kay added sweetener and creamer to her coffee. "But I can see L.J.'s side, too.''

"Oh, really? I thought you were my friend. Are you taking Jared's side now?''

"I'm not taking anybody's side," Kay said. "I'm afraid you two are in a no-win situation. He wants what you aren't willing to give and you want what he's incapable of giving.''

"You think I'm crazy for not marrying him, don't you. You think that any woman in her right mind would jump at the chance to be Mrs. L. J. Montgomery.''

"I don't think you're crazy." Kay sipped her coffee. "But I do believe that you aren't being totally honest with yourself about why you won't marry him.''

Munching on the dill pickle slice she'd taken off the top of her sandwich, Paige narrowed her eyes, glaring at Kay.

Kay unwrapped her ham-and-cheese sandwich. "Have you ever considered the possibility that you're punishing him for not loving you just as you are, for wanting to remold you into a different woman?''

"Punishing him...? Where did you get such an idea?" Paige spluttered.

"L.J. doesn't love you because he can't. He doesn't believe in love. Has no idea what being in love is all about.''

"That pretty much sums up his views on the subject."

"Well, I'd say that you aren't being honest about whether or not you want to marry him. Instead, you've been punishing him for not loving you by keeping him from getting what he wants. Namely, you and the baby. And he's been so determined to have his own way, trying to steamroll you into agreeing to marry him, that he hasn't given your needs much consideration.''

"Is there a reason for this amateur psychiatric evaluation?" Paige asked. "Are you about to give me some incredibly brilliant advice?"

"If L.J. doesn't know how to love, and his love is what you want, then you should teach him how to love." Kay bit into her sandwich.

"Teach him how to love?" Was it possible, Paige wondered, to teach someone how to love? "Just how do you suggest I go about doing it? Hypnotize him? Put a spell on him?''

"I haven't figured out the whys and wherefores," Kay admitted. "But if the only thing keeping you from marrying him is his not loving you, then I should think you could figure out a way to—''

"You have to have a heart in order to love," Paige said. "And I seriously doubt that L. J. Montgomery has a heart.''

"Ms. Summers?" The masculine voice came from the doorway. "May I see you in my office as soon as you finish your lunch?''

Kay and Paige snapped around immediately, both gasping silently when they saw Jared standing just outside the lounge. Turning to face Paige, Kay rolled her eyes upward and mouthed a rather expressive expletive.

"Yes, certainly, Mr. Montgomery," Paige said. "I'll be there shortly."

Jared stared directly at her, but Paige realized that he was looking through her. His eyes were void of any emotion. Without saying another word, he turned and walked down the hall.

"Well, that was an uncomfortable moment, wasn't it?" Kay placed her hand on Paige's shoulder. "I wonder how long he'd been standing behind us listening to our conversation?"

"I have no idea," Paige said. "But I'm sure he heard me tell you that I don't think he has a heart."

"He called you Ms. Summers. That doesn't bode well. I wonder what happened to him while he was in Texas."

Paige gathered up her half-eaten lunch, shoved back her chair and stood. "I guess I'll find out when I get to his office." Paige dumped the remains of her meal in the garbage.

She stopped by the rest room to freshen her makeup and buy enough time to calm her screaming nerves. She had no idea what Jared was going to say, but her feminine instincts warned her to be wary. His cool, controlled facade could well be nothing more than another tactical maneuver to put her off guard.

The door to his office stood wide open. He sat perched on the edge of his desk, his arms crossed over his chest, waiting for her like a commander prepared to issue orders to his subordinates. She took a deep breath, counted to ten and marched right into the lion's den, fully prepared to fight to the death, if need be.

"Thank you for cutting your lunch short," he said.

"What I have to say is very important to me, and I hope a great relief to you. After our discussion, please return to the lounge and finish your lunch. You need proper nourishment."

"I'll eat something on my afternoon break," she said. "Now, Jar—Mr. Montgomery, why did you ask me to come to your office?"

"Sit down, please."

When she sat down in the chair in front of his desk, he shifted his hips and turned to face her. "First, I want to apologize for embarrassing you the way I did when I made a scene at Josephina's the other night. I was way out of line." He spoke directly to her, but his gaze focused on the framed map hanging on the wall behind her.

She wondered if he was being honest or if this contrite behavior was just an act. "Yes, you *were* out of line. You had no right to—"

"That's what I want to talk to you about," he said. "I want to define exactly what my rights are concerning you and our child. I flew off to the ranch right after I left Josephina's because I needed some time to sort things through and put the whole situation into proper perspective."

"I see. Well, you aren't the only one who's been giving a great deal of thought to the situation." Leaning forward, Paige clasped her shaky hands together. "Things can't go on the way they have been. You can't continue disregarding my feelings in your efforts to get what you want."

He looked directly at her then. "I agree."

Paige's mouth fell open. "You agree?"

"I've considered our situation from every angle and taken your needs as well as my own into consideration," he told her. "You've made it perfectly clear that you don't want to marry me. I accept your decision, and I won't ask you again."

"You won't?"

"No." Glancing away from her sharp scrutiny, he cleared his throat. "I've offered time and again, and you've refused me time and again. So I've come up with another plan that will enable me to take care of you and our child and still allow both of us our freedom."

"You've come up with a plan?" she asked. "What sort of plan?"

"I'd like to be present when our little girl is born, and I want to be a part of her life from that moment forward." Jared slid off the edge of the desk. "I intend to take care of my daughter. I'll have my lawyer arrange generous child support payments in exchange for very liberal visitation rights.

"I want you to consider allowing me to sign over my home here in Grand Springs to you. For you and the baby. And I'd like to set you up in business. Being your own boss would enable you to take the baby to work with you at least part of the time."

Stunned by Jared's rational solution to their problem, Paige sat there speechless for several minutes. Was this the same man who'd been damned and determined to marry her? Was this the same jealous, possessive, macho jerk who had done everything but brand her with a hot poker in order to lay claim to her?

"What happened to change your mind?" she asked. "You were so adamant about our getting married."

What had happened? Hell, Jared had realized how out of control he was. L. J. Montgomery always controlled the situation. He never allowed the situation to control him. But Paige's unexpected pregnancy had thrown him for a loop, knocked him off center and hurled him into a succession of illogical, emotional, irrational actions. He had allowed his obsession with Paige Summers to nearly wreck his life. He had become so determined to make her marry him that he'd given her complete power over his life. And no one, least of all, some stubborn, ungrateful working girl was going to have him jumping through hoops.

After a great deal of thought, he had come to one conclusion. He didn't trust Paige. He didn't trust any woman. Hell, he didn't trust people in general.

He wanted to marry Paige and be a father to their child. Her repeated refusals to accept his proposal could be genuine. But denying him what he wanted could also be a ploy. There was only one way to find out. Call Paige's bluff. If she thought he was no longer determined to marry her, she might do an about-face and reveal her true colors. He had to know the truth.

So starting today, he was taking back control of his life. If Paige turned out to be a conniving, manipulative little schemer, then he could return to his sensible five-year plan, reach all his professional goals and then choose an elegant, sophisticated lady, one fully prepared to be L. J. Montgomery's wife. She would marry him gladly and appreciate all that his wealth and social position offered her.

Of course, if Paige was on the up-and-up, he'd have to find a way to convince her how foolish her romantic notions of love were. He didn't expect to love his wife. And he didn't expect her to love him. A cold, clammy uneasiness spread through Jared's body. What did it matter to him that his future wife wouldn't love him? After all, he didn't believe in love.

"Are you all right?" Paige asked. "You look like you're in pain."

Shaking his head to dislodge any cock-and-bull notions about love, Jared curved his lips into a halfhearted smile. "I'm fine," he assured her. "And as to what changed my mind about our getting married...well, let's just say that I came to my senses in time."

"Are you saying that you don't want to marry me?"

"I was willing to do the honorable thing and marry you since you're carrying my child," he said. "I realize now that you're right. Neither of us can get what we want from a marriage to each other. You'll eventually find some man who will be able to give you the love you need, and in five years, I'll choose my proper mate."

"I don't know what to say." Paige felt as if she'd been hit by a two-ton truck. This was the reaction she had halfway expected when Jared first learned that she was pregnant. But not now. Not after he'd spent weeks pursuing her, showering her with gifts and attention, and pleading with her to be his wife.

"You don't have to say anything, except that you agree to my terms. I'm prepared to give you what you asked for in the beginning, and that was for you to be allowed to continue working here at Montgomery's until the baby is born. I won't interfere in your life, other than as your employer and as Angela's father. I think you'll agree that I do have a right to be concerned about my child."

"Yes, of course you have a right. It's just that I—"

"We can meet with my lawyer tomorrow and iron out all the details concerning child support and visitation. And whenever you decide about the house, just let me know."

"I won't need a house," she said. "My apartment has a small room that I use for storage. I can turn that into a nursery."

"Fine." He nodded his head. "But later on, in a year or so, if you decide you want the house or one of the new condos Montgomery's is building, you can let me know."

"All right."

"What about allowing me to finance your business?" he asked. "I'd be doing it as much for Angela as for you."

"I'll think about it. But if—and that's a big if—I allow you to help me buy my doll shop and set me up in business, I'll consider it a loan and I'll repay it with interest."

If Paige was acting, she was giving an Academy Award-winning performance, Jared decided. But it was too soon to tell. He had to stick to his plan and wait it out, until he was certain he could trust Paige.

"All right. We'll consider it a loan, if that's the way you want it."

"That's the way I want it."

Paige seemed to be disappointed that he'd given up his pursuit to marry her. But he was relatively certain that she was merely in a state of shock over his abrupt change of heart, and that once she had time to carefully consider his new plan, she would readily agree. Unless her reluctance to marry him really had been an act.... Time would tell. If he had misjudged Paige, she'd give herself away soon enough. If marriage without a prenuptial agreement had been her goal all along, then she'd be forced to pursue him from now on.

"Is that all?" she asked. "Is our discussion concluded? May I leave?"

"Will you meet with my lawyer and sign the agreement tomorrow?"

"Not tomorrow. I'll want my own lawyer to take a look at the agreement first." Paige stood on unsteady legs, willing herself not to stumble on her way out of his office. She held out her hand. "Agreed?"

"Agreed." He gripped her hand in his, shaking it soundly. But he didn't want to let her go. He wanted to pull her into his arms and kiss her. He wanted to add an amendment to their agreement. One that said she would be his lover for as long as he wanted her.

He might not trust Paige, but he couldn't deny the desire that raged inside him. That hot desire could easily be his downfall if he didn't control it. A shrewd woman would know how to use it against him.

Paige jerked her hand out of his grasp. Their gazes met

and held for one long, endless moment, then she looked away and turned, hurrying toward the door.

"Oh, one other thing," Jared said.

She stopped in the doorway but didn't turn around. "I'm driving into Denver next Tuesday for a business meeting. It'll be an overnight trip. I'll need you to go along. As my secretary."

"Overnight?"

"Separate rooms, I promise."

"Strictly business?"

"Business and friendship," he said. "It will make things a lot easier all the way around if you and I can be friends." He crossed the room, halted a foot away from her and reached out, placing his hand on her shoulder. Fighting the urge to take her in his arms and ravish her, Jared squeezed her shoulder gently. "We can put off signing the agreement until after our trip to Denver. We can take that time alone to discuss our child and her future. What do you say?"

"I'll think about it and let you know."

She walked away, through her office and out into the hallway. Jared had the oddest notion that she was rushing off in tears. Surely he was mistaken. Why would she be crying? She'd gotten what she wanted. Or had she?

Even after they were under way, heading south to I-70, Paige wasn't sure she'd made the right decision. But in the week following Jared's return from his Texas ranch, he had neither said nor done anything to suggest that he wasn't one hundred percent sincere about their new agreement. Except for his occasional comments about the baby, he maintained a completely professional attitude toward her. He was her courteous, considerate employer and she was his competent, loyal employee.

Her doubts followed her all the way to Denver as they

connected with I-70, which took them directly into the Mile-High City.

"Why don't we simply fly to Denver in the company jet and return immediately following the business meeting?" she had questioned him before they left town.

"To be perfectly honest, Paige, I want some time alone with you. Away from the office and away from Grand Springs," he'd said. "You and I have some major decisions to make about our lives and our daughter's life. I thought this trip would give us the opportunity to get to know each other a little better...as friends. If we're going to raise a child together, we should at least be friends, don't you think?"

He was right, of course, and although her instincts cautioned her that she might be heading into trouble, she agreed to make the trip with him.

During the two-and-a-half hour drive in Jared's new Jeep Grand Cherokee, he kept up a running conversation on various subjects. Gradually Paige realized that the two of them actually had quite a lot in common, despite the vast difference in their backgrounds. They enjoyed skiing, horseback riding, camping, canoeing and fishing.

"I had no idea you were such an outdoor girl." He looked at her as if seeing her for the first time. "I assumed a woman whose passion is buying, selling and restoring dolls wouldn't be into macho stuff like camping and fishing."

"You forget that I grew up with a very macho father and two gung ho younger brothers. In my family, I either learned to enjoy macho stuff or I got left out."

When Jared put on a Garth Brooks CD, they discovered that they both loved country music. And that led to a discussion about music in general, which revealed their mutual enjoyment of classical and their dislike for hard rock.

They arrived in Denver at ten-thirty, just in time to

freshen up before Jared's eleven o'clock appointment. Five minutes into the business meeting with a group of potential investors, Paige realized that her presence was unnecessary. The minute the meeting ended, at a quarter to twelve, she confronted him. He admitted that requesting her secretarial skills for the business trip had been a ruse.

"I knew that if I was totally honest with you and told you that I wanted to bring you to Denver on a shopping trip, you would have balked at the idea," he told her.

"A shopping trip?"

"For maternity clothes, and for a complete layette, for everything our baby will need."

"But, Jared—"

"Come on, Paige. This is something I want to do for you and our child."

"I don't know...."

"Look, honey, as the baby's father, I not only have certain rights, but certain obligations, too. Don't you agree?"

"Yes, of course. It's just that—"

"Even if we aren't going to marry, I want to fulfill my obligations."

"All right," she reluctantly agreed.

He took her to lunch at European Café on Market Street, a three-story renovated brick warehouse decorated with antique carved-oak paneling. They dined on one of the chef's specialties, filet mignottee "monsieur Louis" and discussed the Lamaze classes they agreed to take together.

They spent hours at Cherry Creek North, checking out the wonderful boutiques and stopping for a late afternoon dessert at one of the sidewalk cafés strung along First, Second and Third Avenues.

Jared made every decision. He chose every item for her and the child. As much as she loved having a new maternity wardrobe, she would have enjoyed it more if she'd been able to choose it herself.

This is what it would be like being married to Jared, she told herself. You aren't even married to him and he's already running your life to suit himself!

They filled the back of the Jeep with boxes of maternity clothes and matching accessories, and Jared made arrangements to have all the items he had purchased for the baby shipped to Grand Springs.

By the time they arrived at the Brown Palace Hotel on Seventeenth Street in downtown Denver, it was after six in the evening and Paige was exhausted. When the bellhop opened the doors to their suite, Paige's mouth fell open. Stopping just inside the sitting room, she surveyed the fine antique furniture, lamps and mirrors. She had never seen anything quite so luxuriously elegant outside the pages of a magazine.

"Take the lady's bag in there," Jared instructed the bellhop, then turned to Paige. "Why don't you go on into your room and take a nap before dinner? I know you're exhausted. I'm afraid I let you overdo it today."

"We're sharing a suite?" Paige asked.

"Separate bedrooms," he reminded her.

"Oh, yes, of course." The bellhop opened the door to her room and carried in her small overnight bag. Paige followed, pausing in the doorway to turn and smile weakly at Jared. "I am tired. I think I'll take a short nap."

"Rest as long as you'd like," Jared said. "I've planned a late dinner here in the suite. I thought that would be better for you after such a tiring day."

"Yes, thank you. Dinner here would be nice."

Once alone in her bedroom, she closed the door and took a deep breath. Even at his best, Jared was the most aggressive, overwhelming, take-charge man she'd ever known.

Despite wearing low heels, Paige's feet ached from the hours of shopping. She kicked off her shoes, removed her coat and fell across the four-poster bed. Looking straight up, she gasped when she saw her mirrored reflection staring down at her.

Scooting off the bed, she glanced around the Victorian-style room while she undressed down to her slip. There was no telling what this suite cost per day, she thought, but then what did it matter to a man as wealthy as Jared.

She lay on top of the bedspread, nestled her head in the crook of her arm and dozed off to sleep, thinking about Jared. Jared with the mesmerizing green eyes. Jared with the devastating smile. Jared with the hard, lean body. Jared. Jared. Jared.

Jared reclined on the sofa. A half-finished rusty nail on the rocks rested on a coaster atop the coffee table, within arm's reach. A copy of the *Denver Post* lay on the floor at his side. He had accomplished a great deal today, far more than just touching base with some potential investors. Of course, his main objective had been to persuade Paige to accept his offer of a maternity wardrobe and a complete layette for Angela. She had protested at first, but then once the shopping bug bit her, she'd been unable to resist temptation.

What woman could have resisted spending his money? This was the first time in Paige's life that she'd been able to afford the best of everything.

After seeing, firsthand, what it could be like as his wife, with unlimited resources, would Paige start pursuing him? Now that he wasn't begging her to marry him, would she realize that she wanted to accept what he was offering— marriage without love—once she'd signed the prenuptial agreement protecting his assets in case of a divorce?

The ringing telephone roused Jared from his memories of a pleasant afternoon. He picked up the receiver. "Montgomery. Yes, that's right. Eight-thirty. No, I don't want any champagne. I ordered sparkling cider. The lady is pregnant. Just make sure everything is perfect."

He glanced at his watch. Seven-fifteen. He hadn't heard a sound from Paige's room since they first arrived. In sock feet, he crossed the sitting area, eased open her bedroom door and pecked in. Lying there on her side, in her half-slip and bra, her long red hair spread out across the pale bedspread, Paige looked like a sleeping beauty. Warmly flushed. Soft and delicate. Small, vulnerable and helpless. And sexy as hell.

He had told this woman he wanted them to be friends, and he did. But he wanted more. Paige had given herself to him once, freely, completely, going wild in his arms. But he now realized that her total abandon with him that night in the elevator had been uncharacteristic behavior for Paige Summers. She wasn't the type of woman who went around having sex with strangers, and he'd bet his last dollar that he was the only man who'd ever made her lose complete control.

He knew for a fact that she was the only woman who'd ever made him lose complete control. And that fact scared the hell out of him. He refused to allow anyone to have that kind of power over him.

Jared's sex hardened instantly and he cursed himself for wanting Paige. And why this woman, more than any other? What was so damn special about her? He could pretty well have his pick of women—everyone except the woman he wanted most. In every former relationship, no matter how passionate he felt about the lady, he never completely lost control. He made the rules. He said when things started and when they ended. And he'd never been enamored for more than a couple of months at a time.

But Paige Summers had changed everything. One wild, impetuous encounter with her in a stalled elevator had wreaked havoc on his orderly life. She'd turned him into a crazed lunatic, panting after her, begging her to marry him. And now, when he thought he'd finally taken back control of his life, he found himself longing for her more than ever.

Easing quietly across the room, he looked down at Paige. Her lush, Madonna-like femininity took his breath away. Her full, round breasts, already enlarged and preparing to nourish his child, strained against the lace cups of her bra. Her once flat stomach now bulged slightly, cradling the baby girl they had created together in their passion.

Unable to resist the lure of her beauty, Jared sat down on the bed beside her. He ran the back of his hand gently across her cheek. She stirred, sighing deeply, then opened her eyes and smiled.

"It's nearly seven-thirty," he told her. "We're having dinner in an hour. I thought you might want to freshen up first, maybe even take a bath."

She stretched lazily, like a newly awakened kitten, then glanced down at her undressed state. "Oh, I—I—" She crossed her arms over her breasts.

Jared pulled her hands away, grasped her wrists and lifted her arms over his shoulders as she rose into a sitting position. Her breasts brushed across his chest. She sucked in a startled breath.

"I've seen you in less," he said. "Don't be embarrassed." He found it difficult not to take advantage of their intimacy, not to draw her into his arms and kiss her. But he didn't dare. If he gave in to his desire for this woman, he'd be lost. And this time, he might not have the strength to regain control. Rising slowly from the bed, he took her hands into his and dragged her across the wrinkled spread.

"I've ordered a platter of fresh seafood. I remembered from our lunches together how much you like seafood."

She knew she should feel uncomfortable standing there in her underwear while Jared discussed their dinner menu, but she didn't. Somehow it felt natural to be alone with him, in her bedroom and partially undressed.

"I think I will take a bath and change clothes," she said. "I feel pretty grimy after all that shopping and then my nap."

"Take all the time you need." Reluctantly he released her hands.

Before he closed the bedroom door behind him, Paige rushed into the bathroom. She had to escape, had to get away from Jared before she made a fool of herself. No matter how many times she told herself that she couldn't possibly be in love with a man like Jared, her heart and her body told her the exact opposite.

She had no control of the sexual attraction she felt for him, the pure animalistic lust that overpowered them both. She didn't want to love Jared. She'd tried not to care about him. He was arrogant and overbearing, qualities she disliked, but he was also a strong, dependable man with a sense of honor she admired. He might think himself incapable of love. but she knew better. He had shown her how very caring and generous he could be.

Unfortunately, even with all his millions, Jared lacked the most important thing in the world. Love. And it was obvious to Paige that he was a man greatly in need of love. Perhaps that was why she was so drawn to him on an emotional level, why despite all his faults, she wanted to give him the one thing his money could never buy.

Dinner arrived promptly at eight-thirty. The waiter placed the meal on the table, arranged the small centerpiece bouquet and lit the candles. Jared turned off all the lights, except one table lamp, allowing the candles to create a cosy, comfortable atmosphere. All this scene needed was music, he thought, and remembered the digital clock radio on his nightstand. He flipped hurriedly through the stations until he heard the incomparable strains of a Strauss waltz.

At precisely eight-forty, Paige entered the sitting room. The sight of her in a dusty rose cotton dress with an empire waist and embroidered bodice took Jared's breath away. She'd left her hair loose, and the mane of burgundy silk cascaded down her back.

How the hell was a man supposed to control his baser instincts when he was presented with such a ravishing temptation? He'd been a fool to think that he could spend the night alone with Paige, even in separate bedrooms, and not want to make love to her.

The moment Paige observed the dimly lit room, the elegant dinner, complete with flowers and candles, her stomach tightened painfully. When she heard the soft, sweet music floating through Jared's open bedroom door, she halted abruptly.

"You look lovely," he said.

She stared at him. He was smiling at her, damn him. Didn't he know what his smile did to her? It turned her knees to jelly and set free a hundred tiny butterflies in the pit of her stomach.

He held out his hand and her instincts told her to flee, to turn around, run back into her bedroom and lock the door.

Had he set this romantic scene intentionally? If so, why? Had he been lying to her when he'd promised not to pursue her, not to ever again ask her to marry him? Or did Jared have another scenario in mind? Were his motives less honorable?

But during the next hour, she couldn't fault his actions

in any way. He was the perfect gentleman, engaging her in conversation while they enjoyed the delicious meal. They discussed the legal document Jared's lawyer had drawn up concerning their child and tentatively agreed to the terms.

"Are you sure you don't want your dessert?" Slicing off a piece of the chocolate cheesecake with his fork, Jared coaxed her to take a bite as he waved the sinfully rich concoction under her nose.

"Don't tempt me anymore," she pleaded. "With my inherited tendency to gain weight easily, I could end up looking like a baby whale by the time I deliver. You should see the pictures of my mother when she was expecting me."

Jared laid his fork on his plate. "Are your parents upset that we aren't going to get married?"

"Mama understands." Paige wiped her mouth with her linen napkin, then folded it and laid it beside her plate. "Daddy's another matter. He's so old-fashioned. He just doesn't want his unmarried daughter to have a baby and be a single mother. Besides, he likes you. He and Austen think I'm being a foolish female and that I'll regret not..." She lifted her glass and downed the last drops of chilled water.

"Do you think that there's even the slightest chance your father and brother are right?" Jared asked. "Is there a chance that you might regret refusing to marry me?"

Grasping her folded napkin, she twisted it tightly. "Oh, it's not just my father's and brother's opinion, but Kay's, too," Paige admitted. "They all think I'm nuts for not agreeing to marry you. After all, you're everything a woman could want. Rich, successful, handsome, intelligent—"

"And your baby's father."

"Yes, and my baby's father."

Jared reached across the table, removed the wrinkled napkin from her grasp and took her hand in his. "Do you think that someday we'll both regret not marrying?"

"I honestly don't know." Their gazes met and held. Paige's heartbeat accelerated. "Do you think we will?"

"Maybe." He caressed her knuckles with his thumb. "Probably. The first time Angela asks us why we didn't get married."

Tilting her chin, Paige shook her head. Her long, loose hair bounced back and forth across her shoulders. She closed her eyes and bit down on her bottom lip. "You're determined to name our little girl Angela, aren't you." Opening her eyes, she glanced across the table at him and laughed softly.

God, she looked delectable enough to eat. Her light olive skin all creamy perfection. Her cheeks glowing with healthy vibrance. Her lips moist and pink and inviting.

Still holding her hand, Jared rose from his chair, rounded the table and drew her up and into his arms. She made no protest, verbal or physical, simply waited for him to make the next move.

"I think we can dance to this music." His lips brushed her ear as he whispered to her.

She responded by placing her left hand on his shoulder and stepping closer into his embrace. Her mind told her that she shouldn't be doing this. Her heart told her that she should.

"We're playing with fire, aren't we, honey?" Pressing her closer, allowing her to feel his arousal, he lowered his head and pressed his cheek against hers. "I don't want you to think that I set this evening up to seduce you. I didn't. At least not consciously."

"I believe you." Laying her head on his chest, she listened to the hard, sturdy beat of his heart. "You've been kind and gentle and understanding. You've done everything you could to make this day special for me.'' She looked up at him at the precise moment he looked down at her. ''You can't help it any more than I can, this insanity between us.''

''You know how much I want you.'' He held her gaze with his as surely as his strong arms held her soft, ripe body.

''Yes, I know.'' She gazed longingly into his eyes. ''You want me as much as I want you.''

''Paige.'' He closed his eyes, blocking out the sight of her, willing himself not to lose control. Burying his face in her hair, he breathed in the sweet, fresh scent of her.

He kissed her throat. She groaned. Holding her in his arms was like possessing a little bit of heaven, but knowing he didn't dare make love to her was pure hell.

''We can't do this to ourselves, honey.'' Leaning into her, Jared opened his eyes and brushed his lips across hers. ''It's tearing me apart wanting you the way I do and knowing our making love again is the worst thing we could do to ourselves.''

''I know. I know.'' If he didn't kiss her—completely, thoroughly—and soon, she thought she'd die from the wanting.

''You need a man who can love you for the wonderful person you are. I can't give you that.'' He caressed her buttocks. Cupping her firmly, he lifted her enough to fit her femininity against his throbbing sex. ''All I can give you is this.''

His mouth covered hers. She parted her lips, accepting his probing tongue. Easing her hand up the back of his neck, she threaded her fingers through his thick, dark hair and held his head down, encouraging him to deepen the kiss. The world around them disappeared, replaced by a sensual haze, and the only thing that mattered was getting closer, giving more, taking more and appeasing an insatiable hunger.

Swooping her into his arms, Jared carried her to the sofa and sat down, holding her in his lap. With great urgency, he unzipped her dress and lowered it to her waist, all the while kissing her, taking her breath away with the frenzy of his caresses.

She stilled his hands as he eased her bra straps down over her shoulders. "Please, Jared, don't. I can't let you make love to me and then later pretend…" She had almost said *pretend I don't love you and that it doesn't matter that you don't love me.* "We've already decided that we aren't going to get married, so if we make love now, after you've spent so much money on me today, it will make me feel as if you've bought and paid for me."

"Dammit, Paige, you know it isn't like that!"

"It would be so easy for me to give in to what we both want," she admitted. "But afterward, I'd hate myself. And I'd hate you, too."

He eased her off his lap and onto the sofa, then stood and glared at her. "Have it your way!" Without a backward glance, he stormed off into his bedroom and slammed the door.

Paige stumbled as she made her way across the sitting room, a sudden burst of tears almost blinding her. If only things were different. If only Jared loved her the way she loved him. But he didn't. If only he could accept her for the woman she was and not expect her to change to suit him. But he couldn't.

She didn't dare put herself in a position to be hurt even more. She had given in to her deepest desires once, without considering the consequences. Now she was in love with a man who didn't love her. And she was five months pregnant with his child.

Seven

"I'm sorry, Paige. I let things get out of hand last night," Jared told her. "What happened was my fault, and I had no right to get angry with you and storm off the way I did."

"It wasn't all your fault," she said. "I'm as guilty as you are. There just seems to be this magnetism between us that we can't resist."

"Do you suppose we can still be friends?" he asked. "For Angela's sake?"

"We can try...for the baby's sake."

He didn't offer his hand to her for the traditional deal-making handshake, nor did she offer hers. Jared had come to realize that it was dangerous for them to touch, and he suspected that she had come to the same conclusion. Paige might be faking her reluctance to marry him and her disinterest in his wealth, but the one thing he knew she wasn't faking was her desire for him.

He took her to breakfast at Ellynton's in the hotel before they headed back to Grand Springs. Their return trip, if a bit strained, was pleasant enough. But she seemed as relieved as he was when they arrived at her apartment.

"You go on in," he told her. "I'll unload everything."

Smiling, Paige nodded agreement. She needed rest, especially after not sleeping more than a few hours last night. It had been sheer torment to reject Jared, to sleep alone in her bed, knowing he was only a few steps away. Had she been wrong to deny them both the pleasure they so desperately wanted?

Jared gathered up an armful of packages and followed her into her apartment. She held the door open for him.

"Where do you want all this stuff?" he asked.

"Just put it down in here," she said. "I'll unpack everything later."

He stacked the boxes in a corner of her living room, then returned to the Jeep for a second load. After he brought in the remainder of their purchases, he hesitated in the doorway.

"Take the rest of the day off from work and get some rest." He surveyed her from head to toe. She was so beautiful. So desirable. So tempting.

"Thank you. I am tired."

He hovered in the doorway, looking at her with hungry eyes, and she knew what he wanted. What they both wanted.

"I'll see you tomorrow," Jared said.

"In the morning, at the office."

"Call me if you need anything."

"I'm sure I won't need…I'm fine."

"Take care."

"I will."

He walked away. She closed and locked the door. Wrapping her arms around herself, she bit down on her bottom lip in an effort not to cry. But tears filled her eyes. She had put herself in a no-win situation. No matter what she did about her relationship with Jared, she couldn't be happy. She could never be happy unless he loved her. Truly loved her for the woman she was.

The next day Paige arrived at the office wearing one of her new maternity dresses, a hunter green woolen sheath, adorned with brass buttons. The dress was a bit sophisticated for her tastes, but Jared had insisted it was perfect for her.

Kay asked her a dozen questions about the trip to Denver the minute she entered the employees' lounge. Paige removed her coat, hung it on a rack and retrieved a carton of orange juice from the minirefrigerator.

"We've agreed to be friends," Paige said.

Kay eyed her skeptically. "You two are kidding yourselves if you think you can be nothing more than friends. Anyone who sees the two of you together can sense the tension between you. It's thick enough to cut with a knife."

Kay's statement proved prophetic. With each passing day, the tension between Jared and her intensified to such a degree that everyone else in the office steered clear whenever the two were together. Although they were both polite to the point of nausea, they were not becoming friends. If anything, their relationship became more strained, so that by the end of the week following their Denver trip, they were barely speaking.

If she didn't need her job so badly and the company's good insurance plan even more, Paige would quit and end this daily torment. How long could she and Jared go on this way, tiptoeing around their real feelings? Was it going to be like this for the next four months? And what about after the baby was born? When would it stop, this hungry, desperate need? Would she go on loving Jared forever, even after he married someone else? Someone truly worthy of being L. J. Montgomery's wife.

The row of figures on the computer screen blurred together as Paige gazed at them through misty eyes. She was so absorbed in her own misery that she didn't hear the two men enter her office, until one of them cleared his throat.

"I'm Detective Jack Stryker," the tall blond man said.

Blinking several times to clear away her tears, Paige

looked up into a pair of blue eyes. "Yes, how may I help you, Detective Stryker?"

"Paige Summers?" the other man asked. He, too, was blond and attractive, but seemed less rigid than his partner.

Paige studied him quickly, his short, no-nonsense haircut, his cool gray eyes and his broad, rugged body. "Stone? Stone Richardson?"

"Yeah," Stone said. "I thought that was you, Paige, but I wasn't sure. I haven't seen you in…what…three or four years?"

"Not since Kevin and I broke up," Paige said. "Do you ever hear anything from Kevin now that he's living in California?"

"No, I'm afraid not. We lost touch. The last I heard he was working for some big marketing firm out in L.A."

"Look, I hate to break up old home week," Stryker said, "but we're here on official business. Maybe you can take Ms. Summers out for lunch one day."

"Sorry, Jack." Grinning, Stone winked at Paige. "We need to see L. J. Montgomery."

"Concerning what?" Paige asked, an uneasiness quivering inside her stomach.

"An official matter," Stryker told her.

Paige announced the two detectives and showed them into Jared's office. Just as she started to leave the room, Detective Stryker asked Jared a question that stopped Paige's exit.

"What do you know about Olivia Stuart's death, Mr. Montgomery?"

"Only what I read in the paper," Jared said. "Why are you asking me? What could I know about the woman's death? She was killed on my first day here in Grand Springs. The day of the power outage." Jared glanced across the room at Paige, who stood silent and unmoving just inside the open doorway.

"Don't you think that's an odd coincidence, that Mayor Stuart was murdered on your very first day in town?" Stone Richardson asked.

"A coincidence, perhaps," Jared admitted. "But hardly damaging evidence that I know anything about the woman's death. Besides, it's my understanding that the police have the murderer in custody."

"Joanna Jackson is awaiting trial," Stryker said. "But she was just a hired hand. We're looking for her boss. Someone with a motive to want to see Olivia Stuart dead."

"And you think I have a motive?" Jared grunted. "I didn't even know the woman."

"Mrs. Stuart's last word was *coal*," Stone said. "Does that mean anything to you?"

"Absolutely nothing." Jared shook his head.

"We realize that we might be grasping at straws, Mr. Montgomery," Stone admitted, "but in trying to find a connection between the mayor's last word—coal—and her murderer, we discovered that your real estate and land development company has been buying up land and making inquiries into Grand Springs's past mining history."

Jared laughed heartily. "Hell, boys, don't you think that's stretching it a bit to make a connection between me and the mayor's death?"

Turning sharply, Paige took several tentative steps into Jared's office. "Montgomery Real Estate and Land Development has made it a policy to look into the past mining history of all the areas in which they invest. One of the reasons is because Mr. Montgomery thinks it makes sense to always explore alternative energy sources," Paige told the police detectives. "For you to imply that his actions have any connection to Olivia Stuart's death is ludicrous!"

"It's all right, Paige," Jared assured her. "These men are simply doing their job, following every lead and exhausting every possibility."

"The very idea that anyone would think Jared capable of hiring someone to commit murder is outrageous." Paige glared at Stone Richardson. "You're wasting the taxpayers' money harassing an innocent man when the real killer is still out there loose somewhere."

"Paige, we aren't accusing Mr. Montgomery of anything. We just—"

Storming across the room, Paige pointed her finger in Stone's face. "You don't have a clue as to who hired Joanna Jackson, and with everyone, from the governor on down, demanding results, you have to do something to earn your paychecks. So what do you do? You malign a fine, upstanding businessman, whose plans for Grand Springs can create new jobs and give our community's economy a real boost."

Coming up behind her, Jared grabbed Paige by the shoulders. "Thank you for coming to my defense, Ms. Summers. I appreciate your loyalty."

Paige's cheeks flushed. She glanced from Stone, who smiled sheepishly, to Jack Stryker, who looked down at the floor. "I'm sorry. I overreacted," Paige said. "It's just that I know what sort of man Mr. Montgomery is."

Jared was both startled and touched by Paige's adamant defense of him. Recently, he'd begun to think she hated him. Obviously, she didn't.

"Well, boys," Jared addressed the detectives, "have you ever thought that Mayor Stuart's last word might not have been *c-o-a-l,* but *c-o-l-d?* If she said the word as she was dying, it's possible that she felt cold, and her last word had nothing to do with her murderer."

"It's a possibility," Stone said. "We have to admit that all our *c-o-a-l* leads have hit a dead end."

"I don't think we need to take up any more of your time." Stryker offered his hand.

Jared shook hands with both detectives and saw them

to the door, then turned his attention to Paige, who tried to ease past him. He grabbed her wrists.

"Look at me, Paige."

Her cheeks flushed with embarrassment. Releasing her left wrist, Jared lifted his hand to her face and stroked her cheek. Jerking free of his hold, she ran into her office. Jared followed her, cornering her behind her desk.

If he could trust what his senses told him, if he could believe his own eyes and ears, then he could accept Paige at face value for the romantic, loving, sweet innocent she appeared to be.

Dear God, would he be a fool to continue doubting her? Or would he be a fool to think that she truly loved him?

"You lit into those detectives like a spitting, clawing she-cat." Grabbing her chin, he tilted her face, forcing her to look at him. "Thanks for jumping to my defense, honey. After the cold shoulder I've been getting from you this past week, I'd just about decided that you hated me."

"I don't hate you." *I love you, you big dope,* she wanted to shout at him. *I love you so much it hurts.*

He skimmed his thumb tenderly across her bottom lip. "Maybe we'd both be better off if you did hate me. The way things are…"

She closed her eyes, accepting the inevitability of his kiss, longing for and yet dreading the sweet agony. Intense desire spiraled up from the depths of her trembling body when his lips covered hers. Paige melted against him. Jared tensed. Ending the kiss abruptly, he released her chin.

She was pregnant with his child. She wanted him. He wanted her. No matter how many problems marriage wouldn't solve, it could, at least, give him two things he wanted. Legitimacy for his daughter. And Paige in his bed every night.

Of course, theirs wouldn't be an ideal marriage. But he was more than willing to give it a try—if Paige would ever accept their relationship for what it was and not what she wished it could be. She was putting them both through hell, and for what? Because she wanted him to love her? Or because she thought if she denied him long enough, he'd marry her without a prenuptial agreement?

He had always pictured his wife as a tall, cool, sophisticated blonde from a wealthy family. Someone who, like him, would consider marriage a mutually satisfying business arrangement. But the woman carrying his child was a voluptuous, earthy redhead, who said she believed in romantic love. Was he overly optimistic to think he could change this woman, make her over into his ideal?

"I promised that I wouldn't ask you again," he said. "And I won't. But you could ask me, honey. All you'd have to say is, Jared, will you marry me?"

If only it were that simple, Paige thought. But no matter how wonderful being Jared's wife might be for a while, sooner or later, the marriage would fall apart. The hot sex would bind them together at first, and later their child would unite them, but eventually Jared would look at her and see that she wasn't the woman of his dreams, the wife he had wanted at his side, the accomplished, sophisticated, socially prominent partner he had planned to share his life with. And when the day came that he realized he couldn't change her, he would resent Paige, perhaps even grow to hate her.

And eventually, his inability to love her would break her heart and she would hate him.

"Ask me, honey," he repeated his request. "Ask me to marry you."

"I can't."

She ran from him, not daring to look back. She didn't slow her pace until she entered the ladies' room. Leaning against the wall, she covered her face with her hands and burst into tears.

* * *

When Paige returned to her desk, eyes dried and face washed clean of her smeared makeup, she found Kay waiting for her.

"Are you all right?" Kay asked.

"Yes, I'm fine. Why?"

"Because when Jared called me into his office before he left, I noticed that you were conspicuously absent from your desk." Kay glanced down at her watch. "That was fifteen minutes ago, and it's not afternoon break time. Besides, Jared was roaring like a wounded animal, issuing orders right and left. He couldn't wait to get out of here. And your eyes are red and swollen. You've obviously been crying. So, I assume something happened between you two."

"Jared left? For the day?" Paige stared at Jared's closed office door.

"For the weekend," Kay said. "He said he was going to Aspen."

"Was he going alone?" Paige asked, really not wanting to know the answer if Jared had taken along a companion.

"He didn't fill me in on his personal plans." Kay laid a comforting hand on Paige's shoulder. "Want to tell me what happened?"

"Nothing new." Paige slumped down into her cushioned swivel chair. "I want him. He wants me. I love him. He doesn't love me. And despite what he's said, he still thinks marriage will solve our problems. I know that our marriage would end in disaster and we'd wind up hating each other."

Paige moped around the office the rest of the day, then drove directly from work to her parents' home and ended up spending the night. Her mother listened with loving patience, consoling Paige and trying to convince her that Jared wasn't enjoying a cosy weekend with another woman.

"I hope he *is* with someone else," Paige told her mother. "Some beautiful, skinny model or some rich and famous movie star."

She said it, but she didn't mean it. The very thought of Jared with another woman ripped her heart apart. But she might as well get used to the idea of other women in Jared's life. After all, he wasn't the type of man who'd stay celibate for long.

On her way back to her apartment on Saturday morning, Paige stopped by the Decorating Center and purchased paint and wallpaper border. Then she spent the day cleaning out the small storage room that she'd filled with many dolls from her collection. Part of her collection remained at her parents' home, but when she'd moved into her downtown apartment three years ago, her father had built shelves along one wall to house more than two dozen of her prized dolls.

The room was small, but certainly large enough for a nursery. The baby bed, chest, stroller, car seat, high chair and bassinet Jared had purchased in Denver would arrive next week, and unless she cleared out this room, there would be no place to put them. Thank goodness, she wouldn't have to remove her dolls. They made a perfect background for a baby girl's room.

Paige would make sure that her little girl had more than enough huggable, squeezable, drag-around dolls, but she would teach Angela from an early age which dolls were toys and which were treasured untouchables.

Angela? Now *she* was calling their baby Angela. She couldn't believe it. Jared had brainwashed her. *Damn Jared. Damn him for getting me pregnant. Damn him for making me love him. Damn him for not loving me. Damn him for going off on a ski trip with someone else.* Paige stomped her foot. Damn Jared for everything!

She spent Saturday evening removing the dolls from the

shelves in the storage room and placing them on the floor in rows against her bedroom wall. Once the spare room was bare, she applied the first coat of pale pink paint. She finished the job on Sunday afternoon, and by the end of the day, she could envision how completely perfect this tiny space was going to be for Angela.

Yes, Angela. Jared had named his daughter and the name had stuck. Paige finally admitted to herself that she couldn't imagine calling her baby girl anything else.

Just as she climbed off the ladder at the end of the day, a fluttering sensation rippled inside her. Gasping, she grabbed the ladder with one hand and placed her other hand over her tummy. Tears sprang into her eyes. Angela moved again. Slowly, cautiously, Paige stepped down off the ladder and slumped to the floor, covering her belly with both hands, as tears trickled down her cheeks. Their little girl had moved inside her. She wanted to share the moment with Jared. But she couldn't. He wasn't here. He wasn't even in town.

Exhausted, but filled with a sense of accomplishment, Paige crawled into bed on Sunday night. She couldn't help wondering what Jared was doing right at that minute. Was he en route, returning to Grand Springs? Or had he stayed over another night in Aspen, sharing a bed with some willing woman? Groaning loudly when images of Jared making passionate love to some willowy blonde flashed through her mind, Paige pulled the covers over her head and prayed for dreamless sleep.

The ringing telephone woke her at five o'clock the next morning. Only partially awake, she reached for the phone and knocked her alarm clock off on the floor.

"Hello?"

"Sorry to wake you," Greg Addison said.

"Mr. Addison?"

"Yes, Paige, it's me. I know this is a godawful hour to

wake a person, but Jared insisted I get in touch with you immediately.''

"Jared? Is something wrong?" Paige sat up in bed, bracing her back against the headboard.

"Jared had a skiing accident yesterday afternoon," Greg said. "He's all right. Just a badly sprained ankle. He'll have to stay off it for a few weeks.''

"Please tell him..." Paige paused momentarily. Tell him what? Tell him that she was sorry he hadn't broken his damn fool neck? Tell him that he deserved to be in pain since she'd spent the entire weekend in misery imagining him with another woman? "Tell him I hope he gets better soon.''

"In typical Jared fashion, he's being a royal pain in the butt about this." Greg chuckled. "They released him from the hospital around midnight and he flew straight back to Grand Springs and called me to come to the airport and drive him up here to his place on Eagle Ridge.''

"I don't suppose Jared will come into the office today, will he?" Paige asked.

"I was getting around to that," Greg said. "Jared insisted I call you so you can get an early start. The doctor doesn't want him putting any weight on his ankle for a while, so he's going to be working at home for at least a week. He wants you to come out here this morning.''

"Oh. I see." She didn't want to spend the day alone with Jared in his home. It would have been difficult enough seeing him at the office, wondering every time she looked at him if he'd spent the weekend with another woman. But to be alone with him? No, she couldn't do it. But she had to. It was her job. "I understand. Tell Jar— Mr. Montgomery that I'll be there by eight. But I'll need directions.''

"No need for directions," Greg told her. "I've been

instructed to come get you and deliver you personally to the great man's door.''

"It seems he's thought of everything," Paige said. "I'll be ready by seven, Mr. Addison.''

Snow covered the mountaintops, their sharp peaks piercing the blue sky. The aspens and cottonwoods stood tall, proud and barren, like emancipated sentinels guarding the verdurous evergreens. A heavy frost coated the land. The farther they drove up the mountainside, the denser the early morning fog and more concentrated the fine mist.

Greg whipped his Explorer into the circular gravel drive in front of Jared's enormous three-level log home. Perched on a sloping hillside, surrounded by towering ponderosa pines, the wood-and-glass structure blended with the rugged, north central Colorado terrain. The glass face of the A-frame core of the sprawling cabin reflected the frost-tipped trees as they shivered in the cold November wind.

"What do you think of the place?'' Greg asked. "Impressive, huh? Jared doesn't do anything by half measures. Nearly five thousand square feet of house and over fifty acres, all for a single man living alone.''

"It's fabulous.'' Paige surveyed the massive structure as she opened the door and got out of the Explorer. This was the house Jared had offered to give her?

Wooden stairs led upward to the second level, joining the first tier of decks that spiraled around and upward like a garland on a Christmas tree.

"The front door's straight up those stairs.'' Stepping outside, Greg pointed toward the double glass doors, flanked by floor-to-ceiling windows across the expanse of the A-frame section. "He's waiting for you. I think he's expecting you to prepare his breakfast.''

"Oh, really. When did meal preparation become part of

my secretarial duties?'' Paige stuffed her gloved hands into the pockets of her quilted thermal parka.

"I'm not issuing orders, Ms. Summers," Greg said. "But I'll warn you that he's not in a good mood, so you might want to give him a little leeway and—"

"Pamper the poor invalid?"

Greg chuckled. "Yeah, something like that."

"Aren't you coming in?" Paige asked.

"No, thanks. I've got a ton of work waiting for me at the office." He glanced meaningfully up at the cabin. "Besides, I've done my tour of duty. Now it's time for you to earn *your* hazardous duty pay."

"Thanks for warning me."

Paige squared her shoulders, stiffened her spine and marched up the steps. Turning the brass door handle, she found the front door unlocked.

"Hello? Jared?" she called out to him, but received no response.

Entering the foyer, she gasped as her mind assimilated the massive grandeur of the cabin's interior. Pine log walls reached upward toward the cathedral ceiling. A hand-carved staircase led to an upper balcony. The hardwood floors glistened as the early morning light, descending from an enormous skylight, spread across the polished surface.

"Jared." She called to him again.

"I'm in here," he said.

Going in the direction of his voice, she entered the living room. Stopping suddenly, she glanced around the thirty-by-thirty-foot area. Jared, wearing faded jeans and a long-sleeved cotton shirt, sat in a large navy blue corduroy recliner, his leg resting on a matching round ottoman. A pair of crutches lay propped against a square wooden table beside the chair.

"What the hell took you so long?" Tilting his head to

one side, he glared at her. "I was getting worried. Thought maybe that light drizzle out there had turned to sleet and Greg had had a wreck."

"The rain has almost stopped," Paige said. "And it's not late." She checked her watch against the mantel clock. A roaring fire burned brightly in the huge rock fireplace.

"It's after eight," he told her. "And I'm starving. Do you suppose you could scramble me some eggs or something? I haven't eaten a bite since lunch yesterday."

And just who did he have lunch with yesterday? she wondered. "Maybe you should have had Greg bring out a cook for you instead of a secretary."

Jared rolled up the newspaper he held and slapped it across his palm. "Dammit, Paige, don't play women's lib with me this morning. You're not just my secretary. You're supposed to be my friend, aren't you? Is it too much to ask a friend to fix me a little breakfast?"

"As a friend, I'd be glad to fix your breakfast." She unzipped her gray ankle-length parka and removed her purple knit cap and gloves. "But as a friend, I'm warning you that, after breakfast, your disposition had better improve or I'm out of here."

Sticking out his lip in a little boy pout, Jared looked at her pathetically. "Have pity on me, honey. I'm an injured man in pain. I haven't had any sleep in twenty-four hours. Haven't eaten in eighteen." And haven't had sex in five months. But he could hardly say that to her, could he? If he admitted that he hadn't been with another woman since the evening they met, she'd know just what a powerful hold she had on him.

"You poor baby." She tossed her parka, gloves and cap across the back of one of the two red-navy-and-gold plaid sofas that formed an L in front of the fireplace. "Since you seem to be in need of pampering, why didn't your

weekend ski bunny come back to Grand Springs with
you?''

"My what?" Turning sideways in the recliner, Jared
stared at Paige. Lovely, vibrant, scowling Paige. How
could a pregnant woman in a nondescript gray-and-tan pin-
striped jumper look so damned sexy?

Paige thought Jared looked too sleek and tanned and
gorgeous for a man who'd spent hours in a hospital emergency room. With his long, lean, powerful body sprawled
out in the comfortable chair, he projected an aura of pure,
unadulterated masculinity.

"I was referring to the woman you spent the weekend
with in Aspen.''

"Oh. That woman.''

Jared grinned. Paige's stomach quivered. He laughed.
She frowned.

"Just what's so funny?" she asked.

"You are," he said. "What gave you the idea that I
spent the weekend with some woman? Or should I say
who put the idea in your head?''

"No one put the idea in my head. I just assumed that
you... Are you saying that you didn't spend the weekend
with a woman?''

"Would you care if I had taken some cute little *snow
bunny* with me to Aspen?''

"Why should I care? We're not married. We're not engaged. We're not—''

"Lovers? No, honey, we're not any of those things, are
we." Jared glanced meaningfully at her stomach. "So why
didn't I spend the weekend with another woman?''

"Are you telling me that you didn't?" Paige mentally
scolded herself for feeling so relieved. "You spent the
weekend alone?''

He could lie to her and see how she reacted. Or he could
be honest with her, the way he wanted her to be honest

with him. He could take a chance and trust her. God knew he wanted to trust her.

"Did I mention that not only am I tired, sleepy and hungry—" he paused for effect "—but that I'm also lonely and horny as hell?"

Amusement rose in her throat and erupted in an uncontrollable giggle. "You're awful. Do you know that? You're absolutely awful."

But you love me, anyway. God, where had that thought come from? He didn't really believe Paige loved him, did he? But maybe she did. Maybe she— Hell, what difference did it make? He didn't want her to love him, he just wanted her to— To what? Marry him. Be his lover. Allow him to train her how to be Mrs. L. J. Montgomery.

"So, will you fix this awful guy some breakfast?" he asked.

"If you promise to behave yourself today and not give me any trouble." She took several steps toward the foyer, then paused and turned halfway around. "Where's the kitchen?"

"Go out into the foyer, down the hall past the stairway. It's straight back. You can't miss it." When Paige headed toward the foyer, Jared called out, "Hey, you *can* cook, can't you?"

"You'll just have to wait and see," she told him, then disappeared down the hallway.

The kitchen was as enormous as the living room and opened up onto a rear deck that overlooked a small stream. The arched, paneled ceiling loomed a good fourteen feet overhead and recessed lighting combined with a wide expanse of windows to illuminate the interior.

Twenty minutes later Paige served Jared a plate filled with crisp bacon, scrambled eggs and buttered toast. She watched in amazement while he devoured every bite and finished off three cups of coffee.

"You were starving, weren't you?"

"I'm a big boy, in case you haven't noticed," he said. "It takes a lot to fill me up."

"I'll clean the kitchen, and then we can start work."

"Fine. But before you do that, help me into the den. I've got things set up in there. A computer that's linked to the ones at the office, a fax machine, a second phone line. Everything we'll need."

Jared eased his feet off the ottoman, reached for his crutches and stood, balancing his weight on his uninjured foot.

Paige rushed to his side. "What can I do?"

"Just follow along behind me and make sure I make it into the den without falling flat on my face." He started the slow, cumbrous trek across the living room and out into the foyer. "I'm not used to maneuvering like this."

"You're doing fine," she assured him.

She helped Jared settle into his den-cum-office, a large, open room with another rock fireplace and double doors opening onto a patio.

They worked together all morning in a mutual sense of camaraderie, each trying to stay on the other's good side. Occasionally, Jared's temper flared, especially after the mild pain medication wore off and his ankle ached.

Before preparing lunch, Paige insisted Jared take a couple of his pain pills. When she carried a tray laden with their lunch of soup and grilled cheese sandwiches into the den, she heard Jared snoring. Pausing in the doorway, she shook her head and smiled. The map he'd been studying lay across his chest, lifting and falling with each steady breath he took. His head rested on his shoulder. His foot with the sprained ankle had slipped off the small, cane-bottom footstool he'd used as a prop.

After setting the tray on the massive oak desk, Paige walked over to Jared and knelt down beside him. She lifted a rectangular pillow off the empty rust red leather chair across from where Jared sat, placed the pillow on the footstool and lifted his foot to rest on top. She picked up the neatly folded, Navajo-print, cotton throw off the end of the wide rock hearth, shook it loose and arranged it over Jared's sleeping form.

Leaving him to rest peacefully in front of the warm fire, Paige took the tray back to the kitchen and ate her lunch alone. Later, she returned to the den and cleared away the work she and Jared had begun that morning. She reorganized Jared's home files, which were a mess, explored the huge kitchen, which she found stocked with enough food to see a dozen people through a rough winter, and finally settled down with a geology report on the Rocky Springs Ranch, a large section of property just outside Grand Springs that Montgomery Real Estate and Land Development had recently purchased.

Jared woke at four-thirty and found himself alone in the den. Someone had wrapped him in a cotton throw. Paige? Of course, Paige. He called her name. No answer. Where was she? Surely, she hadn't phoned Greg and he'd already taken her back into town.

Unsteadily, Jared made his way down the hall. His rubber-capped crutches would have allowed him to move in relative quiet, but with all his weight bearing on one booted foot, his hampered walk drummed noisily along the wooden floor.

"Paige, are you still here?"

"In the kitchen," she said loudly. "I just put a pan of lasagna in the oven for your dinner."

He found her at the sink, her hands in soapsuds up to her elbows and a dish towel thrown over her shoulder. He grinned. So this was what the phrase *domestic goddess* really meant. Paige looked right at home in the kitchen. In his kitchen. Preparing his dinner. A primitive masculine sense of *Paige was in his kitchen and all was right with the world* overwhelmed him. It was only a short mental leap from *Paige in his kitchen* to *Paige in his bedroom*.

"What would you say if I asked you to stay here with me this week?"

Dropping the plastic mixing bowl into the soapy water, Paige whirled around and gazed at Jared, her mouth open in an astonished gasp. "I can't."

"Why not?" He pulled out a chair from the kitchen table and sat, propping his crutches against the wall directly behind him.

"You know why not," she said.

"What if I promise to be on my best behavior? What if I sign an agreement, in blood, that—"

"I can't stay here. I have things to do at home. I'm working on the baby's nursery. Anyway, all that stuff you bought in Denver is being delivered this week."

"So I'll call and have the delivery delayed until next week," he said. "You have plenty of time to get the nursery ready. Besides, I thought you were going to let me give you this house. For you and Angela."

"I never agreed for you to give me this house." Paige jerked the dish towel off her shoulder, dried her hands and marched over to Jared. "My staying here is out of the question." She flipped the dish towel back over her shoulder.

"Look, honey, I'm going to be working from home the rest of the week. You'll have to drive out here early every morning and drive back into town late every evening, maybe sometimes at night. It would make a lot more sense for you to move in for the week."

"But what would people—" She paused midsentence, realizing what an idiotic statement she'd been about to make.

"See, you can't think of a logical reason not to stay here."

He was right, of course. The whole world knew they'd been lovers, knew she was pregnant with his child. There was no logical reason for her not to move in for the week. But there were several illogical reasons. She was in love with Jared, and therefore very susceptible to him on an emotional level. And then there was the ever-present sexual attraction that fairly crackled between them as if they were two live wires.

"I'll stay," she said. "But only if you agree not to touch me."

Laughter rumbled up from his chest as he shook his head. Paige glared at him.

"I mean it. I don't want you to even shake my hand."

The laughter died inside him. They were in an impossible situation. He and Paige. They were an unfeasible combination, but a combustible one. Even knowing how wrong they were for each other, how easily they could destroy each other, they could not extinguish the passionate fire that blazed anew each time they touched.

"I promise that I won't touch you...unless you touch me first. I'll force myself to resist you. Do you think you can resist me?"

"Why you egotistical, macho—"

"Now, honey, don't get yourself all riled up."

Paige realized that he had issued her a dare—*do you think you can resist me?* A dare she'd be a fool to take. But then, where Jared was concerned, she'd been a fool since the first moment they met.

"I'll need to go home and get some things," she said. "I can hardly wear these same clothes the rest of the week."

"Call Kay and have her go to your place and pack what you need. Greg will bring your bag when he comes out in the morning for our meeting. He's going to Florida for a couple of weeks to handle some problems in my office down there and I need to brief him before he leaves.''

"But I can't sleep in my clothes, and I don't have a toothbrush and—''

"I have extra toiletries. Half a dozen new toothbrushes still in their boxes." He looked her over from head to toe. "I'll loan you a pair of pajamas for tonight. The top should be just about right for you as a gown.''

Paige groaned. Her gut instincts told her that she'd live to regret giving in to her desire to be with Jared. Just one week, alone with the father of her child. A week to share a life with him. To pretend that...

"If you don't keep your promise, I'll leave immediately," she warned him. "And I'll never trust you ever again.''

"I swear I won't touch you, unless you touch me first.''

"Then I don't have anything to worry about, do I.''

He smiled, that damn killer smile of his. "Nope, I guess you don't.''

Eight

Had she made a deal with the devil, agreeing to stay with Jared for the rest of the week? He had promised not to touch her—unless she touched him first. Would he keep his promise? And could she spend the next few days with him and not succumb to her own desires?

Despite the chilling autumn wind that whistled around the corners of the three-level cabin, the interior was cosy-warm. Paige snuggled beneath the cranberry red coverlet, soft, thick blanket and flannel sheet. The wind disturbed her. The creaking, house-settling noises disturbed her. The moonlight-illuminated shadows falling across the windows disturbed her.

Tossing and turning in the queen-size, pencil-post bed, Paige longed for sleep, but sleep wouldn't come. No matter how hard she tried, she couldn't forget that Jared was in the room across the hall. He was so very near and yet so very far away. Distance did not separate them. Only the strength of his promise and her iron-willed determination kept them apart.

When he'd shown her into this room, one of five guest bedrooms in the sprawling log cabin, why hadn't she insisted on another room, farther from his, even one on another floor? Why had she so readily agreed not only to stay with him all week, but to sleep directly across the hall from him?

He had issued her a dare—I won't touch you if you don't touch me first—and there was no law saying she had to accept his dare. But she had, and she'd done it without thoroughly thinking through the whole situation. She'd been so damned and determined to prove to him that he wasn't irresistible and that she could and would hold out against his devastating charm, that she hadn't taken into account her own desperate desire for him.

She could deny the truth all she wanted to, but the truth was still the truth. She was in love with Jared Montgomery and probably had been since they'd made love in the elevator. She had tried to convince herself that her cowboy stranger and L. J. Montgomery were two different men. But they weren't. They were just two different sides of the same man—a man that she now believed she had been destined to love. And even if Jared didn't know it, she was his destiny—the woman he was meant to share his life with, the woman he was meant to love.

Paige wanted Jared as she had never wanted another man. The sexual electricity between them was like nothing she'd ever experienced.

She needed him in her life, caring for her, surrounding her with his protection, loving her completely. If only she could find a way to reach his heart, to break through the protective barrier that he'd built around his deepest feelings.

Was she longing for the impossible, for a man who believed himself incapable of loving, a man who didn't even believe the romantic emotion existed, to love her as she loved him?

She was a fool!

Kay was wrong, wasn't she, Paige wondered, if she thought you could teach another person how to love? Love was an emotion, a deep, heartfelt need, not a lesson that could be taught and learned.

Paige had been surrounded by love her entire life. Conceived in Walt and Dora Summers' passionate love. Born into the safe, secure love of two devoted parents. Raised in a home filled with genuine, abiding love.

But what if the circumstances of her life had been different? What if, as Jared, she'd never known real love? Would she be capable of opening up her heart to another and bestowing upon him life's most basic yet most precious gift? Jared didn't believe in love because he had never loved or been loved.

A loud crash came from across the hall, followed by several thunderous bumps and a string of expressive curse words.

Paige sat straight up in bed. Jared? The noise had come from his room, hadn't it? She threw back the covers, turned on a bedside lamp and got up. Had Jared fallen? Was he hurt? Did he need her?

She rushed across the room, opened the door and ran across the hall. Standing barefoot at Jared's bedroom door, she knocked loudly.

"Jared, are you all right?"

"How the hell should I know?" He responded in an angry roar. "I'm lying flat on my back on the floor in this pitch-black room!"

Paige flung open the door and immediately flipped on the light switch, which activated brass lamps on the nightstands that flanked his king-size bed. The soft, low-wattage lamplight caressed the forty-five-foot-square area, gilding every inch of the room with a transparent golden glow.

She entered his room, then stopped abruptly after taking only a couple of tentative steps. The sight of Jared, wearing nothing but the pajama bottom that was the mate to the black silk top she wore, took Paige's breath away. He lay sprawled out on the wooden floor, halfway between his bed and the bathroom. The tip of one crutch peeked out from underneath the bed. The other crutch, which lay on a knotted brown area rug, pointed toward the French doors to the right of the massive rock fireplace.

Momentarily mesmerized by Jared's long, lean body, Paige stared at him, scanning every muscle. She noted the width of his naked shoulders, the strength of his powerful arms, the thatch of curling dark hair that covered his broad chest, narrowed to a seductive, thin line and disappeared beneath the waistband of his pajamas.

Flattening his palms against the floor, Jared lifted himself into a sitting position and braced his body with his arms. He looked up and saw Paige standing just inside the doorway. Every muscle in his body tensed. His heartbeat drummed in his ears. His sex hardened instantly.

She was beautiful beyond words, beyond reason. Like a vision out of his most erotic dream. She stood there, her skin glistening in the golden light, her mahogany red hair spread out over her shoulders and down her back, her full breasts pushing against the black silk and her nipples tightened to pinpoints. His pajama top hit her mid-thigh, revealing the long, creamy expanse of her slender legs. She stared at him, her brown eyes filled with undisguised longing.

He groaned, the sound beginning deep inside him, at gut level, rising in his throat and erupting from his lips on one long, agonized breath.

"You *are* hurt!" Paige hurried to Jared, knelt at his side and laid her hand on his shoulder. "What happened? Did you injure your sprained ankle?"

A knot formed in his throat, the tension threatening to choke him. He swallowed, dislodging the emotional knot, then glanced meaningfully at her hand resting on his naked shoulder. "I was on my way back from the bathroom. One of my damn crutches got tangled up in that stupid rug—" he nodded to the guilty object "—and the next thing I knew I landed flat of my back and the crutches went fly-ing."

"Do you think you can get up if I help you?" Leaning over him, she slipped her arm around his waist. "Or are you in too much pain to move?"

He was in pain, all right, but not the kind of pain she meant. He was mad as hell about taking a spill, but the only thing he'd hurt in the fall was his pride. However, he *was* in pain. He ached with a purely primitive male need that the very sight of her had brought to torturous life.

"I'm okay, honey. Help me stand up." He eased his arm around her shoulders, boosted himself upward with his other arm and stood on one shaky leg. "Help me get back in bed."

Without a moment's hesitation, Paige assisted him. Allowing him to lean heavily on her, she led him slowly toward his massive bed.

"I'm sorry I made so much noise that I woke you," he said. "I know how important getting plenty of rest is for you and the baby."

"I wasn't asleep," she admitted, then immediately wished she hadn't been so honest. He would wonder, wouldn't he, why she was still awake in the middle of the night?

"I was having a difficult time getting to sleep, too." He tightened his hold around her shoulder. "I kept thinking about you being right across the hall. Were thoughts of me being so close keeping you awake?"

Shivers of awareness rippled along Paige's nerve endings. Her femininity tightened and released, tingling with anticipation. "I should have gone back to my apartment tonight. Then both of us would have gotten a good night's sleep."

"But if you'd gone home, I'd have been all alone," he told her. "With no one to help me."

When they reached the edge of his bed, Paige removed her arm from around his waist, then stepped out from under his big arm. Wavering on one foot, Jared held out his hands to her in a pleading gesture.

"You don't need me," she said. "Just sit down." She nudged him in the middle of his chest.

He grabbed her wrist, and as he fell backward onto the rumpled covers, he pulled her down on top of him. "But I do need you, honey." Placing his hand at the base of her spine, he eased it over her buttocks and down her bare legs.

Squirming against him, she issued a weak protest. "No, Jared. Please." His sex pulsated against her feminine mound, igniting a gush of warm, damp heat. "You promised."

Easing his hand up and under the silk pajama top, he cupped her hip. She moaned. Gazing into her dreamy brown eyes, he slipped his fingers inside the elastic waistband and slid her beige lace panties down her hips. "You touched me first," he reminded her.

While he kneaded the firm flesh of her buttocks with one hand, he grasped the back of her head with the other and drew her face to his. "I didn't break my promise." He whispered the words against her lips.

"You don't play fair." Her breath mingled with his. "I touched you because you needed my help."

He ran the tip of his tongue across her bottom lip. She sighed. He smiled. "But you did touch me first, honey, and there were no stipulations to our deal."

"This won't change anything," she told him. "No matter what happens—"

He silenced her warning with his mouth, covering her lips with his, tasting her sweetness as he pressed his tongue between her teeth. She opened for him, like a flower to the sun, giving him free access. Accepting him, welcoming

him into her moist warmth, she became a willing partici-
pant. She had fought a long, hard battle, struggled dili-
gently not to give in to her own wanton desires, but in the
end it all came down to this—this simple, desperate need
to be one with the man she loved. And she did love him.
Oh, how she loved him!

Paige's hot body melted into his, like thick liquid metal,
adhering to the solid mass beneath her. He lifted her hips,
shifting her up and down, rubbing her intimately over his
throbbing sex. As his tongue thrust deeply into her mouth,
she reciprocated, beginning a dual dance of passion. He
ate at her mouth, devouring her, and she wrapped herself
around him, longing for more. So much more. The frenzied
kiss ended when Jared released her mouth and took a deep,
hard breath. Paige licked her swollen lips.

She felt just as she had that evening in the elevator when
she'd given in to her most primitive longings. Only Jared
could make her feel this way. Only Jared had the power
to ignite the fires within her and set her body aflame. Only
Jared's possession could consume the blaze and render her
to sparkling embers that he alone could set afire again.

Grasping her waist, he lifted her off his sweaty chest.
Paige spread her fingers through his damp chest hair. He
groaned. His sex hardened painfully, her very touch taking
him to the edge.

Lifting her up so that she rested on her knees above
him, he dragged her panties down as far as he could. Bracing herself with her arms, she lifted one leg at a time and
finished removing the sheer lace briefs. She sat on top of
Jared, her femininity resting on his silk-covered arousal.

He looked up at her as she smiled down at him. Her
cheeks flushed a seductive pink, her pupils dilated, dark-
ening her eyes from brown to black, and her kiss-swollen
lips sighed his name.

"Jared."

That one word branded him, burning into his soul. There was no turning back now, for either of them. The madness had taken over, the pure animalistic need to mate.

With trembling fingers, he grasped the silk pajama top, ripping it apart, popping the line of pearlized black buttons in his haste to undress her. He spread apart the dark, shimmery material and bared her breasts.

She shuddered when he exposed her breasts to the air. Her nipples puckered into jutting points. Her flooded femininity ached. Her heavy breasts throbbed.

When he grasped her breasts in his big hands, she cried out from the relief his touch gave her and from the still hungry need eating away at her insides. He massaged her breasts, teasing the nipples, until Paige thought she would die from the agonizing pleasure of his masterful touch.

Lifting his hips, he jerked his pajama bottoms down over his hips and to his knees, then wriggled them to his ankles and kicked them off onto the floor.

Taking her hips in his hands, he positioned her, aligning her body to his. With one quick, powerful lunge, he took her, his strong, upward thrust filling her completely. Crying out her pleasure, Paige tossed her head backward and her long red hair brushed her hips.

"Ride me, honey. Hard and fast."

She obeyed his command, giving herself over completely to the pursuit of her own needs. Rising and falling, she rode him with mindless abandon, spiraling out of control as her senses ruled her, every sensation heightened by their physical union.

She smelled the musky, earthy aroma of their hot, sweaty bodies. She heard their labored breaths and the wet, undulating rhythm of their lovemaking. She saw the taut, fast-building passion on Jared's face and knew he saw the same in hers.

Leaning over him, her breasts pressing against his chest,

she licked a moist line up his throat to his lips, tasting the rich, hot dampness of his skin.

When she braced herself with her arms, positioning her breasts invitingly over his mouth, Jared thrust upward into her, stealing her breath, and latched onto a nipple, sucking greedily. Every nerve in her body screamed for release.

Paige gasped for air as Jared tormented one breast and then the other, sucking, laving, nibbling. While one hand aided his mouth, he used the other to urge the acceleration of her pace, leading her into a frenzy. She became a sizzling mass of sensations, a being completely ruled by her passion.

When her body tightened and then released, plunging her into a maelstrom of pure sexual fulfillment, Jared allowed her time for completion before he flipped her over onto her back and took his own pleasure, hammering into her. Fast and furious, he emptied himself. His big body shivered with release. They clung to each other, their breathing ragged and harsh, their bodies sticky with sweat.

Slipping off her, Jared pulled her into his arms, cradling her head against his shoulder. He kissed her forehead.

"Jared—"

He placed his index finger over her lips. "Don't say anything, honey. Don't spoil what we have right now."

She snuggled against him as he drew the covers up and over their naked bodies. He was right. Now was not the time for talking. Tomorrow would be time enough.

Paige drifted into a peaceful sleep, draped securely in Jared's arms.

Jared awoke shortly after daybreak, and for one brief moment he couldn't believe that Paige was sleeping beside him, warm, naked and sated from their lovemaking. For the past five months he had longed for her, wanted her, needed her in a way he'd never needed another woman.

What was it about this one woman that made him want her so?

He smoothed his hand over the quilted coverlet, gripped the edge and pulled the covers away from her body. She was ripe and voluptuous, her body temptation personified. Her large breasts beckoned his mouth with their fullness. The cinnamon thatch of hair covering her mound tempted his fingers to explore the depths of her body.

And her little round tummy protruded slightly, just enough so that he could tell his child lay nestled inside. He kissed her belly. Paige stirred, moaning softly. He licked a circle around her navel. Squirming, she opened her eyes and smiled. He lifted his head.

"Jared?"

"I want to make love to you," he said, and before she could reply, he kissed her belly again.

She grasped his shoulders, urging him to come to her. He eased upward far enough to capture one begging nipple in his mouth and clasp the other nipple between his thumb and forefinger. When he had her writhing beneath him, he lowered his head and painted a damp trail from her breasts to the apex between her thighs. Urging her legs apart, he lowered his head and sought the secret heart of her. She gasped loudly when his tongue laved her intimately. Gripping his shoulders, she held on for dear life as Jared brought her to the brink and, with one final caress, plunged her headlong into rapture. While the aftershocks rippled through her, Jared mounted her, thrusting deeply into her wet body. All the while he lunged in and out, he claimed her mouth repeatedly in quick, smoldering kisses, the musky, feminine taste of her still on his lips.

He groaned when the force of his powerful climax hit him. Within minutes, she joined him, experiencing a second, even more earth-shattering release.

He rolled her over on top of him and they went to sleep again, still joined, their naked bodies lying atop the covers.

When Paige awoke the second time, she was alone in bed. A blazing fire warmed the room and morning sunshine flooded through the French doors and numerous windows. She stretched, then groaned. Her body ached from their passionately strenuous lovemaking.

Sitting up in bed, she glanced around the room in search of Jared's pajama top and her panties. She saw the pajama top lying on the floor, at the side of the bed. Reaching down, she retrieved the black silk shirt, slipped it on and tied it beneath her breasts in a loose knot. She finally spotted her panties, curled into a wad at the foot of the bed. Snatching them off the floor, she slipped into them quickly.

"There's no need to get dressed, honey." Jared stood in the doorway, holding an open basket filled with food, while he braced his body on one crutch. Obviously he had showered, shaved and dressed. His hair was moist, his face smooth. He'd put on a pair of faded jeans and a pullover sweater. "I thought we'd spend the day in bed," he told her.

He brought the basket over to the bed and handed it to her. "Toast. Juice. Fruit. Cereal." He listed the basket's contents. "Sit back and enjoy your breakfast."

Paige accepted the basket, scooted back against the headboard and stretched her naked legs out across the bed. Dropping his crutch, Jared sat down on the edge of the bed, jerked off his sweater and unzipped his jeans.

"What are you doing?" She stared at his broad, hairy chest and remembered the feel of him pressing against her, rubbing her breasts, igniting her passion.

He unzipped his jeans. "I'm getting back in bed with you."

"No, don't. I—I haven't had a bath." She glanced down at the basket. "I haven't eaten breakfast."

He removed his jeans and tossed them aside. Paige sighed with relief. He wore a pair of black briefs.

"Eat up, honey." He removed the cap from the mug and lifted the juice to her lips. "When you finish breakfast, I'll give you a bath."

"You'll give me a—"

He pressed the mug to her lips. She sipped the fresh-squeezed orange juice.

"How on earth did you manage to climb the stairs on one crutch and carry a basket, too?" Paige asked.

"It wasn't easy, honey, but for you, I'd do anything."

She couldn't stop the grin that spread across her face when she remembered all the things he'd done for her and to her during the night. "What time is it?"

"What difference does it make?"

"I thought you were expecting Mr. Addison this morning."

"I was," Jared said. "Greg has been here and gone."

"Oh, my goodness. It must be late."

"Only a little after ten," he told her. "Now, eat your breakfast like a good little mother."

She didn't think she could eat a bite while he sat there staring at her, his gaze fixed on her breasts. But once she took the first bite, she found she had a ravenous appetite.

When she finished eating the cereal, Jared lifted the basket and set it on the floor, then reached out for Paige. She drew away from him.

"What's the matter, honey? Don't tell me you're shy this morning."

"No, not exactly."

Grabbing her hand, he tugged gently. "Well, come on, and let me give you your bath."

"No, Jared. I don't think I'm ready—"

"After last night, you're ready for anything and you know it. What's wrong, have you never let a man bathe you before?"

"No, I haven't," she admitted. "Just how many women have you bathed?"

"Ah, so that's it, huh? You're jealous of all the other women I've known."

"I am not jealous of all the other women you've known," she said adamantly. "Just how many women have there been?"

He fell across the bed, laughing so hard he clutched his sides in pain. Paige lifted a pillow and hit him repeatedly. Grabbing her wrists, he wrangled the pillow away from her and tossed her flat on her back. Straddling her hips, he gazed down at her and flashed her his brilliant smile. She lashed out at him, slapping his chest and shoulders. Manacling both of her wrists, he held them over her head. She squirmed, but he held her in place.

"There's never been anyone like you, Paige. Never."

Frowning, she glared up at him. He lowered his head and brushed his lips across hers. She thrashed her head from side to side. He buried his face in her neck as he rubbed himself intimately against her. Moaning softly, she instinctively lifted her hips in invitation.

Jackknifing into a sitting position, he eased off the bed, balanced on one foot and dragged her to her feet. "You're tempting me, honey, but I'm determined to give you a bath before I make love to you again."

"Jared, I do not want you to give me a bath. We need to talk. We need to...oh!" Paige pulled one hand free and placed it over her stomach. "Oh, my."

"What's wrong? Are you in pain? Is something wrong with the baby?" Fear knotted Jared's stomach and coated his palms with sweat.

"No, I'm fine. The baby...Angela...Angela moved."

She grabbed Jared's hand and laid it on the rounded swell of her belly. "I've felt her fluttering around inside me for a couple of days, but just then it was more than a flutter."

Tears glistened in Paige's eyes. Jared knew he'd never seen anything as gloriously beautiful as this woman, her seductive body just beginning to show signs of ripening with his child.

"Angela moved?" He wondered if Paige realized that she'd called their daughter Angela.

She placed her hand over his. "Just hold your hand there for a few minutes. Maybe she'll move again for her daddy."

The bottom dropped out of Jared's stomach. *For her daddy.* For him. Oh, God in heaven, please let her move. Let me feel her alive inside her mother.

"Come on, Angela, give a little flutter for Daddy," Jared coaxed as Paige maneuvered his hand over her belly.

As if on cue, the baby moved. Jared drew in a deep breath. "Damn!" Emotions he had never known rose from the very depths of his soul. Emotions he could not—dare not—name.

Kneeling in front of Paige, he clasped her hips in his big hands and drew her belly forward. He kissed the tiny mound that cradled his daughter, then stood and draped his arm around Paige's shoulders.

"We're going to take a shower together," he said. "A long, hot shower."

On a rational, cognitive level Paige knew that she and Jared needed to talk, to discuss what was happening between them. But on a purely emotional level, heightened by physical pleasure, Paige made no protest when Jared showed her the way into his private bathroom.

He opened the door to the enormous glass-and-chrome shower and they stepped inside. Leaning against the tiled wall, Jared pulled her close, enjoying the feel of her body against his. He quickly divested her of the silk pajama top. She removed her panties and helped him take off his briefs. Standing in front of him, she trembled with desire and anticipation. He had schooled her body in exquisite pleasure and it longed for another lesson.

Water jetted down against their bodies from all four sides of the shower. Squealing, Paige flung herself into Jared's arms. While rivulets of water cascaded down their bodies, Jared held her close, kissing her passionately.

He lathered her with soap and washed every inch of her, taking his time as he concentrated on her breasts, and then her buttocks, finally parting her legs to cleanse her intimately.

Jared pleasured her with his mouth and hands and taught her to pleasure him. The slow, sweet loving grew in intensity until passion claimed them. They emerged from the shower glowing with joyous satiation. Wrapping themselves in two of Jared's plush robes, they went into the bedroom, gathered up Jared's crutches and ventured downstairs.

They spent the rest of the day together in a sexual fog, lovers with no past and no future, living only for the wondrous present. They prepared a late lunch together and sat on a rug in front of the fire in Jared's bedroom, feeding each other, nibbling on each other's fingers.

"Move in with me," he said, cupping her chin in his hand.

"I can't. I—"

"Then stay for the rest of the week, as we had planned. Only sleep in my bed."

Jared wanted her to live with him, to be with him whenever he wanted her, and he wanted her all the time. It seemed the more he made love to her, the more he wanted her, the deeper she became entrenched in his life, possessing him as no woman ever had.

She had given herself to him without demanding anything of him. She hadn't been denying him sex to manipulate him as he'd feared. Paige wasn't playing games, wasn't trying to up the ante.

Why had it taken him so long to realize that she really was just what she appeared to be? Why had he allowed what one woman had tried to do to him seventeen years ago to keep him from trusting Paige?

Because it had been easier to distrust her, to assume she was like most of the other women he'd known, than to accept the fact that she loved him. Being loved by Paige scared the hell out of him.

She was hardly a suitable wife for L. J. Montgomery. But by God, she would marry him! He was not going to spend his life without her. She was a diamond in the rough, one he could polish to brilliant perfection.

"All right. I'll stay until Sunday." Paige wrapped her arms around his neck.

"And then?"

"And then we'll see," she said.

"Yes, we'll see," he agreed.

Paige wondered if she could teach Jared how to love her in a week. Would she be able to open up his heart and plant the seeds of an emotion he didn't believe existed? If she couldn't teach him to love her, would she be able to walk away at the end of their time together and survive a broken heart?

They made love again and again as if it were their last twenty-four hours on earth. And when one day ended and the next began, they slept in each other's arms, sated and happy, secure in the certainty that they would have five more days alone together.

Nine

Paige had never known such happiness as she experienced with Jared that week, and when Sunday afternoon arrived and their time together came to an end, she had never known such sorrow. They had worked side by side every day, slept in each other's arms every night and shared every moment of their special time alone together. Not once had they marred the beauty of the past week by discussing the future. But it was time for her to return to her apartment in Grand Springs, and they couldn't delay the inevitable forever.

Standing by the fireplace in his bedroom, Jared watched her pack her suitcase. When she glanced his way, he averted his gaze. He didn't want her to leave.

"What time did you tell Kay to pick you up?" he asked.

"At four," she said. "I thought that would give us time to drive down the mountain before it gets dark."

He checked his watch. "We have less than an hour."

"I'll see you at the office tomorrow." She zipped her burgundy suitcase.

Using his crutches, Jared took several tentative steps toward her. "Don't leave. Stay with me."

"Oh, Jared." Breathing deeply several times, she willed herself not to cry. She'd known she was taking a chance, risking a broken heart, by staying with him. She had placed her hopes and dreams on teaching Jared to love her. She'd failed. Not once had he mentioned the word *love,* not even in their most passionate moments.

"Please, honey. Stay."

"Why do you want me to stay?" *Dear God, let him tell me that he cares. If only he could say that he thinks he's falling in love with me, it would be enough.*

"Why?" He stared at her, an incredulous look on his face. "Because we're good together, you and I. We're damn good together."

Hell, it could take years to have his fill of her, to reach the point where he didn't want her day and night with an insatiable hunger. If only she'd marry him...

Closing her eyes, desperately trying not to cry, Paige bit down on her bottom lip. She had to agree with him. They *were* good together. But didn't he realize that what they shared was special, that the chemistry between them was experienced by only the luckiest couples in the world?

"This week together has been wonderful," she admitted. "The most wonderful week of my life. But—"

"No buts, honey. You want to stay. You know you do." With his gait hampered by the use of the crutches, he made his way slowly across the room. When he reached her side, he sat down on the edge of bed, propped his crutches on the footboard and held out his hand.

She lifted her suitcase, placed it on the floor, then sat down beside Jared and put her hand in his. "It would be so easy to agree to stay here with you, but I can't. These past few days together have been days out of time, moments we've stolen from our real lives. We've been pretending that everything is all right, that we don't have any problems."

He brought her hand to his lips and kissed it, then held it against his cheek. "Isn't what we've shared this week enough for you? God, Paige, don't you realize how good it is between us?"

"Of course I realize how good it is." She slipped her hand out of his grasp. "But I want more. I want it all. Not just the fantastic sex. Even marriage isn't enough without the love and happily-ever-after that goes with it.''

"Why can't what we have be enough for you?" Jared clenched his jaw.

"Is it enough for you?" Paige asked.

"Yes, it's enough. It's more than enough. Hell, it's more than I ever thought I'd have.''

Jared's brutally honest admission touched her deeply. How little *had* he expected? Had he really thought he could marry a woman and spend a lifetime with her not only without love, but without passion? Poor, poor Jared. His plans to find a suitable mate, marry and produce an heir had been logical, unemotional, sterile plans.

"Before we met..." She paused, trying to choose the right words, words that wouldn't frighten him. She wondered if perhaps not only did Jared not believe himself capable of loving someone, but that the very thought of love scared him. "Hasn't it ever been like this for you before? I mean...haven't you ever felt about another woman the way you feel about me?''

Grabbing her shoulders, Jared turned her to face him. "Dammit! What do you want me to say? Do you want me to admit that you hold a power over me that no other woman ever has?''

"I want you to be honest. With yourself, as well as with me.'' *Tell me you love me.*

"All right. The honest truth is that I want you more than I've ever wanted anything in my life, but I hate needing you this way. I've always had control over every aspect of my life. You make me lose control. You make me crazy!''

Even though he couldn't tell her that he loved her, Paige wondered if perhaps the feelings he did have for her were closer to love than anything he'd ever felt. Had their week together strengthened his feelings for her even more than she had hoped? Had Kay been right after all, about teaching Jared how to love? If so, this might be the first step in the learning process.

Leaning her head to one side, she rubbed her cheek across the top of his hand that held her left shoulder. He loosened his grip, ran his hand down her arm and circled her waist.

"I need to go back to my apartment for a few days," she told him. "I can't think rationally when we're together all the time. Whether or not I should move in with you is a major decision."

Jared cupped her chin in his hand. "Are you saying that you're considering moving in with me?"

"Yes, I'm considering it. But if I do decide to live with you, it will be only until Angela is born." *Or it can be for the rest of our lives, if you learn to love me.*

"Ah, honey, you've made me a happy man."

"I haven't decided yet. I think this is something we both need to take time apart to consider. In a few more months, I'm going to be big and fat and...and we may not be able to have sex. Be sure this is what you really want."

He kissed her, hard and fast, then smiled. Paige's stomach did an evil flip-flop.

"I don't care how big and fat you get," he said, then patted her stomach. "You'll be getting larger as my baby grows inside you. And even if we can't have sex later in your pregnancy, there are other ways to make love."

Don't blush, dammit, she told herself. Don't blush! "I need a few days to think about it."

"Take a week, if you need to, as long as you decide to live with me."

Jared toppled them both over into the bed, and within moments they were lost to the passion that neither could control. They were still in bed when Kay arrived. Jared dressed hurriedly and went downstairs to answer the door, while Paige freshened up and put on her clothes.

The house was empty without Paige, and Jared was lonely. Although he'd been alone most of his life, he didn't think he'd ever been really lonely before. Except, maybe, for a while after Grandpa Monty had died. He had missed that old man for a long time. Hell, sometimes he still missed him.

Even though his parents had given Jared everything money could buy, they'd never spent much time with him. As a child, he'd been cared for by a succession of nannies and servants, people paid to see to his needs. As an adult, he'd changed very little about his lifestyle, depending on employees to keep his business and his ranch running smoothly. Even though he made friends easily, he never knew what they liked better, his money or him. And always in the past, he had chosen women with whom he could have unemotional, uninvolved relationships that he could end effortlessly.

But Paige was different from any woman he'd ever known. And the way he felt about her was different. Stronger. More intense. He'd never really needed anyone before—he'd made sure of that. But Paige had hit him like a ton of bricks. A chance encounter in an elevator had turned his life upside down. After making love to Paige, nothing else would ever be the same.

As much as he wanted her, Jared hated his weakness. Paige made him vulnerable. She had taken his sane, orderly, well-planned life and thrown him into utter chaos.

Here he was rich, powerful, not bad-looking and reasonably young. With the snap of his fingers, he could have a hundred women at his beck and call. But he didn't want those hundred women—he just wanted one. One feisty, stubborn, romantic redhead, who had him spinning his wheels while he waited for her to make a decision.

Using a cane for support, Jared paced back and forth in his den. How long was it going to take Paige to come to her senses, to realize that there was no logical reason for them not to live together, for them not to marry?

She had moved back to her apartment three days ago, and even though he'd seen her every day at the office, it wasn't enough. He wanted her in his home, in his bed, in his arms, every morning and every night.

Resting one foot on the hearth, Jared tossed today's issue of the *Grand Springs Herald* into the fire, then lifted the brass poker and stoked the burning logs. Paige should be here with him now. They could be discussing the Rocky Springs Ranch development or the Florida beachfront condos that Montgomery's was building. They could be talking about Lamaze classes or deciding on a middle name for Angela. They could be making love on the rug in front of the fireplace.

Jared viciously jabbed at the logs, then threw the poker down on the hearth. Three days. Three damn days! That's all it had been since he'd made love to Paige, and here he was half out of his mind. Wanting her. Needing her. Missing her.

When the phone rang, Jared glared at it. He had no intention of breaking his neck to answer it. For the past three evenings, every time the phone rang, he'd been certain it was Paige. And every time, he'd been wrong.

Moving at a snail's pace, he walked across the room. The phone continued ringing. He lifted the receiver.

"Hello."

"Jared, this is Austen Summers."

"Austen?" Paige's brother? "Is Paige all right? Has something happened to her?"

"Paige is okay." Austen took a deep breath. "We—

that is, the family, Mama, Paige and I, are at Vanderbilt Memorial. We think Dad's had a heart attack.''

"Good God!''

''I thought you'd want to know. Paige is pretty upset. You know how nuts she is about—'' Austen paused. ''We—that is, Mama thinks Paige needs you.''

''I'll leave immediately,'' Jared said.

''We're still in ER.''

''I'll be there as soon as I can.''

Paige couldn't remember ever being this scared. Her big, strong, invincible father had doubled over with severe pain shooting down his left arm and pressing against his chest. Heart attack, the medics had thought, but Dr. Howell had corrected that diagnosis.

''From the evidence, I don't think he's had a heart attack,'' Noah Howell told them. ''We're going to run some tests to make sure, but my guess is that Mr. Summers has a blocked artery.''

''What does that mean?'' Dora asked. ''Can you operate and fix the problem?''

''If it is a blocked artery, I'll send him to St. Joseph's in Denver for a procedure called balloon angioplasty, which will surgically repair the blood vessel.''

Paige sat alone on a vinyl sofa in the ER waiting room. Austen leaned against the wall, his arms crossed over his chest and his vision focused on the floor. The staff had allowed their mother a quick visit with their father.

''It's all right if you want to cry,'' Austen said. ''I'd cry myself if I could.''

''We need to be strong for Mama,'' Paige told him. ''She's the glue that holds this family together, but without Daddy, she'd be lost.''

''He's not going to die!'' Austen slammed his fist into the side of the sofa.

Paige jumped. "No, of course he's not going to die." She needed to convince herself as much as her brother that their father was going to live. The very thought of losing him was more than she could bear.

It would be so easy for her to fall apart, to dissolve into a puddle of tears, but that was the last thing her mother needed right now.

Dora Summers emerged from her husband's ER cubicle. Paige shot off the sofa and rushed to her mother's side. Austen walked toward them, but stayed back several feet.

"Your daddy's all right. He—he isn't hurting anymore. They've given him something." Tears gathered in Dora's eyes. "They're going to take him upstairs to ICU and monitor his condition overnight."

Paige hugged her mother. "Daddy's tough. He—he—"

"It's all right, sweetheart," Dora said. "You go ahead and cry if you want to. Don't hold it in and make yourself sick. That wouldn't be good for you and the baby."

"I'm okay, Mama."

"Your daddy is worried about you. He kept asking how you were doing. He said not to let you get all upset. He doesn't want you staying here at the hospital all night."

"But, Mama—"

"You know how Daddy is about us. He thinks he has to take care of us, even—" Dora's voice cracked and tears streamed down her face. "Even when he's lying flat on his back in a hospital."

"Mama, I won't get any sleep if I go back to my apartment. I'll be all alone and worried sick."

The automatic emergency room doors behind them opened. Dora glanced over Paige's shoulder. Jared Montgomery marched into the waiting area.

"I don't think you'll have to go home alone." Dora turned her daughter toward the ER entrance.

Jared! He dropped his cane to the floor and opened his

arms to her. She flew across the room to him. Encompassing her in his embrace, he held her close, stroking her back with tender care.

"Oh, Jared. How did you know I needed you? Daddy—Daddy is—" The dam holding her emotions in check burst, flooding her eyes with tears and sending sobbing shivers through her body.

"It's all right, honey. I'm here." He continued his comforting caresses as he kissed her forehead and cheeks. "I'll make sure that your father has whatever he needs. Only the best for Walt Summers. I can have doctors flown in from anywhere in the world."

"Jared, Jared." She fell apart in his arms, secure in the knowledge that he would hold her together and keep her safe.

"Come on, honey. You need to sit down." When he draped his arm across her shoulders, she slipped her arm around his waist.

Austen picked up Jared's cane and held it out to him.

"Thanks."

"They think Dad's going to be okay," Austen said. "Dr. Howell is keeping him overnight in ICU to monitor him. They'll run some tests tomorrow to determine if the diagnosis of a blocked artery is correct."

Dora patted Jared's hand that held his cane. "Thank you, dear, for offering your help. If Dr. Howell is right about Walt's condition, they'll send him to St. Joseph's in Denver for some sort of surgical procedure."

"What can I do to help, Mrs. Summers?" Jared asked.

"You can take Paige home with you and make sure she gets a good night's rest. Her father is worried about her and the baby. He'll do much better knowing that you're taking care of his little girl." Dora smiled at Jared and then at Paige, who leaned her head on Jared's shoulder. "My Walt is so old-fashioned."

"Dad just can't get used to the idea that modern women can take care of themselves," Austen said.

"Sometimes we all need a little taking care of, you know." Dora sighed. "I've rather enjoyed having a strong man to lean on from time to time."

Jared squeezed Paige's shoulder. "Well, honey, will you let me take you home?"

Paige was torn between her desire to stay at her mother's side, standing vigil over her father, and the certain knowledge that by going with Jared she would do her father more good than if she stayed here at the hospital and caused him to worry about her.

"Yes, I'll let you take me home," she said. "But you have to promise to bring me back to the hospital first thing in the morning."

"I promise."

"Go on," Dora told them. "Austen will stay here with me, and if I need you, he'll call."

Paige hugged her mother and then her brother. "If there's any change in Daddy's condition—"

"I'll call you immediately," Austin assured her.

"Get your coat and wrap up good and tight. I know it's freezing out there," Dora told Paige, then turned to Jared. "Take care of her. For—for her daddy."

The mantel clock in the living room struck eleven o'clock. Paige sat curled up on the larger of the two sofas that were arranged in front of the fireplace. Jared handed her a cup of warm milk, laced with a dash of cinnamon. Curling up her nose, she frowned when she accepted his offering.

"You did sprinkle cinnamon on it, didn't you?" She glanced down at the cup she held.

"Just as you requested." Jared knelt beside the sofa,

lifted Paige's feet, one at a time, and removed her shoes. "Drink it all and then I'll put you to bed."

Paige shivered. The cup trembled in her shaky hand.

"Are you cold?" he asked. Before she could reply, he removed the navy afghan from the back of the other sofa and draped it around Paige's hips, covering her from waist to toes. "Is that better, honey?"

"Yes, fine, thank you." She sipped the warm milk. Disgusting. Totally disgusting, even with the dash of cinnamon.

Jared eased down beside her, hooked the curved handle of his cane across the back of the sofa and stretched his arm around Paige's shoulders.

She took another sip of the warm milk, then set it on the end table. "I'll finish it later." Laying her head on Jared's shoulder, she cuddled against him. "Thank you. You've been very good to me tonight. I appreciate it."

He cupped her chin in his hand. "Ah, honey, don't you know how easy it is for me to be good to you? All I want is for you to let me take care of you and Angela."

She cried softly, quietly, while Jared held her in his arms, soothing her with his gentle touch. He asked nothing more of her than to allow him to take care of her—her and their unborn child. And despite her own inner strength and independent nature, Paige was glad that she wasn't alone. Glad that she had someone to lean on, someone to take care of her, if only for this one night.

But what about all the days and nights ahead? She had planned to raise her child alone with her parents' help and support. And her mother had offered to baby-sit until the baby was old enough for play school. Paige hated the idea of leaving her baby with strangers, but to be honest, she hated the idea of leaving her baby with anyone.

Now she was five-and-a-half months pregnant and facing motherhood alone. No husband to love her. And no child-care assistance from her mother for quite some time, if her father's health deteriorated. The last thing on earth she wanted was to be a burden to her parents.

Paige couldn't let her pride stand in her way. Not now. She needed someone to be there for her, and Jared was more than willing. She'd be a fool not to accept his offer and move in with him.

Living with him didn't mean she had to marry him, although marrying him *would* solve her immediate problems. But could she marry him without love and risk not only their future, but their child's future, as well?

Her eyelids drooped. She yawned. Jared kissed her forehead.

"Come on, *Mommy,* let me put you to bed before you fall asleep here on the couch." He retrieved his cane, stood and braced himself, putting most of his weight on his un-injured leg. Reaching down, he grasped her hand and pulled her off the sofa. The navy afghan fell to the floor. Stepping over it, she slipped her arm around Jared's waist.

Before exiting the living room, Paige picked up her bag from the coffee table and draped it over her shoulder. When they reached the second-floor landing, she halted.

"I don't want to be alone," she told him. "I'd like to stay with you. I need you to hold me. Just hold me."

Jared sucked in a chest-tightening breath, pulled her into his arms and held her. His big, strong arms trembled every so slightly.

He led her into his bedroom and sat her down on the edge of his bed. "I'll get you something to sleep in." He rummaged around in a dresser drawer until he found a pair of cotton flannel pajamas he'd never worn. He couldn't even remember what he was doing with them. Maybe someone had given them to him as a gift.

He tossed the green-and-blue plaid top to Paige. "Here,

honey, put this on.'' He draped the bottoms over his arm and headed toward the bathroom. "Take your time."

Fifteen minutes later when he returned, freshly shaved, barefoot and wearing only his flannel pajama bottoms, he found her sitting on top of the covers, her back to the headboard. She held something in her hand. As he neared the bed, he realized that she was looking at some photographs.

"What have you got there?" He sat down on the edge of the bed, leaned his cane against the nightstand and propelled himself upward to sit beside her.

Her hands trembled as she held out the pictures, offering them to him. "They're the sonogram pictures. I've been carrying them around in my purse for six weeks." Guilt overwhelmed her. These were the first pictures of their daughter, and she had selfishly kept them to herself. He had every right to be upset with her for not sharing them with him before tonight.

"The sonogram pictures of Angela?" he asked.

He stared at Paige, but his gaze wasn't the accusatory glare she had dreaded. Instead it was a look of tenderness—a look of love. Did Jared love their baby?

Jared's hand shook when he took the pictures from her. He studied each snapshot, turning them in every direction. He blew out a long, deep breath. "Whew! It's amazing, isn't it? There she is, not even fully developed inside you, but she's already a baby girl. Our baby girl."

"Oh, Jared." Paige caressed his cheek. "I'm sorry that I haven't already shown you these pictures. I had no right to keep them from you. It's just that I—I—"

"It's all right, honey. You're showing them to me now."

After looking at the fuzzy black-and-white pictures of his daughter for quite some time, Jared finally laid the sonogram photographs in a neat little stack on the nightstand, then turned and pulled Paige into his arms. She quivered with soft, silent sobs as she melted against him, allowing her body to dissolve into his. He held her, gently soothing her.

Jared loves our baby. Jared loves our baby. She repeated the words over and over until they became a litany. If Jared could love Angela, he could love Angela's mother, couldn't he? It wasn't that Jared was incapable of love, it was simply that he had no idea what love was. He probably didn't realize how deep and profound his feelings for their child were.

"Jared?"

"Hmm-mmm?" He kissed her cheek and nuzzled her ear.

"Thank you."

"For what, honey?"

"For caring about me and Angela." Closing her eyes, she sighed.

Jared held her in his arms until she fell asleep, then he eased her under the covers and pulled her close to him again. Didn't she know, he wondered, that he couldn't help caring about her and Angela? It wasn't that he wanted to care so damn much, he just couldn't help himself. Paige Summers had to be the easiest person in the world to— To what? To want? To need? To care about?

And Angela. The precious little girl he and Paige had created one wild, reckless night. Oh, he cared about his daughter, all right. He couldn't even begin to describe the way he felt about his child. She was a part of him. Blood of his blood. Bone of his bone. But she was also a part of Paige. Beautiful, smart, funny, endearing, adorable Paige. Being Paige's child made Angela all the more special.

Why don't you admit it? he asked himself. You love your little girl! Maybe you've never loved another soul as long as you've lived, but you love the child growing inside Paige's body.

He laid a possessive hand over Paige's belly. In the silent darkness of night, with Paige sleeping in his arms and his daughter fluttering softly against his palm, Jared whispered, "I love you, my little Angela."

Ten

Jared woke as the first faint glimmer of morning light painted the dark sky with streaks of pink and lavender. Gray shadows of towering trees danced on the windowpanes. Rousing languidly, he scratched his chest and yawned. He felt a warm, sweet weight against his back and remembered that Paige had spent the night.

Easing over onto his back, he laid his arm across the top of her pillow and glanced at her. How could any one woman be so damned beautiful? Groaning softly, she cuddled to him, lifted her hand and laid it on his stomach. Every muscle in his body tensed. Every nerve tingled with awareness.

He wanted to make love to her. Slowly, tenderly caressing every inch of her lush body. He had wanted her last night, but it hadn't been the right time. She had needed his strength, not his passion, and he had tried his best to comfort and support her.

Turning his head so that he could look at her, drink his fill of her while she was unaware of his scrutiny, Jared watched Paige while she slept. She rested against him, safe, secure, trusting him completely. She was so young, so lovely, and yet such a complicated woman. By comparison, most of the accomplished, sophisticated women who were a part of his world were simple to understand. Like him, they weighted people's worth, as they did everything else, in dollars and cents.

He had never had room in his life for sentimentality or

romance, and certainly not love. But Paige seemed to treasure the concepts that he had always scorned.

Be tough. Get them before they get you. Show them who's boss. Men don't cry. Love is for fools. His father had instilled those ideas in Jared's head long ago. Rules to live by.

His father had died rich, powerful and unloved. A man whose marriage was a farce, he had sought pleasure in other women's beds. Larry Montgomery had smoked too much, drunk too much and lived too hard. And when he died, not even his own son had shed a tear.

Is that what you want? Jared asked himself. To wind up like your father?

Paige stretched her arms over her head, arched her back and yawned. Her eyelids fluttered. As she gazed up through barely open slits, her vision not quite focused, she smiled when she saw Jared looking down at her.

"Good morning." Reaching up, she slipped her arms around his neck and drew his head down for a quick kiss.

He rubbed her nose with his. "It's barely daylight. You should be sleeping."

"I don't want to waste any more time sleeping." She ran her hand over his shoulder and down his arm, caressing his hard, tense muscles. "I've missed you." Gliding her fingertips across his chest, she teased his tiny male nipples, bringing them to attention.

Jared sucked in his breath. "I've missed you, too, honey. You'll never know how much."

"Show me." Her voice was syrupy slow and smooth, tinged with just a hint of her mother's Southern drawl. "Show me how much you've missed me."

Jared whipped the covers to the foot of the bed and surveyed her long, slim, naked legs, her narrow feet and her honey-pink toenails. Rising up and over her, he bridged her hips with his legs, bracing himself on his knees. She lay beneath him, pliant, patient and pulsating, as she gazed longingly into his eyes.

She had never known what true passion was until she met Jared. This never-ending, gut-wrenching need. This insatiable hunger. This deep, all-consuming desire to love and be loved.

Jared was the most magnificent man she'd ever seen. Big, lean and powerful. And totally male to the very marrow of his bones. Her soft feminine body yearned for the hard masculinity of his. Her female scent, her inviting stare, her aroused sighs sent a message his body could not ignore.

He undid the top button of the baggy flannel pajama shirt she wore. Paige smiled. He undid the second button. She opened her mouth on a silent moan. He undid the third. She licked her bottom lip. He undid the fourth and final button. She quivered.

He lifted the sides of the shirt, separating them and exposing her breasts. Her chest rose and fell with each heated breath, keeping time with the rapid beat of her heart. He caressed her throat. Leisurely stroking her collarbones, he teased her with quick forays across the tops of her breasts, dipping his finger in the deep crevice between.

Arching her back, she lifted up, straining toward his touch. Cupping her breasts, he lowered his head and kissed first one shoulder and then her other. She shivered and sighed.

Easing his hand down her stomach, he pressed his palm against her lace-covered mound. She bucked, pressing her body intimately against his fondling hand. He tormented her with his hands and mouth, petting her without ever giving her what she wanted, what she was panting for.

Her nipples puckered into tight, aching points. Her full breasts throbbed. The core of her femininity tightened and released in a tingling, staccato rhythm.

"Please, Jared. Please," she begged.

"Please what?"

"Touch me."

He delved his finger between her breasts and licked the hollow of her throat. "I am touching you."

She squirmed beneath him, lifting her hips and rubbing herself against him. "You know what I want."

He lowered his head to her breast at the same time he slipped his fingers inside her panties. When he laved her nipple with his tongue and massaged her intimately, she cried out from the exquisite, torturous pleasure.

Getting out of bed, he manacled her ankles and slid her across the bed until her hips rested on the edge. He slipped her panties off her body, then divested himself of the flannel pajama bottoms. Approaching her, naked and trembling with the force of his desire, Jared spread her thighs apart and raised her legs to straddle his shoulders.

"Tell me what you want?" Cupping her hips, he lifted her up and into him, stopping just short of entering her.

"I want you inside me. Now." She reached for him, but he brushed her hand aside. "Please."

"Yes." He plunged into her. "Now!"

She gasped, amazed anew by the fullness, the power, the incredible completeness of his possession. In the days they had spent apart, her hunger for him had only increased. She wanted him now more than ever before, wanted him as she had never wanted anyone else.

Embedding himself deep within her, he dug his toes into the bedside rug, ignoring the pain in his ankle. He tightened his leg muscles and clutched her hips.

And then the mating dance began, savage in its intensity, wanton in its maneuvers, pure animal passion by its very nature. As he pounded into her, her desire spiraled higher and higher. With each forceful lunge, he brought her closer and closer to the pinnacle.

Their earth-shattering releases came simultaneously. Jared cried out when his hit him, the strong, masculine cry of a conqueror who had been conquered. Moaning deep in her throat, Paige panted as wave after wave of fulfillment claimed her.

Jared drew her up off the bed and into his arms, his mouth taking hers in a greedy, hungry kiss, devouring her with his passion. She clung to him, her body fluid and boneless, as the aftershocks echoed through her.

Their bodies still joined, their arms linked around each other, Jared and Paige tumbled onto the bed. They lay together in sated silence, exchanging languid caresses as they drifted off to sleep.

Waking first an hour later, Paige showered, dressed in the clothes she'd worn yesterday and went downstairs to the kitchen. She telephoned the hospital and spoke to her mother. Learning that her father had spent a restful night and had already been taken for tests, she felt a great sense of relief. Her father was going to be all right. She would not allow herself to believe otherwise.

Using his cane, Jared entered the kitchen just as Paige flipped the last pancake off the grill. Coming up behind her, he eased one arm around her waist and patted her tummy.

"How are my girls this morning?" He nuzzled Paige's neck.

"We're hungry." Hoisting the plate of pancakes over her head, she pivoted around, stood on tiptoe and planted a kiss on his lips. "Here, take these and go sit down. Angela and I are starving for pancakes with maple syrup."

While they ate, Paige gave Jared a report on her father's condition. "Regardless of what the tests show, I have no doubt that Dr. Howell will send Daddy to Denver."

"I'll have my plane standing by," Jared said.

"You're going to fly Daddy to Denver?"

"I'll fly the whole family," he told her. "My jet is at the Summers family's disposal."

Reaching across the table, she covered his hand with hers. "Do you have any idea how wonderful you are?"

A slight flush stained Jared's tan cheeks. Good God! He hadn't blushed since he'd been a kid. Paige Summers, red-headed witch that she was, affected him in some of the oddest ways. His mouth curved into a lopsided grin.

"Who, me?" he asked sheepishly.

She squeezed his hand. "Yes, you." Tears gathered in her eyes. "You're generous and kind and caring... and...and I love you, Jared Montgomery."

Her declaration of love shouldn't have taken him by surprise, but it did. He felt as if someone had punched him in the gut. He didn't love her, couldn't love her, despite how much she'd come to mean to him. But damn his self-ish black heart if he wasn't glad that she loved him.

He no longer had any doubts as to the sincerity of her love. The only doubt that remained in his mind was whether or not he could persuade her to marry him.

"Paige...honey...I—I—"

"It's all right, Jared," she said. "I don't expect you to confess your undying love for me. It's just that I've been falling more and more in love with you these past few weeks, and somehow today seemed the right time to tell you."

"If you love me, then why won't you—" He had prom-ised that he wouldn't ask her again. Besides, he already knew the answer to his question. Paige wouldn't marry a man who didn't love her, and as long as he was incapable of saying and meaning those three little words, she would never be his wife.

"I can't marry you, Jared, and you know why." She stroked her thumb across his knuckles. "But I will move in here with you...until...until after Angela is born." She loved him. She wanted to be with him. And she had less than four months to accomplish her goal—teach Jared to love her.

In his haste to get up, he almost knocked over his carved-back oak chair. Grabbing it by the seat, he righted it quickly. "Ah, honey, that's the best news I've heard in a long time." Lifting his cane from where he'd hooked the handle on the table's edge, he approached her and held out his hand. "I promise you that you won't be sorry you've given me the opportunity to really take care of you and Angela."

And Jared, my dearest Jared, you won't be sorry that you've given me the opportunity to continue your lessons in love.

Rising from her chair, she placed her hand in his and happily allowed him to draw her into his embrace. She laid her head on his chest and listened to the slow, steady beat of his heart while he caressed her tenderly.

He might not call what he felt for her love, but she suspected that it was the closest thing to love he'd ever known.

Paige's father was transferred to St. Joseph Hospital in Denver later that day, after Dr. Howell informed the family that he'd made arrangements with the head of cardiology to perform Walt's angioplasty. Paige suspected that Jared's influence had gained her father the attention of such a highly renowned physician.

"The angioplasty is a fairly routine procedure," Dr. Howell had told them. "Afterward, with a change of diet, more exercise and mild medication, Walt will probably feel better than he has in years."

Jared flew the family to Denver on his private jet and stayed at Paige's side every moment. He accompanied her when she went in to see her father.

"I'm counting on you to take care of my girl," Walt said. "She's a bit stubborn, like me. But she's worth her weight in gold, just like her mother. You'll know how I feel once that little granddaughter of mine is born and she wraps herself around your heart."

"I promise I'll take care of Paige," Jared assured her father. "And our baby."

A few minutes later in the waiting area, Paige introduced Jared to Bryant and wasn't surprised when her twenty-year-old brother bristled and refused to shake hands. In their recent phone conversations, Paige had tried to convince Bryant that Jared wasn't an evil, older-man seducer of young virgins. But she'd been unable to change her loving, protective brother's opinion that L. J. Montgomery was a playboy millionaire who had taken advantage of his sister.

But sometime between that first introduction and the family's return flight to Grand Springs the next day, Bryant's hostility changed, if not to friendliness, at least to cordiality.

"I guess he's not as bad as I thought," Bryant admitted. "He seems to genuinely care about you."

"He does care," Paige said. "He cares a great deal about me and our baby."

"Then why won't you marry him? It's plain to see that you're in love with him."

"But he isn't in love with me."

"If he isn't, then he sure as hell is giving a great imitation of a man in love." Bryant hugged Paige to his side. "He's possessive, protective, and he looks at you like you're the only woman on earth."

Paige held Bryant's words in her heart, praying that he was right. But if Jared did love her, could he accept her as she was? Or would he, as Kevin had done, try to re-create her, try to mold her into his idea of the perfect wife?

* * *

Once they had Walt Summers settled in at home and he was taking an afternoon nap, Dora shooed her brood out of the house.

"Your father needs his rest," she said. "And that means peace and quiet. We don't need you boys roughhousing around here all afternoon. Go somewhere and find something to do." Dora turned to Paige. "And you, young lady, go home. If your father wakes and finds you hovering over him, he'll be upset. His major concern is for you and the baby."

Jared suggested a late lunch at Randolphs, but Paige craved a hamburger and fries. Although she usually chose the healthiest foods possible, today she yearned for something greasy and fattening. Jared indulged her appetite by ordering exactly what she wanted, plus a chocolate milkshake.

Paige swallowed the last french fry, then slurped down the remainder of her shake. Chuckling, Jared picked up a napkin, reached across the booth and wiped the chocolate stain from the side of her mouth.

"I ate like a pig, didn't I?" Paige patted her tummy. "But I think Angela enjoyed our sinful meal as much as I did."

"I'm sure she did." Jared gathered up the leftover debris from their lunch, stacked all of it on a tray and deposited it in the garbage on their way out of the fast-food restaurant. He'd finally gotten the hang of walking with a cane but was glad he wouldn't need it much longer.

Within minutes of their entering the highway, Paige realized Jared wasn't headed toward the Wellman Building, but in the opposite direction, blocks from the office.

"Where are we going?" she asked. "I thought we were going in to the office for a few hours."

"Greg and Kay can hold down the fort for another

day.'' Stopping the Jeep at a red light, Jared glanced over at Paige. ''I have a surprise for you.''

''What sort of surprise?''

''A big surprise.''

She couldn't imagine what big surprise he had in store for her. How much more could he give her? She had enough maternity clothes for two women and enough baby clothes and paraphernalia for three infants.

Jared turned off Main Street onto a side avenue, where a variety of specialty shops occupied a row of newly renovated buildings.

''Where *are* we going?'' Paige looked from side to side, searching for some clue to their destination.

''Just wait and see.'' Flipping on the blinker, he turned the Jeep into a small parking lot, adjacent to an empty building. ''We're almost there.''

''Almost where?''

He pulled the Jeep to a stop, then opened the driver's side door. ''Wait right there, honey.''

What was going on? she wondered. What was Jared up to now? Uncertainty and anticipation tingled simultaneously inside her, creating giggles in her throat. When Jared opened the passenger door and helped her out, she grinned at him. He had a look on his face like that of a little boy on Christmas morning.

''Close your eyes,'' he told her as he took her by the hand.

''You've got to be kidding.'' The giggles she'd been holding in check suddenly erupted.

''Humor me, Paige. Close your eyes.''

''Oh, all right.''

Closing her eyes, she allowed him to lead her around the Jeep, out of the parking lot and down the sidewalk. He stopped abruptly, released her hand and moved around behind her. Draping his cane across his wrist, he grasped her shoulders, then turned her to face the empty building. He knew this was going to be a surprise, he just hoped it was a surprise that made Paige happy.

He'd never worried much about making someone else happy, but lately, doing things that pleased Paige, things that made her smile, had become very important to him. If owning a doll shop meant so much to her, he would willingly indulge her need for a hobby.

"All right, honey, you can look now."

Paige opened her eyes. "Oh, my goodness!"

The outer brick walls of the old two-story building had been painted a light gray, and all the accents, including the shutters, were a muted Colonial blue. Empty display windows flanked each side of the solid-glass front door. A large ornate sign, lettered in a matching blue, hung over the entrance. On the left side of the words reading The Dollhouse was a painting of a Victorian dollhouse, and on the right side was a painting of an antique doll.

"Do you like it?" Jared asked anxiously. "Anything you want changed, just tell me and I'll have it fixed by tomorrow."

"Is this…is this mine?" What had he done? Paige shook her head in disbelief.

"The place is all yours. I bought the building for you early this week." He stuck his hand into his pants pocket, brought out a doll-shaped key ring and handed it to her. "They redid the outside when the whole street was renovated, and I've had the inside gutted, so you can start fresh and do whatever you want with the place."

The key chain rattled in Paige's quivering hand. "You don't mean that you're giving me this building?"

Jared laughed, then took the keys out of her hand and unlocked the front door. "Of course I am."

"But, Jared, I can't—"

"Come on inside." Leaning on his cane, he led her into

the vast downstairs area that had been stripped bare to the outer brick walls. "I know it doesn't look like much right now, but once you decide exactly what you want done with the place, I'll get carpenters and plumbers and electricians in here to—"

"Jared, I can't accept this building as a gift."

Swirling around, gripping the key chain in his hand, he stared at her. "Of course you can. This is your dream, isn't it? What you've always wanted. Your own doll shop."

"But I can't let you buy it for me."

As he continued staring at her, his forehead wrinkled and his eyes narrowed. "Why the hell not? I've got so much money I couldn't spend it all in ten lifetimes. Why can't I buy the mother of my child something that she's always wanted?"

"Oh, Jared, what am I going to do with you?" She realized that he honestly didn't understand, that to him this building was a little gift to make her happy and nothing more.

"If you don't like it, then I'll find you another place," he said.

"I love it," she admitted. "This building is so big. I can do so much with it. And it's in a fabulous part of town." How could she accept his generous gift and still maintain her pride and independence? "I'll pay you for the building."

"You'll what?"

"I have nearly eight thousand dollars saved that I can give you in one lump sum, and then when The Dollhouse starts showing a profit, I can make monthly payments to you."

Jared rubbed his chin and grunted. He didn't understand Paige Summers. Other women had taken his gifts without hesitation and held out their hands for more. But not this woman. Not this proud, stubborn woman with her middle-class morals.

"Don't be silly, honey." He laid the key chain in the palm of her hand and folded her fingers over it. "Keep the eight thousand and put it toward renovating the interior of this place."

"Jared, I can't accept this kind of gift from you. Please, try to understand."

He realized that was just the problem. He didn't understand. Not really. But he didn't want to argue the point with her. Not now. There would be time enough for that later. He was sure he could bring her around to his way of thinking. After all, when she became his wife, she would have to adjust to a whole new way of life.

"We'll work out all the details to your satisfaction later," he said.

Paige sighed with relief, then threw her arms around Jared's neck and hugged him enthusiastically. "Thank you."

Releasing her fierce hold around his neck, she grabbed his hand and urged him to follow her farther into the downstairs interior. "If I start work as soon as possible, I might get everything in shape before the baby's born," she said. "Then I could have a spring grand opening. Maybe late April or early May."

"Honey, I can get workers in here and whip this place into shape in no time flat."

"No, Jared." She drew his hand to her face, rubbed her cheek against it, then kissed his wrist. "I want to do the rest. Hire workers. Make the decisions. Even put the finishing touches on everything myself."

"All right. Whatever you want." He was willing to pacify her—up to a point. If taking charge of the project, even doing some of the hands-on work herself, made her happy, he would gladly let her have her way. "Will you let me help you put the finishing touches on everything?"

She squeezed his hand. "Did I hear you correctly? Is L. J. Montgomery actually offering to do manual labor?"

Jared grinned. "For you, honey, I'd do just about anything." He intended to keep her happy, to give her whatever she wanted, so that she would give him what he wanted most. For her to marry him.

"I will pay you back. Once The Dollhouse starts making a profit."

He chuckled. "Honey, if you were my wife, there would be no need for you to pay me back, would there? And no need to worry about making a profit. A lot of my associates' wives have hobbies. Some even run little businesses like this that make excellent tax write-offs."

At first, she couldn't believe that she'd heard him correctly, then she tried to convince herself that he hadn't meant what he'd said. But he had meant it. Jared had given her this building as a toy, a little hobby that would keep her entertained while he took care of his business—important business.

She hadn't even agreed to marry him, and already he was casting her in the mold of other millionaire businessmen's wives.

On the ride home, Paige decided that she would accept Jared's generous gift, regardless of his motives for buying the building for her. She'd show him that The Dollhouse would be more than a hobby for her and a tax write-off for him. She'd make a success of the business, no matter what she had to do.

If there was any hope for Jared and her to have a future together as husband and wife, he would have to not only love her, but love her enough to allow her to be herself. And that meant she would make her own decisions.

Was she wishing for the impossible? Could she really expect Jared to alter his way of life to accommodate her, when she had no intention of changing herself to suit him?

"You're awfully quiet over there," Jared said as they drove up the mountain. "What are you thinking about?"

"I'm thinking about how I want to organize the space at The Dollhouse," she said. "I want one room upstairs just for American-made dolls. Everything from the ones produced in the late-nineteenth and early-twentieth century, like Joel Ellis dolls, all the way up to today's Barbie dolls."

"From what I've seen of your doll collection at your parents' home, I'd say you have enough stock to open a business tomorrow."

"Well, I might put some of my personal collection on display and even sell a few, but I plan to keep most of them to pass along to Angela one day."

"What if my daughter doesn't like dolls?" Jared asked jokingly.

"Not a chance!" Paige playfully socked Jared's arm.

He listened to her plans until he parked the Jeep in the circular gravel drive at the cabin.

"I hope I can find enough musical dolls and automata to create a separate section for them." Paige made no protest when Jared opened the door, removed her seat belt and buttoned her coat. "All I have in my collection are a few medium-priced 'pull toys' and a couple of *marottes.*"

Jared helped her out of the Jeep. "What the hell is a *marotte?*" Taking her arm, he hurried her up the stairs and onto the deck as fast as his limping gait allowed.

"A *marotte* is a stick doll, usually with a bisque head," she told him as he unlocked the front door and quickly ushered her inside and out of the cold night air. "A *marotte* has a head and a plump upper body, but it's not a whole doll."

When they removed their coats, Jared hung them in the closet. "Go warm yourself by the fire and I'll fix you some hot tea and me some coffee," he told her.

"All right. Thanks." She walked into the living room while he headed toward the kitchen. "I think I'll phone the folks and check on Daddy," she called out to Jared.

He knew she couldn't wait to tell her parents about The Dollhouse, so he took his time preparing their drinks. When he returned to the living room, he found her still on the phone with her mother.

"I love you, too, Mama," Paige said, then hung up the telephone and turned to Jared, her mouth curving into a warm, welcoming smile.

How easy it was for Paige and her mother to openly express their emotions, to say "I love you" at the end of their conversation. Jared couldn't imagine telling Joyce Montgomery that he loved her. She was his mother, but there were times when he wasn't even sure he liked her. What would it have been like, he wondered, to have grown up as a part of the Summers family?

He was glad that his daughter would belong to Paige's warm, loving family and grow up as Walt and Dora's adored grandchild. He hadn't even told his mother about the baby, but when he did, she'd be outraged at first. And if she finally accepted the fact, she'd probably send a gift. Something expensive and totally useless.

Jared set the tray holding Paige's cup of tea and his coffee mug on the end table to her left, and walked across the room to the rolltop desk.

"How's your father?" Jared asked.

"He was asleep, but Mama said he's doing just fine. She promised to wait and let me tell him all about The Dollhouse in the morning."

Jared opened the long, narrow top drawer of the desk, reached inside and pulled out two large envelopes. "I want

to go ahead and give you the deed to the building downtown and…'' He hesitated, uncertain exactly how to go
about explaining the contents of the second envelope. He
didn't want to do anything to make Paige unhappy. And
two extravagant gifts in one day might be one gift too
many.

''Oh, is that what you've got there?'' she asked. ''You'll
need to get your lawyer…what's his name? Mr. Mc-
Cafferty?…to prepare an agreement for my loan payments
on The Dollhouse.''

''I thought… Never mind, we'll iron out the details
later,'' he said, knowing it was useless to argue with her
at this point. Jared's brow wrinkled.

''Is there something wrong?'' Paige lifted her teacup
and sipped the warm, sweet liquid.

''I have something I want to show you. Upstairs.''
Maybe it would be easier to present her with the second
gift once she saw the surprise on the second floor.

''Not another gift?'' She laughed, but when he didn't,
she placed her tea back on the tray, then stood and walked
toward him. ''You have to stop buying things,'' she told
him. ''I have everything I need, and so does Angela.''

''Just come with me. Please.'' Jared found that buying
expensive gifts for a woman who didn't expect them was
a real pleasure.

She let him lead the way to the second floor, but balked
when he stopped in front of the closed door to the bedroom
next to his. ''My gift is in there?''

''Sort of.'' He placed the two envelopes under his arm,
then reached out and grasped the brass door handle.

''What do you mean, sort of?''

Without reply, he turned the handle, opened the door
and flipped on the light switch. Paige's eyes widened and
her mouth opened to a circle as she sucked in an astonished breath.

She couldn't believe her eyes. The bedroom that only yesterday morning had boasted a set of sturdy pine twin beds, matching dresser and chest, beige walls, tan carpet and plaid curtains was now a completely furnished pastel nursery.

"When—when did you have this done?" Floating into the room, her mouth still agape, Paige stared at the pink, blue and yellow hearts wallpaper border. A pale shade of pink paint coated the walls of the large nursery.

"Do you like it?" He stepped into the room but stood just inside the doorway.

"When? How? Yesterday when we left for Denver this was a guest room."

"I called Marcy Dailey from the airport and told her what I wanted and that the job had to be finished by this evening."

"Marcy Dailey!"

Jared crossed the room as quickly as he could, putting more weight on his injured ankle than he should have. But he ignored the pain shooting up his leg. "Now, honey, don't get ticked off because I had Marcy pull things together for us. She's the best decorator in town."

He smiled at Paige. She frowned at him.

"I had only one date with Marcy," Jared said. "I haven't seen her again."

She didn't care about the date he'd had with Marcy Dailey. Didn't he understand that the reason she was upset had nothing to do with his having dated Marcy and everything to do with the fact that he had hired a professional to decorate the baby's nursery?

Misunderstanding the cause of Paige's wrinkled brow and clenched teeth, Jared said, "I kissed her good-night and left her at her door. I swear." He held up his hand in an oath-sign. "And it was a closemouthed kiss."

Pacing around the room, Paige ran her fingertips over

every piece of furniture, and her gaze inspected every detail of the perfect nursery. She paused beside the white Jenny Lind crib, the one Jared had picked out and bought on their Denver shopping trip.

"The room is beautiful," she said. "All the things that were in boxes at my apartment and all the furniture and stuff you bought in Denver are right here."

"Then you approve?"

What was she supposed to say? How could she tell him that despite the perfection of the nursery, she was disappointed that he'd allowed another woman to create the room for their daughter. She turned to face Jared. "Why did you do this? Why did you fix a nursery here at your house?"

Jared jerked the two envelopes out from under his arm and held them out to Paige. "Not my house, honey. Not anymore. This is your house now. Yours and Angela's."

"What!" She stared at the envelopes but didn't touch them.

"I deeded this house over to you. And I'm putting one of the new condos downtown in your name, too." He looked at Paige, his eyes pleading with her to accept this second extravagant gift.

So, she thought, Jared had her life all mapped out, the major details planned. What was he trying to do—buy her? He had purchased a building for her doll shop and would financially back her new business. A hobby for the little wife. Now he was putting some of his property in her name. Was he trying to bribe her with expensive gifts? Was using his money the only way he knew how to show affection?

He was giving her a golden life on a silver platter, and she knew she should be grateful. There were only two possible problems with this wonderful life. Only two questions to which she needed an answer before she committed herself to him for a lifetime. Did he or did he not love her? And would he or would he not accept the fact that she had no intention of turning herself into his idea of a suitable wife?

Jared was, without a doubt, the most exasperating, over-bearing, stubborn man in the world. And one of the most generous and caring, too, she reminded herself. Despite all his high-handed tactics, she couldn't help loving him. "Lawrence Jared Montgomery, what *am* I going to do with you?"

"Well, honey, if you really want an answer to your question, I have a suggestion."

"You do?"

His killer smile turned her knees to jelly. She bit down on her bottom lip. He dropped the two envelopes to the floor, reached out and grabbed her around the waist. After nuzzling her neck, he kissed her earlobe, then whispered his suggestion, using rather explicit language.

Despite her misgivings, despite the warning signals going off in her brain, Paige couldn't resist Jared. Even if she could never marry him, she loved him desperately. And she wanted him.

"You're bad," she told him. "Really, really bad. You know that, don't you?" Paige patted his bottom.

Grabbing her hand, he stilled her movements, then slid her hand around to the front of his slacks. "But I can be good. Really, really good. Come with me and I'll show you just how good."

Eleven

In the days following her father's surgery, Paige and Jared settled into a routine. They worked together at the office every day as employer and employee. In the evenings Jared helped Paige at The Dollhouse, and they often ordered takeout for dinner. And at night, they slept in each other's arms. They had become friends as well as lovers. But two words were never mentioned. *Love* and *marriage*.

They spent Thanksgiving Day with her parents. Everyone stuffed themselves with Dora Summers's scrumptious Southern food, the four men completely wiping out the savory corn bread dressing.

Paige marveled at the way Jared seemed to enjoy being a part of her family. Her parents had welcomed him warmly, treating him as if he were a third son. Jared and seventeen-year-old Austen became fast friends, and by the end of the Thanksgiving weekend, Jared had won over Bryant.

Paige and Jared didn't discuss the future beyond Angela's birth and the spring grand opening of The Dollhouse. Instead, they lived in the present.

Paige knew that they couldn't go on this way indefinitely—pretending everything was all right. Even though they lived together as if they were husband and wife, they were no closer to marriage than they'd been three months ago. And she wondered how much longer she could go on hoping that Jared would learn to love her.

She knew he still wanted to marry her, but true to his

word, he didn't ask again. He understood that she would never marry him without love. Why was it so difficult for him to love her—Paige Summers—just the way she was?

Without telling Paige, Jared hired Marcy Dailey's rival to decorate the house for Christmas. When the man showed up, Paige promptly dismissed him and confronted Jared.

"I don't want some interior designer decorating my house for Christmas," Paige said. "This *is* my house, isn't it?"

"Of course it's your house, honey. I just thought hiring someone to decorate would make things easier for you."

"Well, your family probably always hired someone to put up a Christmas tree and hang garlands and prepare the food." Just the way he'd hired someone to decorate Angela's nursery! "But in my family, we do it ourselves!"

Jared gave in to her wishes without a fight and insisted she spare no expense in decorating *her* house for the Christmas season. That's the way he kept referring to the log cabin—as her house. A couple of times he called it *our* house, then quickly corrected himself. She wished the cabin was *their* house, that they could create a real home for Angela.

Huge pine-and-holly wreaths hung on the double front doors. Pine boughs tied with Yuletide green-and-gold plaid ribbons decorated the den, where Paige had placed a nut-garland swag across the fireplace. A three-foot, fresh-cut pine tree, decorated with country craft ornaments and multicolored lights, took a place of honor on the side of Jared's gigantic oak desk.

In the living room, Paige had used red velvet ribbon to accent the pine-and-holly garland draped over the top and down each side of the massive rock fireplace. Various sizes of white candles, interspersed with pinecones and greenery, covered the mantel. Red and white poinsettia plants lined the row of banisters across the open second-story landing.

And an eight-foot blue spruce placed in front of the wide expanse of living room windows twinkled with the glow from hundreds of miniature white lights. A flame-haired angel in white perched atop the tree, guarding an array of her crystal, porcelain, cloth and gold-plated sisters who hung from every branch.

After leaving the office early, Jared and Paige decided to forgo working at The Dollhouse and instead stopped by her parents' home for dinner. They stayed for a while after their meal, but headed home before the weather turned nasty. According to the six o'clock news report, a winter storm would sweep across Colorado tonight and tomorrow.

Once home, they went straight into the living room. Jared built a fire in the fireplace while Paige turned on the Christmas tree lights and a floor lamp on the opposite side of the room. She loved the homey holiday atmosphere she had created all around them.

Kicking her shoes off on the floor, she sat down beside Jared on the larger of the two living room sofas. She snuggled her back against his chest as he pulled her into his embrace, circling her body with his arms.

"I think we should have Mrs. Clark here on a daily basis after Angela is born." Jared tenderly rubbed Paige's full, round tummy. Now, in her sixth month of pregnancy, she had blossomed. Even her slender face had filled out.

"Mrs. Clark is here twice a week already," Paige said. "Do you think Angela and I are going to be so messy that we'll need a full-time housekeeper?"

"I think that, for a while, you'll need a little extra help." He kissed her cheek. "Knowing you, you'll want to spend every moment with Angela, not waste your time worrying about housework. Besides, once The Dollhouse opens, you won't have time to do anything around here."

"Jared, how can I accept another gift from you? And that's what having Mrs. Clark here on a daily basis would be."

He ran his hands up and down her arms, caressing her softly through her blue silk blouse while he nuzzled her neck. "It's only natural, as Angela's father, that I want to take care of her and her mother, isn't it?"

"Yes, I suppose it is."

"All right, then." He nibbled on her earlobe. "Honey, you're going to have to get used to the fact that your baby's father is a very wealthy man and I intend to spend a great deal of money giving my daughter the best life has to offer."

"And you're going to have to accept the fact that I'm not accustomed to having everything I want just handed to me." Paige tilted her head back so that she could see his face. "I might feel differently if we were...if we were married, but we aren't. And...well, just chalk it up to my middle-class morality, but I'm beginning to feel like a kept woman."

Laughter rumbled from Jared's chest. Turning her in his arms, he smiled at her, then lowered his head and kissed her. By the time he ended the kiss, she was breathless and her lips were pink and puffy.

"Being a kept woman is your choice, not mine," he said teasingly. "You can make an honest man of me, just like that." He snapped his fingers. "Ask me the right question and we can plan a Christmas wedding."

His lighthearted comments caught her off guard. He hadn't mentioned marriage in quite some time. Not since he'd promised not to propose again. "If you can say the right words, I'll ask you the right question."

Tightening his hold around her body, his muscles

tensed. "We're still at an impasse, aren't we, Paige. Dead-locked by our own inabilities to compromise."

She wanted to cry. But she wouldn't. What good would it do? All the tears in the world wouldn't change their situation. Only Jared's change of heart could do that, or should she say only his discovery of a heart. A heart capable of loving and of willingly proclaiming that love.

"But we have compromised," she told him. "We've agreed to be friends. And lovers. And we plan to rear our child together, to give her a mother and father who both love her and will always be there for her, making sure she has the best."

He wanted to say that married parents were what would be best for Angela, but he didn't say it. What good would it do? Nothing he said or did was going to change Paige's mind. "Yeah, you're right. We have compromised, haven't we. We even have the legal documentation to prove it."

He had gotten just what he'd wanted, hadn't he? Paige had accepted the terms his lawyer had stipulated. She had taken what they'd offered and hadn't asked for anything more. Not for herself or for Angela. And heaven help him, if she'd asked for the moon, he would have given it to her.

The odd thing was that he wasn't so sure anymore exactly what he wanted. It sure as hell wasn't marriage to a sophisticated socialite who would willingly marry L. J. Montgomery for his millions. It wasn't the sterile, loveless relationship his parents had had. It wasn't some well-bred, cool, regal lady to play queen to his king.

"Someday you'll find a suitable wife," Paige said. "And I'll find someone who'll love me just as I am."

The only problem with that scenario, she decided, was that she would never love another man. She'd go to her grave loving Jared. And if she couldn't find a way to teach him how to love her, she'd never get what she wanted most out of life.

Why couldn't she have fallen in love with a less complicated man? Why had fate given her such a difficult task? What she had wanted was a sweet, easy-going guy who was ready for love and marriage. Instead, what she'd gotten was a magnetic, powerful dynamo who didn't believe in love.

"I've decided to go ahead and furnish one of our new condos on Ponderosa Avenue for you," Jared said. "We'll be putting them up for sale right after the first of the year." With his arms wrapped tightly around Paige, he reached for her hands that lay folded in her lap. "As a matter of fact, I think we should move in there for the last month or so of your pregnancy. It's closer to the hospital. And we won't have the twenty-minute drive up the mountain every day."

"I think that's a good idea, but there really was no reason for you to give me this house and a condo in town."

"With a condo in Grand Springs and a cabin on the mountain, you and Angela will have the best of both worlds."

"When I start working at The Dollhouse on a regular basis, I'll probably stay in town most of the time."

"Are you still planning on taking Angela to work with you every day?" Jared asked.

"Yes, I am," she told him.

"You know it would be easier if we hired a nanny for Angela."

"We've had this discussion before and the answer is still no! You might have been raised by a nanny, but I intend to raise my child myself."

"Why do you have to be so stubborn?" he asked. "Everyone I know has a nanny for their children."

"Everyone at your socioeconomic level, Mr. L. J. Montgomery, but not ordinary working people like my family." Pulling her hands out of his, she straightened her spine and eased away from him, just enough so that her back didn't touch his chest.

"Dammit, Paige, as my wif— As my child's mother, you'll be in that socioeconomic bracket. And if you choose to run a business, you'll be a working mother. If you want to stay home and raise Angela, then stay home. There's no need for you to work."

"Let's get this straight right now—" Turning around to face him, Paige pointed her finger in Jared's face "I'll agree to a housekeeper and I'll even agree to a baby-sitter, but I do not want a full-time nanny. And I will not live off your generosity for the rest of my life. I'm going to work and support myself and Angela and—"

"You're going to drive me insane, Paige Summers! That's what you're going to do."

"I wouldn't drive you insane if you didn't keep trying to change me—if you didn't keep trying to cram your life-style down my throat." She glared at him, her dark eyes misting with emotion. "For heaven's sake, Jared, just let me be myself!"

"Be yourself! I don't want to change you. I just want to make things easier for you."

"Do you really mean that?" she asked.

Did he, he wondered? Since the first time he'd asked Paige to marry him, he'd been trying to figure out a way to mold her into his idea of a suitable mate, someone *appropriate* for a man in his position. But would he really want Paige to change, to be different, to be like those cool, aloof, status-oriented women he'd dated for years?

No. Hell, no! He adored Paige just the way she was. Emotional. Passionate. Loving. Independent.

"Yes, honey. I really mean it. I don't want to change you."

Paige smiled. A shiver raced along her nerve endings. "I believe you." She sighed deeply. He hadn't said he loved her, but accepting her for the person she was certainly was a step in the right direction. If Jared could learn to like and respect her for herself, if he could stop trying to convert her into a multimillionaire's wife, then there was hope that he could learn to love her. Wasn't there?

"I thought we were going to discuss plans for the holidays," Jared reminded her.

"We were, before...well, that's all settled, isn't it? And you're right, we do have a lot of plans to make for this month. Christmas is only two and a half weeks away, and then New Year's is a week after that. And Mama's already been asking me if we're going to spend Christmas Day with them."

"Of course we'll spend Christmas Day with your folks." He'd actually been looking forward to sharing another warm, loving holiday with the Summers family. He could almost taste Dora's sweet potato pie. "I haven't spent a holiday with my mother since I was a teenager. For the past few years, she's gone to Europe with friends right after Thanksgiving and stayed until January."

Paige couldn't imagine what Jared's life had been like. Terribly lonely and sad. And sorely lacking in motherly love, in parental love, in love of any kind.

"Well, I'll call Mama tomorrow and tell her that we'll both be there for all her Christmas Day festivities." Jared laid his hand on Paige's stomach and she relaxed against him. "But I'd like for us to spend Christmas Eve here, if that's all right with you."

"Why wouldn't it be all right with me?" He hugged her with fierce tenderness. "I like having you all to myself, just the two of us alone." As if in protest at not having been included in her father's census, Jared's daughter stirred within Paige's womb. Chuckling, he patted Paige's tummy. "Excuse me, Miss Montgomery, I apologize. I should have said that I like being alone with my two girls.''

''Miss Montgomery?'' Paige had never given a thought to her baby's last name. If she and Jared didn't marry before Angela's birth, she assumed her child would be a Summers.

''Yes, of course, Miss Montgomery,'' Jared said. ''Honey, didn't you read the agreement we signed? Didn't your lawyer go over everything with you? I plan to legally recognize Angela as my daughter and give her my name, even if we aren't married when she's born.''

''Yes, I read the agreement.'' *I read it through my tears.* ''And I'm sure Mr. Bowes explained that stipulation. I'd just forgotten.''

''Well, getting back to our holiday plans,'' he said. ''Just what do you have in mind for us on Christmas Eve?''

''I thought we'd have a nice dinner first, and then exchange our gifts—'' she glanced under the towering blue spruce where Jared had already placed several packages ''—and you are not to buy me anything else. I noticed three of those five gifts have my name on them.''

Propping his chin on top of her head, he nuzzled her hair into disarray. ''After we exchange our gifts, what then?''

''We'll cuddle on the sofa and watch my favorite Christmas movie.''

''You're kidding?''

Swirling around so that she faced him, Paige tilted her chin defiantly. ''No, I am not kidding. Just what's wrong with watching *It's a Wonderful Life* on Christmas Eve?''

''What is *It's a Wonderful Life?*'' he asked.

''Now, you've got to be kidding. Are you telling me that you have never heard of the Jimmy Stewart classic about an angel sent down from heaven to save George

Bailey and show him what a wonderful life he has? If so, you have lived a deprived life and it's high time you were exposed to some holiday magic.''

"No wonder you're such a romantic. Dora spoon-fed you on the silver screen's sentimental hogwash.''

"We *are* watching *It's a Wonderful Life*.'' She crossed her arms over her chest. "It's a tradition in the Summers household. Every year since I was a little girl, we watched it on television at Christmastime. And a few years ago, I bought the video. One for me and one for Mama.''

"All right, we'll spend Christmas Eve doing whatever you want to do. And we'll share Christmas Day with your family. But I want to make our New Year's plans.''

"You do?'' she asked. "What do you have in mind?''

Jared lifted Paige onto his lap, then raised her arm and placed it around his neck. He looked at her surprised face and grinned. "Sit here like a good girl and I'll tell you.''

"I'm always good,'' she said flippantly.

"Ah, honey, don't I know it.'' Jared sighed.

"Oh, you!'' She punched him on the chest. "You know I didn't mean it like that.'' She cuddled up against him and batted her eyelashes. "So, are you going to tell about your plans for New Year's?''

"I'd like to fly you down to Texas and show you my ranch.'' He'd never taken a woman to the ranch. Few if any of his lady friends would have enjoyed a visit to the old homestead he had inherited from his grandfather. "The Circle M is a legacy from Grandpa Monty. I think you would have liked him, and I know he would have liked you.''

"I'd love to see your ranch. I know how much a part of you it is. And if your grandfather was anything like the way you've described him to me, I know I would have liked him, too.'' Hugging Jared, she dotted little kisses all over his face. "I can't think of a better way to start off the New Year than visiting your ranch."

He took her face in his hands, stilling her busy lips. She stared at him, her eyes questioning.

"What?" she asked, knowing he wanted to tell her something.

"You're the first woman I've ever asked to come with me to the Circle M."

"Oh."

They gazed at each other. The mantel clock tick-tocked rhythmically. The logs crackled in the fireplace. The December wind howled through the trees.

The subtle touch of his breath across her lips urged them to open. Tunneling his fingers through her hair, he brought her face to his and took her mouth in a tongue-thrusting kiss of pure possession. Responding passionately, Paige tightened her hold around his neck, then slid her other arm around his waist.

Without breaking the kiss, Jared lifted her in his arms and stood. She clung to him, her body tingling with anticipation.

He carried her out of the living room, into the foyer and up the stairs, his gait unhampered now that his ankle had healed. Kicking open the half-closed door to their dark bedroom, he kissed Paige again, then carried her over to the bed. Placing her on top of the coverlet, he leaned over and began undressing her slowly.

They made love with tender passion, their need for each other overriding all else. When they made love, nothing and no one else existed. Only the two of them, and the earth-shattering pleasure they found in each other's arms.

Two hours later, Jared awoke, left the bed, slipped into his jeans and headed out the door.

"Where are you going?" Paige lifted her head off her pillow.

"I'm going to turn off the lights downstairs and close up, then catch the ten o'clock news. I want to check on that winter storm the weatherman said was headed our way."

Stretching languidly, Paige smiled. "I'm glad tomorrow is Saturday. We can sleep late and stay in bed all day if we want to."

Jared grinned wickedly, then winked at her. "Don't wait up for me, honey. Get your rest."

"I think I'll take a shower before I go back to sleep."

Jared watched her get out of bed, her ripe body gloriously naked, her long red hair hanging provocatively down her back. He felt a twinge of renewed arousal. Hell! Was it always going to be like this? Every time he touched her? Every time he looked at her?

She turned halfway around in the bathroom door, the silhouette of her body outlined by the dim glow from the recessed hall lighting. He sucked in his breath. Six months pregnant, her breasts enlarged, her tummy protruding, and she was still the most beautiful woman on earth.

"Don't stay downstairs too long." The tone of her voice issued an invitation. "You know that after my shower I enjoy you rubbing scented lotion all over me."

"I could just skip the news and take a shower with you," he said.

She turned her back to him, but paused just inside the bathroom, glanced over her shoulder and smiled. He followed her without hesitation, as much a slave to his desire as she was to hers.

An hour later, Jared went downstairs, made sure the doors were locked, turned off the lights and checked the weather channel on the television. A severe winter storm had moved across the western part of the state and would soon sweep into Grand Springs.

When he returned to his bed, he found Paige asleep,

holding his pillow to her body. He eased the pillow out of her grasp, placed it back at the top of the bed and crawled in under the covers. Fitting his body, in spoon fashion, to hers, he nuzzled the back of her head, breathing in the sweet floral scent of her freshly washed and dried hair.

He went to sleep, holding her securely in his arms, his hand laid protectively over their unborn child.

Twelve

Paige woke with a start. Pain sliced through her back and spread out across her lower abdomen. Sitting up, knocking the covers to her knees, she clutched her stomach with trembling hands. Oh, God, what was wrong? What was happening? She gulped in huge swallows of air. The pain intensified, eliciting a loud cry from deep within her. Doubling over, her arms crisscrossing her belly, Paige screamed.

Jared shot straight up. "Paige! My God, honey, what's wrong?"

"Jared...ooh." Clenching her teeth tightly, she tried to resist the spasm that racked her body. Sweat broke out on her forehead and beaded her upper lip. Holding her stomach with one hand, she reached out to Jared with the other. "I'm cramping," she told him. "And it's bad."

"Oh, God!" Fear spread through him quickly, like a fast-acting poison. "Try to stay calm." His voice vibrated with emotion. "I'll call Tony Petrocelli and tell him to meet us at the hospital."

Paige panted, trying to lessen the residue of pain left from the last spasm.

Jared hopped out of bed and switched on the bedside lamp. He headed toward the closet, then stopped dead still when Paige moaned loudly. Pivoting around, he ran to her just as she tried to stand.

"Wait, honey." He eased her back down onto the edge

of the bed. "Stay right here until I get dressed and call the doctor, then I'll help you put on a gown."

She grabbed Jared's arm. "Tell Dr. Petrocelli that I think I've gone into labor."

"You think you're in labor?" he asked. "But you can't be. You're barely six months pregnant."

"I know." Tears welled in her eyes. "If—if I have the baby now, she can't survive." Tears cascaded down her cheeks. "Please, Jared, do something! Don't let me lose our little girl." Tears clung to the corners of her mouth and dripped down her chin.

"You're not going to lose our baby," he told her, damned and determined to make his pronouncement true. "Whatever is wrong, Petrocelli will take care of it once we get you to the hospital."

"The pain has stopped now. Help me up. I don't think I'm bleeding, but I need to check and make sure."

Jared's stomach knotted painfully, and a weak, sick feeling spiraled through his body. He eased his arms beneath her, lifted her and carried her to the bathroom. He sat her down on the commode.

"Don't move," he said. "I'll be right back."

Jared dressed hurriedly in jeans and a shirt, then pulled on his socks. While he hobbled across the room, with one boot on and struggling into the other one, Paige emerged from the bathroom.

"It's all right. I'm not bleeding."

He stomped into the second boot, then rushed across the room and draped his arm around Paige's shoulder. "Any more pain?"

"No more pain. Maybe it was just a false alarm. Who knows, it could have been severe gas pains."

"Whatever it was, we aren't taking any chances." Jared lifted her into his arms again and carried her back to their bed. He jerked the covers off and wrapped the spread and blanket around her naked shoulders. "I'm calling the doctor right now."

"Get me a gown and robe first, please." She smiled weakly. Please, dear God, she prayed. Don't let me have any more cramps. Don't let me go into premature labor. I can't lose our baby. I can't lose Angela!

Jared helped her into a yellow flannel gown and matching quilted robe, then knelt beside the bed and slid her house slippers on her feet. Glancing up at her, he caressed her face. "Still all right?"

She nodded affirmatively. He kissed her on the forehead.

"That's my girl," he said. "What's Petrocelli's number?"

"Maybe we should wait. I hate to wake him in the middle of the night."

"I'm not waiting." Jared lifted the receiver from the phone on the nightstand. "What's his number?"

"Here, let me dial the number. I know it by heart."

Jared handed her the phone. She dialed the number, and when Dr. Petrocelli's answering service picked up, she calmly explained what had happened. Jared pressed his ear to the back side of the phone, listening to the conversation.

"Ms. Summers, I think you should probably go straight to the hospital, but if you prefer, I'll contact Dr. Petrocelli and have him call you. Do you live in town?"

"No, we live about twenty minutes out, on the mountain. Why, is there some problem?"

"I hope not," the woman said. "But it's snowing awfully hard out there, and the latest weather reports say this could be the first really bad storm of the winter season."

Jared grabbed the phone out of Paige's hand. "Tell Petrocelli not to waste any time calling us back. Tell him to meet us at the hospital. We're leaving right now." Jared slammed down the phone, then turned to an open-mouthed Paige. "You'll need your boots and your heavy parka."

"Jared, I don't think this is necessary. I'm fine. I'm—"
Paige gasped as aching ripples spread across her stomach.

"What's wrong? Another pain?" He grabbed her by the
shoulders.

Gritting her teeth, she bore the sharp, searing cramp. She
clung to him, crying. "Something is wrong. Dreadfully
wrong."

Within minutes, he had dressed her warmly and put on
his heavy coat, Stetson and leather gloves. He carried her
downstairs and had her wait in the living room while he
went outside and started the Jeep. The snow was falling
so hard, he could barely see the cabin. He made his way
back to the deck, following the beams from the floodlights
he'd turned on before he went outside.

Grabbing the cotton throw off the sofa, he wrapped it
around Paige, lifted her into his arms and carried her out
to the Jeep.

"It'll be warm in here in a minute," he said. "Just sit
tight, honey. We're on our way. I'll get you to the hospital
as quick as I can."

"But Jared, it's snowing so hard. How will you be able
to see the road?"

"I'll get you off this goddamn mountain if I have to
feel my way, all the way from here to Vanderbilt Memorial."

His insides constricted. His hands trembled on the steering wheel. He couldn't let Paige see how scared he was.
And he *was* scared. Damn scared. He'd read half a dozen
books on pregnancy and childbirth, and he knew severe
abdominal cramping in a woman's twenty-fourth week
didn't bode well. In most cases, labor at this stage of a
woman's pregnancy ended in a premature birth. And the
baby's chances for survival weren't good.

Glancing at the windshield, he wondered why it hadn't
already defrosted, then he looked closer. Ice. Dammit! A

thin layer of ice melted slowly from the glass. If there was ice on the windshield, then there would be ice on the roads. And ice under the snow would make the road down the mountain treacherous.

Gripping the steering wheel with white-knuckled ferocity, Jared closed his eyes momentarily and prayed. *Let me get Paige to the hospital safely, where the doctor can take care of her. Please, please, don't let anything happen to her and our baby.*

The frigid December wind pounded the Jeep, swaying it from side to side. Even the powerful four-wheel drive was at the mercy of the winter storm, little more maneuverable than any other vehicle on the ice-slick mountain road. And with the windshield wipers swiping back and forth at high speed, Jared barely could see a foot in front of him. The strong headlight beams illuminated the snow shower and the white cocoon that enveloped them, but the lights could not penetrate the thick, opaque veil of falling snow.

Jared had turned the radio on, searching the stations for weather bulletins. But when he noticed how upset the storm warnings made Paige, he turned the radio off.

With one hand, Paige held together the cotton throw Jared had wrapped around her. With her other hand, she cupped her abdomen. According to the clock on the dashboard, they had been en route nearly fifteen minutes and she hadn't suffered another cramp. That had to be a good sign, didn't it? Although she suspected she had gone into premature labor, she couldn't be sure. After all, she'd never been pregnant before, never gone into labor before. But what else could it be? What other possible explanation could there be for her cramps?

Paige couldn't see the odometer from where she sat huddled on the passenger's side of the Jeep, but she doubted they had traveled more than five miles. The road's hazardous condition prevented Jared from driving any faster. He kept his eyes riveted to the windshield, and she wondered if he could see any better than she could. She hoped so, because she couldn't see a thing, except a constantly moving, white curtain that obliterated the darkness.

Jared's calm, controlled manner amazed her. He had taken charge in an authoritarian, no-nonsense way, and she had no doubt that he would get her safely to the hospital. Although she sat silently, praying with every breath she took, she was half crazy with worry. It took every ounce of her self-control not to burst into tears.

Jared glanced at her, taking his eyes off the road for a split second. The lighted instrument panel cast a dim glow inside the Jeep, revealing Paige's huddled form. She looked so small, so pale and so very fragile, her long red hair falling in disarray around her shoulders. He wanted to reach out and pull her into his arms, but he couldn't.

"Are you all right, honey?" He barely recognized the hoarse, unsteady voice as his own.

"I think so," she said. "I'm doing a lot of praying, begging God not to let anything happen to Angela."

"So am I, honey. So am I."

He'd never been religious. Hell, he didn't even think of himself as a spiritual person, not the way Grandpa Monty had been, a man one with the world around him. But tonight Jared wanted desperately to believe in a higher power that could protect his tiny, unborn daughter and keep her tucked safely inside her mother's womb long enough for her to survive in the outside world.

Jared prayed. With every breath he took. With every beat of his heart. The thought of losing this baby tormented him. And so unbearable was the thought that something could happen to Paige, that he refused to even consider the possibility. He simply could not imagine his life without her.

Listening to the constant swish-swish-swish of the windshield wipers, Paige closed her heavy eyelids. Overcome by weariness and lulled by the repetitive sound, she dozed off into a light sleep.

The cramp hit her suddenly. Hard. Racking. Powerful. An aching pressure in her pelvis and lower back, spreading quickly down into her groin and thighs. Crying out in agony, she grabbed her stomach and doubled over in pain. Her fingers clawed into the seat belt that held her in place.

Stealing a glimpse of Paige's tortured face, Jared tightened his hold on the steering wheel to steady his shaking hands.

"It's bad, isn't it, honey." God, don't do this! Don't! Please, don't.

"Yes. It's bad." Paige's chin trembled. Her teeth chattered. Despite the warmth from the heater, she suddenly felt unnaturally cold. Pain sliced through her body like a deadly knife. "Jared!"

He eased his foot down on the brake pedal, slowly stopping the Jeep in the middle of the road. After shifting the gear to park and flipping on his emergency blinker, he turned to Paige. "We're only a couple of miles from town." He held out his hand. "Is there anything I can do? If there is, just tell me and I'll do it."

Biting down on her bottom lip, Paige grabbed Jared's hand and squeezed it tightly. She counted to ten, and then ten again, waiting for the contraction to end. Sucking in small, deep breaths, she relaxed as the pain melted and gradually evaporated.

"I'm all right now," she told him, clinging fiercely to his big hand. "The pain's gone. I'm sorry I cried out that way. The pain was terrible and I was so scared." She gazed at him through tear-filled eyes. "Oh, God, I'm still scared."

He gave her hand a quick, hard squeeze, then released

it. "Keep telling yourself that everything is going to be all right. You're going to be fine, and so is Angela."

Hurriedly, he flipped off the emergency blinker, shifted the gear into drive and pressed his foot down on the gas pedal. "We should be at the hospital in another ten or fifteen minutes." Damn this weather! Damn the blinding, never-ending snow! Why tonight of all nights had the worst winter storm in years hit Grand Springs?

When they entered downtown, he couldn't even see the traffic lights until he was almost under them. He spotted several empty stalled cars and trucks, some barely pulled off the side of the road.

What the hell! The red Bronco came from out of nowhere, its headlights piercing through the snow veil as it neared the Jeep. The other vehicle was headed straight toward them. Jared cursed loudly. Paige screamed.

Turning the steering wheel to the right, slowly easing his foot down on the brake, he guided the Jeep off the side of the road and onto a snow-covered embankment. He brought the Jeep to an uneasy stop just as the red Bronco swerved back into the left lane and drove on past them.

"Damn, stupid fool!" Jared unbuckled his seat belt and reached for Paige.

She trembled from head to toe, her big brown eyes staring straight ahead but seeing nothing. Jared grabbed her by the shoulders.

"Paige, are you all right?" When she didn't respond, just keep staring sightless out the window, he shook her gently. "Paige, dammit, snap out of it! Don't you dare go into shock or—" His voice cracked. "Come on, honey. We didn't wreck. We're safe." He caressed her cheek tenderly.

Paige blinked several times, then breathed deeply. "Hurry, Jared. Please. I can feel another contraction starting."

Within five minutes, he pulled the Jeep up at the hospital's emergency entrance, removed Paige from her seat and carried her into the ER. He refused to release Paige when the nurses offered to help her into a wheelchair.

"Just show me where to take her!" he demanded "Is Petrocelli here?"

"Follow me," the young blond nurse said. "Dr. Petrocelli arrived just moments ago."

Jared paced the ER waiting room like a madman, anger and fear welling up inside him until he thought he'd explode. What the hell was taking so long? Why hadn't a doctor, a nurse—anyone—come out and told him something? He hadn't wanted to leave Paige. When she'd clung to his hand so tightly, it had almost killed him to pull his hand from hers and walk out of the examining room.

Glancing at the large utilitarian black-and-white clock on the wall, he couldn't believe it was after four in the morning. He checked the time on his watch—four-thirty-one—and noted the date. December 6. Exactly six months since the day he and Paige met. Exactly six months since they had made mad, passionate love in a stalled elevator during a power blackout. Exactly six months since they had created a child together—a child whose life hung in the balance this winter morning.

"Mr. Montgomery," the nurse called.

He rushed toward her, halting at the entrance to the hallway leading to the examination cubicles.

"Dr. Petrocelli would like to speak to you," she said.

"How is Paige? Is she all right? What about the baby?" Jared ran a trembling hand over his face.

"The doctor will answer all your questions. Come with me, please."

Tony Petrocelli met Jared in the hallway, placed his

hand on Jared's shoulder and looked him square in the eye.

"The news isn't good, is it." Jared asked.

Tony narrowed his dark eyes and shook his head. "I wish I could tell you that you don't have anything to worry about."

"Just give it to me straight."

"Paige is in labor."

"Can't you stop it?"

"We can try," Tony said. "But I can't make any guarantees. Believe it or not, things could be worse. Paige isn't bleeding. The membranes are intact and the cervix hasn't dilated."

"What are you doing to stop the labor pains?"

"She's had only one other contraction since you brought her in, and she said it was mild compared to the others she had, so all we're going to do is monitor her and—"

"What the hell do you mean all you're going to do is monitor her?" Jared bellowed. "If you aren't going to do anything for her, I'll have her transferred by helicopter to Denver!"

"Mr. Montgomery, they can't do any more for Paige in Denver than we can here. Of course, if you and Paige want to—"

"I'm sorry. I—I— Dammit man, can't you understand what I'm going through? That woman and that child are my life. Without them—" Jared choked on the lump that lodged in his throat.

Tony clamped his hand down hard on Jared's shoulder. "Under normal circumstances, when a woman goes into premature labor and her condition is similar to Paige's— carrying one fetus, no bleeding, no dilation—hospitalized bed rest alone, without medication, will check the contractions."

"And if it doesn't?"

"Then we may have to administer a drug that can relax the uterus. I prefer not to use tocolytic agents, except when there is no alternative. New research has raised questions about their safety and effectiveness."

"Is Paige in any danger?" Jared had not wanted to even consider the possibility, let alone voice it aloud. But he had to know. If anything happened to Paige...

"Physically, she should come through this just fine, regardless of what happens. Emotionally, it could be very difficult for her if she loses the baby. Paige wants this child very much."

"So, you're saying Paige isn't in any danger?"

"There are certain risks involved in every pregnancy," Tony explained. "Barring any complications, Paige should be all right. But I'm not God, Mr. Montgomery. I can't give you any one hundred percent guarantees."

"I understand." No guarantees that the labor would stop. No guarantees that if Angela was born now she could survive. No guarantees that there was no danger to Paige.

"I'm having Paige moved into a private room," Tony said. "We'll monitor her closely. The next thirty-six hours are crucial. She needs to be completely free of any worries or concerns. Bed rest and complete relaxation are essential."

"Do you have any idea what caused her to go into premature labor?" Had it been his fault? Had their frequent, passionate lovemaking triggered her labor? Or had the stress she'd endured during the earlier months of her pregnancy created problems?

"In most cases, we don't really understand what causes labor to begin early. Although there are several possible causes, I don't think any of them apply in Paige's case. She doesn't smoke, drink or use drugs. She's young, healthy and free of disease."

"Could stress have caused this...or—" Jared cleared his throat "—having frequent sex."

Tony Petrocelli's lips twitched. He looked sympathetically at Jared. "Both stress and sexual intercourse are possible causes in some cases, but not in most. There's no way to say for certain, but in Paige's case, I'd say probably not."

"May I see her?" Jared asked, his eyes pleading.

Tony patted Jared on the back. "As far as I'm concerned, you can stay with Paige twenty-four hours a day until she leaves the hospital."

A hard knot formed in Jared's throat, preventing him from speaking. Tears welled up in his eyes. He grabbed the doctor's hand, shook it and then released it quickly. Turning around, he ran up the hallway.

"Mr. Montgomery...Jared?" Tony called out.

"Yes?" Jared paused.

"There is a chance, regardless of what we do, that the labor won't stop. If that happens...I've already alerted the neonatal center in Denver to be ready, just in case."

Cold, deadly fear shivered through Jared's body. "If she's born now, what are our little girl's chances?"

"A damn sight better than they would have been only a few years ago."

"But?"

"But still not good for a twenty-four week preemie."

Jared nodded his head, then turned and walked down the hall. Just as he neared Paige's ER cubicle, they wheeled her bed through the door.

"Jared..." Her voice was weak and soft and needy.

Clasping her hand in his, he trotted alongside as they rolled her out of the ER and into an elevator. After what seemed like an eternity, the nurses cleared out of Paige's private room and left the two of them alone.

Leaning over the bed, Jared kissed Paige's forehead.

"Everything is going to be all right. Dr. Petrocelli said a few days' bed rest here in the hospital and you and Angela are going to be just fine."

Paige tried to smile, but the effort failed. She gripped Jared's hand. "I love you, you know. I think I've loved you from the first moment I saw you. I thought you were just a cowboy. A big, handsome cowboy with a smile that turned my knees to jelly."

His shoulders trembled. Tears welled in his eyes and one lone drop trickled down his cheek. How could he have ever doubted this woman? How could he have even considered the possibility that she had deliberately trapped him by getting herself pregnant?

"I haven't done a damn thing to deserve your love. I've fought you every inch of the way. Every moment since we met, I've wanted you and at the same time I've been trying to figure a way to change you into what I thought was the ideal wife for me."

"And have you?" She reached up and wiped the tear from his cheek.

"Have I figured out a way to make you over into the ideal wife? Hell, no!" He squeezed her hand. "I don't want you to change, honey. I've become rather fond of the real Paige Summers, you know."

"You want me just the way I am?" she asked.

"Just the way you are." He swallowed hard, trying desperately to hold back his tears. "Haven't you figured it out yet, Paige? I finally have. You are so much a part of me that I'd die without you."

A large, heavyset nurse, with a hypodermic needle in her hand, entered Paige's room. "Would you step outside for just a few minutes, Mr. Montgomery? What I have to do won't take long, then you can come right back in."

Jared brushed his lips across Paige's. "I'll be right back."

He closed the door behind him, then leaned against the wall. His stomach muscles constricted, his chest ached and his big shoulders shook as tears streamed down his face. Dear God in heaven, if anything happened to Paige, he wouldn't want to go on living. She had become as important to him as the air he breathed.

Paige wanted their baby—their precious little Angela—as much as he did. Maybe even more, if that was possible. What would it do to Paige to lose their daughter? She was such a loving, caring person, so filled with goodness and the pure wonder of life.

He had to be strong. Strong for Paige. If the contractions didn't stop and Angela was born prematurely, they would have to face the real possibility that she could and probably would die.

Balling his big hands into tight fists, Jared raised them toward heaven, threw back his head and moaned, long and low and deep. An agonized and angry but silent cry tore from the very depths of his soul.

Please God, please let Paige be all right and spare our precious little Angela. I love Paige and I swear that I'll spend the rest of my life making her happy.

The nurse emerged from Paige's room. "You can go back in now, Mr. Montgomery. Ms. Summers is doing just fine. She should be asleep shortly." She patted Jared on the arm. "Think positive thoughts."

He nodded affirmatively, then when the nurse walked down the empty hallway, he wiped his face with his fingers and cleared his throat.

When he returned to Paige's room, she opened her eyes and lifted her hand. Sitting down beside her, he took her hand, brought it to his lips and pressed his mouth into the center of her palm.

He held her hand, stroking her wrist, until she dozed off into a peaceful sleep. He pulled another chair up in front of him so that he could prop up his feet. Leaning against the bed, he laid his arm alongside hers and threaded his fingers through her fingers.

Paige slept through the morning, waking when the clatter of lunch trays broke through her sedated fog. Something big and heavy weighted down her hand. Jared's hand. He sat beside her asleep, his head resting on his shoulder.

When she tried to remove her hand from his grasp, he grunted, tightened his hold and eased open one eyelid. Peeping at her, he smiled, then yawned.

"Hello," she said.

Releasing her hand, he lowered his feet to the floor and straightened up in the chair. "Hello, yourself, beautiful."

Paige giggled. "I'll just bet I'm beautiful. No makeup. My hair's a mess and I'm wearing this—" she lifted the front of her hospital gown "—designer outfit."

"Honey, you are the most beautiful woman in the world just the way you look right now."

Paige grabbed his hand and laid it over her stomach. "I haven't had any more contractions. What time is it?"

Jared checked his watch. "Eleven-fifty-two. That means it's been—"

"Over eight hours since my last contraction." Opening her arms, she reached for him, drawing him close when he embraced her gently. "Oh, Jared. Maybe…maybe everything is going to be all right."

"Paige, I know that I promised I'd never ask you again, but—"

"It's all right," she told him, sliding her hips over to make room for him. "Sit down, Mr. Montgomery. There's something *I* want to ask *you*."

Easing down on the bed beside her, he continued holding her in his arms. He lowered his head and captured her lips in a tender kiss. She sighed.

"Jared?"

"Yes?"

"Will you marry me?"

Jared's mouth fell open. He gazed at her in total disbelief. "Repeat the question."

"Will you marry me?"

"I thought you said that you wouldn't marry a man who didn't love you."

She rubbed his nose with hers. "But you do love me, don't you?"

"Yes, I do. Paige Summers, I love you. I love you. I love you."

She melted against him, safe in his loving arms. "I know you do."

"How did you know? I didn't know for sure myself until a few hours ago."

"You told me, silly man."

"But I didn't...I mean, I...when?" he sputtered. "I only told you a minute ago."

"No, you told me this morning, before I went to sleep." Paige kissed his chin, then his neck. "When you told me that I was so much a part of you that you'd die without me, I knew you loved me." And she knew that he loved her for who she was and not the woman he'd once wanted her to be.

"I've been a slow learner when it came to the most important lesson of my life."

At that moment, Walt Summers cleared his throat. Jared and Paige glanced at the open doorway where Dora and Walt stood, arm in arm, both of them smiling.

"How did you know I was in the hospital?" Paige asked. "Jared, you didn't call them, did you?"

"Now, don't go blaming Jared." Dora came bustling into the room. "When we called around this morning and couldn't find you two anywhere, I checked with Dr. Petrocelli.''

''I didn't want you and Daddy to worry,'' Paige said. ''I'm doing much better. I haven't had a contraction in over eight hours.''

Jared kissed Paige quickly, then stood, allowing Dora access to her daughter, but he kept a tight grasp on Paige's hand.

''You were probably too little to remember, but the same thing happened with me when I was nearly seven months along with Bryant. I had to spend the next two months in bed, and your father wasn't allowed to touch me.'' Dora blushed. Walt cleared his throat. ''But Bryant and I made it just fine, and so will you and your baby.''

''Jared and I are going to get married,'' Paige told her parents.

''Just as soon as the doctor says Paige is well enough.'' Jared squeezed her hand.

''So you finally realized that you loved our daughter.'' Walt slapped Jared on the back. ''I was beginning to wonder if you'd ever come to your senses.''

''Is that what we walked in on?'' Dora asked. ''Did he finally propose to you again?''

''No. I proposed to him. And he said yes.'' Smiling with a happiness that made her radiant, Paige gazed adoringly at Jared. ''He loves me, Mama. He really, truly loves me.''

Epilogue

Although disappointed that the wedding couldn't be a large, elaborate affair at St. Veronica's, Dora enthusiastically threw herself into preparations for a small, private ceremony on New Year's Eve, working tirelessly with the wedding director Jared had flown in from Denver.

The living room in Jared and Paige's condo had been stripped bare and decorated to resemble a tiny chapel. Gold and white dominated the scene, with touches of forest green and hints of deep red. Candlelight illuminated the setting, and fresh flowers scented the air. A string quartet created a romantic atmosphere with their classical selections.

Reverend Archibald, in his impressive ecclesiastical robes, held an open white Bible in his hands. Looking out over the small assembly, he smiled. The guest list included Paige's brothers and their dates, Dora's sister and her family, flown by private jet from Mississippi, half a dozen Grand Springs's Montgomery Real Estate and Land Development employees and Dr. Tony Petrocelli, his wife Bethany and their young son Christopher.

Greg Addison, handsome and debonair in his black tuxedo, stood at Jared's side.

"Do you have the ring?" Jared asked his best man for the fourth time in five minutes.

"Yes, I have the ring." Greg laughed. "I've never seen you so nervous. Calm down."

"I've never gotten married before. Nothing has ever

been this important to me. I want everything to be perfect for Paige.''

He had made a vow to God, one that he would gladly keep. For as long as he lived, he would love Paige and devote his life to her happiness.

Bryant and Austen escorted their mother down the aisle and to her seat. Dora wiped away her tears with a lace handkerchief Jared had presented to her that morning.

Kay Thompson preceded the bride down the aisle. Her off-the-shoulder, formfitting sheath of forest green shimmered in the candlelight.

The string quartet played the wedding march as her father led Paige down the aisle. Tears glazed the eyes of big, macho, retired Sergeant Major Walt Summers.

Happiness glistened in Paige's eyes as she looked at her groom, perfectly attired in his black tuxedo. The double-breasted jacket, with satin lapels, and matching trousers had been tailored for an exact fit on Jared's long, lean, powerful body.

Jared smiled at Paige, that devastating smile that always turned her knees to jelly. She loved this man with all her heart and soul, and God in his goodness had seen fit to bless them not only with their mutual love, but with the gift of their little Angela's life.

Jared could not take his eyes off his bride. To him, she was the most beautiful creature on earth. Rare. Precious. A treasure without price.

Paige's empire-waist, scoop-neck gown of cream silk duchess satin featured detailed embroidery of gold bullion, pearls, crystals, bugle beads and threadwork of varying textures. Heavy beadwork accented the elbow-length sleeves and the embroidered bodice.

''Dearly beloved,'' Reverend Archibald said. Paige and Jared gazed lovingly into each other's eyes. ''We are gathered here today to join this man and this woman in the bonds of holy matrimony.''

The brief ceremony ended with a passionate kiss, then Jared swooped his bride up into his arms and carried her into the dining room, where a local caterer had set up the reception. Jared placed Paige on a cream-and-gold brocade chaise lounge and stood beside her, protective and possessive, as they greeted their guests.

Since Paige wasn't allowed to travel and the couple would have to abstain from sex until after Angela's birth, they had postponed their honeymoon.

Paige had taught Jared how to love, opening his heart to the wonder of life. And on their wedding night, alone in their home, Jared taught Paige a hundred and one ways a man and woman can make love.

Angela Dora Montgomery arrived at 9:15 a.m. on Wednesday, March 11, 1998, measuring twenty and a half inches and weighing eight pounds, two ounces. Except for the red fuzz covering her little round head, she was a carbon copy of her father. His eyes. His chin. His mouth, which promised a smile Paige said would one day be as devastating as his. Even her small hands and feet were replicas of Jared's.

The delivery went smoothly, resulting in a tired but happy mother, an exhausted but exuberant father and a beautiful, healthy baby.

From the moment Angela wrapped her tiny hand around Jared's big index finger, she captured his heart. She was the living, breathing proof of the passionate love that he and Paige shared. He had denied his feelings from the moment he and Paige met because he hadn't believed emotions so powerful truly existed. But so fierce was the love he now felt for his wife and daughter that he wondered how he had ever lived without them.

While Paige held their newborn daughter to her breast, Jared wrapped his arm around his wife's shoulder, his big body a primitive symbol of his protection. Words were unnecessary. They exchanged a loving glance that said everything.

*   *   *   *   *

Beverly Barton has a new novel out next month in our Silhouette Sensation® series. If you've enjoyed this book look out for Gabriel Hawk's Lady.

36 Hours

When disaster turns to passion

continues with

THE PARENT PLAN

by Paula Detmer Riggs
also available in August

Here's an exciting preview…

The Parent Plan

June 7

Dr. Karen Sloane was used to working under pressure. But standing alone just beyond the glaring spotlights that bathed Devil Butte in brilliant light, she was close to shattering. Silhouetted by the glow, rescue workers struggled to reach the spot where her eight-year-old daughter, Victoria, was trapped in the entrance of a cave. Torrential rains had tumbled tons of rock and earth from the face of the butte, exposing the dark pit. Vicki was alone in that pit—and time was running out.

Karen had been on duty at Vanderbilt Memorial Hospital when Cassidy had called around ten that morning. She could still hear the raw note in her husband's husky voice. The stark undertones of desperation. Somehow she'd managed to reach the site shortly after Lieutenant Brendan Gallagher and the fire department's mountain rescue unit had begun on the rescue shaft now angling down toward her little girl.

Cassidy had been like a crazy man, shouting at Bren to let him help. If he had to, he'd claw his way to his daughter with his bare hands. Catching sight of Karen half stumbling down the mud-scoured slope, Bren had silently pleaded with her for help. She'd put aside her questions long enough to coax Cassidy away from the knot of grim-faced, dedicated men, but a shiver had transited her spine at the wild suffering she saw in his eyes. For an instant she wasn't sure he even knew who she was, and then his arms crushed her to him. Suddenly he was in control again, his emotions shuttered away as he jerked his hat from his head and placed it on hers then ordered her to take his slicker. It was Cassidy's way. Maybe he never said he loved her in so many words, but a woman knew when she was loved. For all his firmly rooted beliefs and sometimes inexplicable opinions on the way of things, Cassidy was a gentle man at heart.

Karen was sure of it.

With a sigh, she searched for her husband's tall form. Suddenly she saw Cassidy standing alone at the edge of the light, an intensely physical man who expressed himself with actions and kept his own counsel. She took a hasty step, then hesitated, suddenly uneasy. There was a look of stark anger about him that almost frightened her.

A rustle of brush had Cassidy turning suddenly to find his wife moving toward him. She looked tired and worried and terribly fragile, but it was the misery in her eyes that ripped at him in ways she would never understand.

He knew the words she wanted him to say, the promises she was desperate to hear, but he couldn't make himself lie. "I knew better, and I let Vicki go out in this weather anyway."

He reminded Karen of a man at war with an enemy only he could see, and her heart ached for him. "Cassidy, don't." Tears stung her eyes as she reached out to touch him. "You couldn't have known that cave was there. And a mud slide can happen any time, to anyone."

"But it happened here, Karen. On land I thought I knew as well as the back of *my* own hand.

"Cassidy, if you need to blame someone, blame Mother Nature, because it's not your fault."

His gaze pinned her with a ruthless intensity that was

as much a part of him as the aura of command he projected. "You're wrong, Karen," he said in flat, even tones. "It's because of *my* mistake that our daughter is down in that cold hellhole, fighting to stay alive."

"How can you say that?" she protested with a fierce gentleness.

Some powerful, but unreadable emotion blazed in his eyes an instant before the fire was extinguished. "I can *say that* because I let you go back to your precious job when I knew you belonged at home with our daughter. I knew better," he went on mercilessly, his eyes raging, "but I kept thinking you'd come to your senses."

Karen couldn't breathe, so excruciating was the pain sweeping through her. Then her training and education kicked in. Cassidy wasn't himself, that was all. He was acting out of fear and desperation. Later, when their daughter was safe, he would take her into his arms and apologize. She stumbled over some unseen obstacle and heard Cassidy's harsh intake of breath. He was at her side instantly, his strong arm wrapping around her waist to keep her from falling. "Kari, I didn't mean...I don't—"

"Cassidy! Karen!" It was Gallagher's voice. *"We have her! Hot damn, she's safe!"*

March 18

Karen pressed the buzzer twice to herald her arrival, then let herself into the large, redbrick and shiplap sliding house she'd grown up in. "Mom?" she called as she slipped off her jacket.

Sylvia Moore pushed through the double doors that led into the living room. "Hello, sweetheart. A visit from you is just what I needed." She said as she set a tray on the coffee table and handed Karen a cup. "Is something wrong, darling? You look a bit sad this afternoon."

At the sound of concern in her mother's voice, Karen shook her head in what she hoped was a reassuring denial. She would not cry. She *wouldn't*.

There was a weighty silence before her mother said softly. "Karen ? What's wrong?"

Her mother's question pierced Karen's brave front and she had to swallow hard before she could speak. "Oh Mom, I'm so scared. I think my marriage is in terrible trouble, and I don't have a clue how to fix it. Cassidy blames me for Vicki's accident. He's been punishing me for it ever since."

That night so many months ago, Karen had almost lost her daughter. Now she had to find a way to keep the memory from destroying her marriage....

COMING NEXT MONTH

GABRIEL HAWK'S LADY Beverly Barton

The Protectors

Ex-CIA agent Gabriel Hawk was the kind of man Rorie Dean would normally keep at a distance. With a heart of stone and the sexiest body she'd ever seen, he was a danger to her sanity! Unfortunately, he was also the only man who could lead her through a war-torn jungle to rescue her nephew...

SECONDHAND DAD Kayla Daniels

Cop Noah Garrett valued his privacy above anything else. But now a little boy and his gorgeous mother, Caroline Tate, were staying under Noah's roof. The child was a murder witness and Noah had no choice but to keep him safe—but that didn't mean he had to take Caroline to bed...

UNDERCOVER LOVER Kylie Brant

John Sullivan was Ellie Bennett's dearest friend—and now he was her lover. But what she *didn't* know about him was immense. Like his troubled past, his top-secret profession...and that a night with her had nearly blown his cover—something he couldn't allow to happen again!

ROYAL'S CHILD Sharon Sala

Heartbreaker/The Justice Way

Royal Justice would do anything to make his four-year-old daughter, Maddie, happy. So when she insisted they pick up a lone hitchhiker, he went against his better judgement, and stopped for Angel Rojas. But once Angel entered their lives, neither he nor Maddie wanted to let her go...

COMING NEXT MONTH FROM

▼™SILHOUETTE®

Intrigue
Danger, deception and desire

NEVER LET HER GO Gayle Wilson
A FATHER FOR HER BABY B. J. Daniels
REMEMBER ME, COWBOY Caroline Burnes
TWILIGHT PHANTASIES Maggie Shayne

Special Edition
Compelling romances packed with emotion

FATHER-TO-BE Laurie Paige
THE PRESIDENT'S DAUGHTER Annette Broadrick
MEANT FOR EACH OTHER Ginna Gray
PRINCE CHARMING, M.D. Susan Mallery
BABY STARTS THE WEDDING MARCH Amy Frazier
UNTIL YOU Janis Reams Hudson

Desire
Provocative, sensual love stories

A KNIGHT IN RUSTY ARMOUR Dixie Browning
THE BRIDE MEANS BUSINESS Anne Marie Winston
THIRTY-DAY FIANCÉ Leanne Banks
WILL AND THE HEADSTRONG FEMALE Marie Ferrarella
THE RE-ENLISTED GROOM Amy J Fetzer
MIRANDA'S OUTLAW Katherine Garbera

When winning is everything...
losing can be deadly.

HIGH
STAKES
Rebecca
Brandewyne

Angela Marlowe's parents were dead,
murdered by powerful, ruthless men.
Now Angela is starting to put the
shattered pieces of her past together
and finds herself entering a maze of
danger and corruption.
But she is not alone.

Available from July